A MOMMY FOR CHRISTMAS

THE OKLAHOMA BRANDS
BOOK FOUR

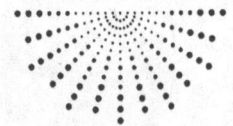

MAGGIE SHAYNE

Copyright © 2011, 2021 by Margaret Benson

Published by Oliver Heber Books

0 9 8 7 6 5 4 3 2 1

Printed with relish.

OLIVERHEBERBOOKS

THE OKLAHOMA BRANDS

November 2005

This book is dedicated to my mom,
for too many reasons to name. She is so much
a part of me and a part of everything I do, and
I see her in myself more and more every day.
I love you, Mom.
~Maggie Shayne, November 2005

November 2013

Only a few weeks after the release of the original version of this novel, my mother passed away after a 14-month battle with pancreatic cancer. The entire time I was writing this book, I was also spending every possible moment with her. I'd moved her into a cabin on my property, so she'd be right next door, and so I could help my stepfather care for her. Near the end, I was being called over there every couple of hours, day and night, and I haven't got one regret about that.

It's only now, holiday season 2013, as I'm re-reading this novel and revising it quite heavily (I was not at my best, creatively) that I realize how much what I was experiencing was reflected in this book. The little boy. The mother he had and the mommy he wanted, an idealized version who would never leave him. His dad, who'd nursed his own mother through cancer as a small child. And Christmas. Christmas, the biggest most spectacularly wonderful day of every single year of my childhood. Christmas was everything, back then. And my mom adored it.

I honestly didn't realize I was working through so many feelings as I wrote this story. Now that I do, I think I've been able to do a better job telling it, delving deeper, and understanding more about myself and my characters these 7 years later.
I think I understand you better now, as well, Mom. And this one's still for you.

Thank you. And Merry Christmas!
~Maggie Shayne (aka Peggy Sue) November 2013

CHAPTER ONE

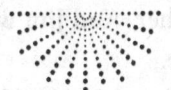

HEN HE FIRST opened the door to her knock,
he thought the woman standing there was a
homeless drug addict. And then he realized she was his wife.

Ex-wife.

For a second he just stood there staring at her. A bag of
bones with stringy once-blond hair and drug-dulled eyes that
used to sparkle like sapphires. Yeah, she was his ex. *And* a drug
addict. The one didn't preclude the other, though if anyone had
told him that five years ago, Jim would have pounded him into
taco filler.

"Hi, Jim," she said, face expressionless. She didn't bother
brushing the rapidly melting snowflakes from her hair or her
shoulders. "It's been a long time."

Four years. Four long years. And now she was back and all
he could feel was panic. "What do you want?" Not Tyler, he
thought silently. Please, God, not that. Not that she would have
a leg to stand on even if she *had* come for their son. She'd signed
him away to save her own skin. After nearly killing him, she
hadn't had much choice about it.

1

"Not even going to invite me in? Say it's good to see me? Ask how I've been?"

"I don't particularly give a damn how you've been." But he wasn't sure how much longer her stick-figure legs were going to hold her, and it was chilly in the hallway. She was so skinny she was shivering. So he stepped aside and prayed Ty would remain blissfully sound asleep in his room. The boy needed a mother, was desperate for a mother. And Jim was working hard to find him one. Just not *this* one.

Angela came inside, staring blankly at the wreath on the door as she walked past it. Real pine. He'd bought it last week and then he and Ty had spent hours decorating it with pine cones and tiny ornaments and a can of spray on snow. And some bells. Ty had insisted he add bells that would jingle whenever the door opened.

He'd have told her all that. But she wouldn't have cared. She was already swinging the door closed behind her—he caught it before it slammed and closed it quietly. Looking around the apartment, she nodded slightly. "Nice place. Way nicer than our old one was."

He shrugged. "I had to find a ground-floor unit. It's easier on Ty."

She nodded, trailing her fingers over the gleaming hardwood finish of a coffee table before sitting down on the couch. He almost winced at her sitting on the furniture. He had a lot of experience with addicts. They were usually dirty, often contagious. And she was an addict. No question. He hadn't seen her in four years, but he'd seen her name countless times.

A second glance told him she wasn't filthy. She'd bathed and her clothes had been washed recently. He thought she might have even run a comb through her hair. Not the usual behavior of the types he dealt with on a daily basis.

"What are you doing here, Ang?" He took a seat in a chair

across from her, hoping she'd get straight to the point. He just wanted her out of there.

She lowered her head. "I need a favor."

"Figures." He didn't try to hide his disgust. "Are you even going to ask how he is?"

Her brows drew together and she seemed momentarily angry—the first hint of emotion he'd seen in those zoned-out eyes of hers. But she bit back whatever she'd been about to say and replaced it with, "How is he?"

"He's wonderful. But he's still suffering. Still in the leg braces. Has physical therapy twice a week and hates it. One more surgery to go, though. Just one more."

She nodded slowly. Didn't ask any questions. Why he felt compelled to fill her in, he didn't know, but he kept on talking.

"We've been through six nannies so far. But they move on, you know. Get boyfriends, lives, less demanding jobs. He's a lot. I'm taking every bit of time off I can get without being fired. Not that I mind. I love being with him."

She drew a breath and studied her hands. Was he boring her with this?

"He's sleeping. But if you want, you can look in on him."

"No." She said it a little too quickly. "That's not why I came."

He turned his head so she wouldn't see the hatred in his eyes, focused instead on the photograph of Ty that hung on the wall near his bedroom. His twinkling eyes and deep dimples and baby teeth eased the rage in Jim's heart. How could Angela not want to see her own child?

Didn't matter. He was glad. Ty didn't need this pile of human refuse in his life. "Right," he reminded himself. "You're here because you need a favor."

She drew a breath, lifted her head. "That's right"

"Hell, Ang, you look like what you really need is a month in rehab. What the hell has happened to you?"

She averted her face.

"You're still using." He didn't make it a question. It had been her damned drug addiction that had almost killed Tyler. She'd been wasted on coke when she'd fallen down two flights of stairs, taking their newborn son with her. If he'd only been more aware, been paying more attention....

"I'm clean. Have been for four weeks straight."

He looked at her eyes and knew better.

"Really. I mean it. I'm changing my life, Jim. I met a guy—a man, a decent man. He's helping me. He...he loves me."

So did I once, he thought.

"He wants to marry me."

"Congratulations."

She drew a breath. "But it might not happen. There are... problems. Legal problems."

He lifted his head slowly. Something about the tone of her voice set off alarm bells in his head. "Who is this guy?"

"Vincent Stefano."

He shot to his feet the minute she said the name, stunned. "What the hell is this, Angela?"

"He's a decent man, Jim."

"He's a porn king, Ang."

"But that's not illegal."

"No, not until it involves kids."

"He didn't do what you think he did. Those photos were planted in his office. He was set up."

"Right." Working on an anonymous tip, he and his partner had executed a search warrant on Skinny Vinnie's office and found an envelope full of photos that made him want to puke. Kids. *Young* kids. "He's a piece of dirt, and he's going away for a long time. So don't make any wedding plans just yet." He closed his eyes and swallowed the bile that rose in his throat. "God, how could you be with a sleazebag like him?"

"I *love* him, Jim!"

"Then you're as sick as he is." He started toward the door.

"You don't understand," she cried, getting up and hurrying behind him. "He's not what you think. He's being framed. And the only thing they have on him now is your testimony."

"Is that what he told you?" He speared her with his eyes. "He's a liar, Ang. I'm not the only cop who saw those photos. And even if I was and I agreed to change my testimony... that is what you're asking for here, isn't it?"

She couldn't hold his eyes, so she lowered hers and nodded.

"Even if I did, there would still be the small matter of those photos locked up safe and sound in the evidence room. Your slimy boyfriend's going down, Ang."

She blinked slowly. "I don't understand. Vinnie said—"

"Just understand this—I wouldn't change my testimony if your damn life depended on it. You got that? Because these are kids. *Kids*, Ang. Kids come way higher on my list of priorities than my drug-addicted ex-wife's love life. Deal with it."

"Damn you, why can't you just listen?"

He went to the door, opened it wide. The bells on the wreath jingled like mad. "Get the hell out."

"I have a chance to be happy, Jim. Don't take it away from me."

"Yeah, it's all about you," he said, holding the door. "I'm testifying against this pervert because I can't stand the thought of you being happy with someone else. You keep believing that."

She leaned toward him, pressed her hands to the front of his shirt. "Don't you care about me anymore? Even a little bit?"

He closed his hands around her wrists to remove them from his chest. "Care about you? You got high and took my baby son down two flights of stairs, Angela. Twenty-four stairs pounded his tiny body. Twenty-four. You broke his little legs in seven places, twisted up his spine, split his head open, and he's still suffering from it. Every time I take Tyler in for physical therapy and listen to him cry in pain and beg me not to make him go through it, I hate you more. That's what I feel for you. Now get out. And if you come within a mile of my son again, I'll find a way to put you behind bars."

She'd backed away from him as he'd pummeled her with his words. When he finished, she lowered her head and moved slowly through the door. "You never loved me. Not really. Not the way he does."

"You think so? Tell me something, Ang, when did you meet this slimeball?"

She stopped in the doorway, head hanging low. "A few months ago."

"Before or after I arrested him?"

"A-after. But it's not—"

"And where did you meet him? Did he drive his Porsche to one of the gutters where you sleep, one of the dives where you drink? Did he walk up to you in his designer suit and ask for a date?"

She shook her head. "It's none of your business."

"Was he a John, Ang?"

She shot him a wide eyed look.

"I'm a cop, you think I don't know? So he picked you up. You, out of every working girl out there. The ex-wife of the cop who busted him. You think that's some kind of coincidence?"

She blinked fast, tears springing into her eyes. "You don't know anything."

"I know he's using you to get to me. And it's not gonna work. You wanna get clean, you do it yourself. Get into rehab. Stand on your own two feet and take control of your life for a change. But don't see this guy as some fairytale prince to your Cinderella. He's trouble, Ang."

Her tears were flowing now. "You're wrong!" she shouted. "You're wrong and I hate you. I *hate* you!"

She surged through the door, ran down the hall to the big double exit doors, getting to them just as they opened and his partner stepped through in a whoosh of snow and wintry wind.

Colby Benton sent a puzzled look at the woman as he stomped his feet and brushed at his sleeves. She pushed past him, out into the snowy Chicago night. The doors swung closed behind her and Colby gave his balding red head a shake, brows raised as he met Jim's eyes.

"Tell me that wasn't a date with one of your mommy candidates," he said. "And if it was, I hope it was a *blind* date."

"Didn't you recognize her, Colby? That was Ang."

Colby's reddish eyebrows went up even farther. "Shit."

"Yeah, that sums it up pretty well." Jim sighed, still staring through the windows in the big double doors, though she was long gone. There was only the steady, swirling patterns made by the snow and shifting wind in the glow of the outdoor lightsFinally he shook himself. "Come on in. I have to go make sure she didn't wake Tyler with all her bull."

Jim turned and walked into his apartment with Colby on his heels. He didn't have to tell his longtime friend to close and lock the door behind him. They were cops, they did some things automatically.

Jim stood for a long moment in Tyler's bedroom. It wasn't dark. He always left a night-light on for his son—a little blue cartoon hound-dog lit by a Christmas-tree lightbulb. The same blue dog and numerous blue paw prints decorated the bedspread, the sheets and the pillowcase. A strip of wallpaper border halfway up the wall sported the same character. There was even a blue "thinking chair" in the corner.

And in the midst of it all, snuggled deep in the covers, lay Tyler. Hair too thick and a little too long and looking like a mixture of honey and amber. Eyes usually sparkling with mischief and intelligence, and so big you could fall right into them, but closed now as he slept. He lay with his lashes resting on his chubby cheeks, hugging a stuffed blue dog. Still sound asleep.

"He okay?" Colby whispered.

7

Jim turned, saw his friend in the doorway and nodded. "Never even knew she was here," he said. He walked softly out of the bedroom, pulled the door closed, but not all the way. Colby handed him one of the beers he'd taken from the fridge, and the two headed for the sofa and sat.

"That's a blessing," Colby said. "He doesn't even remember her, does he?"

"No. He only knows his birth mother had to go far, far away and can't ever be a mom."

Colby nodded slow, sipped his beer as he got comfortable. "Any progress finding him a new one?" He asked it with a slight smile, as if he still wasn't convinced Jim was serious about his ongoing project

"I've crossed the first ten candidates off the list. Have to find some new prospects before I can move on."

Colby blinked. "You're kidding, right? I mean, you're really... auditioning women for this?"

"Dating. As far the women know, anyway. Hell, it's not exactly honest, but I need to find out what they're about before I make any kind of decision here. I need a woman who can love him the way I do. That's a tall order to fill. She's got to be willing to put him first in her life, ahead of everything else. Family, career, friends—"

"You?"

Jim nodded. "Me, certainly. And herself most of all. I don't want another selfish bitch within a hundred miles of Tyler."

Colby seemed to consider that. "I didn't think you were that serious about all this. Hell, Jim, you really mean to get married to a woman you don't love, may not even be attracted to, just to give Tyler a mother?" He searched Jim's face. "It seems kinda... cold."

"Love doesn't enter into it. Sex doesn't have to either. It's about Ty—he's what's important." Jim lowered his head. "I can't be with him all the time. The nannies aren't working out, the physical therapy is torture and all he does is cry. Night after night the kid cries, asking me why he doesn't have a mom. All the kids in his preschool class do, the kids he sees at his doctor's appointments and PT sessions, even the kids on television. He's suffering."

Colby nodded. "But lots of kids don't have moms. He can do just fine without one."

"But he doesn't *have* to. He's suffered enough. Anything I can give that kid to make his life easier, to make it happier, come hell or high water, Colby, I'll damn well do it. Hell, I'm a decent-looking man."

"A stud-muffin, according to the girls in the prosecutor's office," Colby said.

Jim shot him a look and went on with his analysis. "I earn a good living. And I'll tell you, if I can find a woman who'd be the kind of mother Tyler needs, I'd treat her like solid gold."

"Except for loving her. You won't do that."

Jim tipped his head back, looked at the ceiling. "Who'd have pegged you for a sappy romantic, pal? I told you, love has nothing to do with it."

"It isn't gonna work without it, Jim."

"No? Well, it didn't work too well with it, either. I loved Ang. Look where that got me. More importantly, look where it got Tyler." He pursed his lips, shook his head. "Nope. I don't need to love her. Just need her to love my son."

Jim took a pull from his longneck brown bottle and set it down. "So what's up, partner? I know damn well you didn't come all the way over here to talk about my love life."

Colby nodded. "No, you're right. But I have to admit, this whole mommy finding mission fascinates me. We, uh—we have a problem. With the Stefano case."

Jim frowned. "Funny, that's what Ang was here to talk to me about."

Colby looked up fast. "No kidding? What about it?"

"Skinny Vinnie's her new boyfriend. Hooked up with her sometime after we busted him—probably as soon as he made bail and paid a P.I. to check into our backgrounds, looking for some leverage. He's got her asking me to back off on my testimony."

"Yeah? And what did he plan to do about *mine*?"

Jim shrugged. "He told her my word was the only thing the D.A. had on him. I told her he was a liar."

"Oh, he's a liar all right. Maybe not about this, though."

Jim frowned. "What do you mean?"

Colby drew a breath. "Those photos we found in his office have disappeared from the evidence room, Jim. They're gone. They're just... gone."

"We have copies."

"They're gone, too. There's nothing left. So now all the D.A. has on Vinnie Stefano is you and me. We saw the photos, booked them into evidence. We can testify to that, describe them. But even that might not be enough."

"Particularly not if the defense attorney finds out Vinnie's screwing my ex," Jim said, a knot forming in his stomach. "That wouldn't exactly make me an objective, reliable witness, cop or not."

"Nope." Colby took another pull on his beer, draining the bottle. "Chief Wilcox figures Vinnie will be trying anything he can use on us. Blackmail, intimidation, threats, character assassination. Might even try to take us out."

"I wouldn't put it past him," Jim said. "He's got the money and the connections to pull it off, too."

"The chief wants us to get out of town until the trial, Jim."

Jim sighed, glancing toward his son's bedroom. "It's not as easy as all that. I've got Ty. His doctors, his PT. Hell, it's almost Christmas."

"So go someplace you know. Someplace where you can easily set him up with a doctor and physical therapist. Call it a holiday vacation, and we don't come home until January 4th, the day of the trial. That's just under three weeks from now."

"What do you mean *we?* We're going together?"

Colby slapped him on the shoulder. "Hell, you don't think I'm going to let you go without me, do you? I gotta see the way you manage to con some unsuspecting woman into marrying you. A new town will give you a whole new pool of potential brides, won't it?"

"A new town." Jim tipped his head and thought about that. "Or maybe an old town."

Colby stared at him. "What are you thinking?"

Jim went to a shelf, pulled down an old high school yearbook and began flipping through the photos, pausing on the head shots of every girl he'd dated back then. There were a lot of them.

"Thinking of going home for Christmas, pal. Back to Big Falls in the northernest, westernest part of Oklahoma. And one of the girls I left behind."

"Which one?"

"I'll let you know."

Colby rolled his eyes. "You're hopeless, you know that? Hell, that's farther than I wanted to go. But I'm in," Colby said. "I got three weeks' vacation time coming, and Wilcox says you have at least that much. When you wanna head out?"

Jim sighed, thought about Angela, the desperation in her eyes. She'd be back. And she wouldn't be above using Tyler to get her way. "In the morning," he said. "We can take both cars— make it easier to get around once we're down there."

"I'll be here at eight, then," Colby said, rising to his feet.

"Bring breakfast," Jim told him.

～

BEFORE GOING TO his room to start packing, Jim looked in on Tyler once more. His cheeks were starting to lose a little of their baby roundness, his face turning into the face of a little boy. He was an angel. He was Jim's whole life. There was nothing he wouldn't do for his son.

He ran a hand over Ty's silken hair. Then he frowned as he noticed a bit of paper sticking out from under his pillow.

Tugging it out, careful not to wake his son, he looked down at the sheet of oversize lined paper Ty must have got from preschool. He'd drawn on it in crayon. There was a head with squiggles sticking out the top that represented hair. Stick figure arms and legs sprouted directly from the head itself. It had unevenly matched eyes, a round purple nose and a smiling pink mouth. There were squiggly objects all around the figure. Written painstakingly across the top of the page was a single word that made Jim's heart turn the consistency of oatmeal.

Mommy.

His son rolled over and opened his eyes—eyes as blue as the sky back home in Big Falls. "Hey, Dad."

"Hey, Ty. Sorry, pal. I didn't mean to wake you up."

Ty took the drawing from his dad's hands and studied it..

"Ty?"

"Hmm?'

"You draw that picture in school today?"

"Yeah. We was makin' wish pitchers."

"Wish pictures?"

Tyler nodded. "We had to draw a pitcher of somethin' we wanted for Christmas or Hanka."

"Hanukkah?"

"Yeah that. We got two kids that call Christmas Hanka."

"It's not exactly the same thing," he said.

"I know! They get candles 'stead of a tree, and presents every day for a week. Teacher 'splained it." He smiled broadly. "So I drawed a mommy."

"How come you didn't show me?"

Tyler shrugged. "I thought if I put it under my pillow, the tooth fairy might find it."

Jim swallowed the lump in his throat "Tooth fairies don't bring mommies, Ty."

"I know that. I just figgered she might know some other fairies or somethin'. But it's okay if she doesn't. I'm made another one to send to Santa." He sat up a little and pointed at the sealed envelope on his night stand with SANTA written on the front. Then he looked at his picture again. "I made her real pretty, Dad. And look—" he pointed to the shapes on the page all around her "—she has a pony *and* a dog and she knows how to make cookies and she never *ever* gets mad or yells at anybody. She gots a tire swing and a big backyard and she loves little boys. Even the ones who are kinda brokened."

"Ah, Ty..." Jim damn near choked on the lump in his throat as he wrapped Tyler tight in his arms and held him. "You are the best little boy any mommy could ever have, you understand me?"

"Then how come I don't have a mom?"

"Because I haven't found one good enough for you yet," he told his son. "Not because you're broken. You're perfect. You understand? Perfect."

He gave one last squeeze, then gently eased Tyler back onto his pillows and tucked him in. "And it's not up to Santa to pick out the best mom for you, son. That's kinda my job."

"Then he won't bring me one?"

"Probably not. I mean, he's pretty much in the toy business, you know? Moms are people. You see the difference?"

Tyler heaved a big sigh. "Yeah. I see. So *you* have to get me a mom."

"That's the idea."

"But you're so slow, Dad. Most of my friends at school already got moms."

Jim thinned his lips and decided it was time to change the subject. "Guess what we're doin' tomorrow?"

Tyler was instantly distracted. "I thought I was goin' to school and you was goin' to work."

"Nope. We are going on a vacation."

Tyler tipped his head to one side. "We are?"

"Yep. I'm going to take you back to the little town where I grew up. You'll get to see the house I lived in and my old high school and everything."

"Wow! And the waterfall, too?"

"Yep. The waterfall, too."

"Cool." Then he frowned. "But will we be back in time for Christmas?"

"I was thinking we might spend Christmas there."

"But what if Santa can't find me?" Tyler asked, his eyes suddenly huge and extremely worried.

"I'll make sure to let him know where we are, kiddo. Promise." Tyler sighed in relief. "You get some sleep now. It'll be a big day tomorrow."

Tyler held up his arms and puckered up his lips. Jim leaned down for a good-night kiss. Then he left his son to his dreams of the perfect mommy, and went into his own room. But instead of packing, he sat down with his old high school yearbook, a yellow legal pad and a black-ink pen and he got to work on a list of potential mothers for his son.

CHAPTER TWO

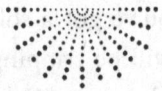

*K*ARA BRAND CAME down the stairs, not touching the garland decked bannister, to find her mother and three out of four sisters waiting for her with the huge Christmas tree as their backdrop. She very nearly turned around and went right back up again. But those smiling, expectant faces wouldn't allow it.

"You look wonderful," her mom said, clapping her hands together. "Except for that doe-in-the-headlights expression. Girl, what are you afraid of?"

Edie elbowed the matriarch gently. "Now, Mom, ease off. It's a big day for her. She's got every right to be nervous." She strode forward, eyeing her younger sister as if she were one of her photographs. "You do look great, hon."

"Yeah, thanks to you." Over the past year her model-turned-photographer sister had made Kara her pet project. She'd nagged her about her walk and her tendency to slouch, grilled her until her entire demeanor had changed. Kara didn't trip over her long legs anymore. She walked surely, deliberately, and had broken the habit of hurrying all the time. She held her chin up and her back straight and she looked people in the eye when she spoke to them. Between that and the fashion coaching, shopping trips, skin-care and makeup tips and a half dozen new hairstyles, Kara almost felt beautiful now. And she'd finally begun to stop thinking of herself as a klutz.

But today she wondered if even Edie's coaching and makeovers would be of any help.

"There's no reason for you to be nervous, Kara," her oldest sister Maya told her. "You've got a solid business plan and no competition. The bank will be tripping over itself to lend you the money." She thinned her lips. "Caleb's still a little hurt that you wouldn't take a loan from us, but—"

"I want to do this on my own, sis," Kara told her. "Just to prove I can."

"Be careful coming out of the bank," Selene told her.

She glanced at her youngest sister's mystical silver-blue eyes and platinum hair and frowned. Selene sometimes...knew things. "Why? What...?"

"I don't know. I just keep thinking it, so I'm telling you."

Kara nodded, clutched her briefcase tighter and glanced at her reflection as she passed the picture window, which had paper snowflakes made by Maya's twins, Scotch taped all over it. She blinked and looked again. God, she would never get used to seeing herself as she was now. Edie's current hairstyle of choice for Kara was a shoulder-length cut that, with a handful of mousse and a little scrunching, turned gently curly. The color was her own dark brown with auburn highlights. She wasn't all that dressed up. Casual chic, Edie said. Trousers with legs so wide they moved like a skirt. Burgundy button blouse. A cameo her mother had given her rested at her throat for luck.

She drew her gaze away and forced her feet to carry her to the front door, grabbed a jacket, and accepted the hugs of her family. Then she got into the car and drove into the festively decked downtown area of Big Falls, where every lamppost had a lighted wreath, and every shop window, a holiday display, for her appointment with Mrs. Terwilliger at the bank.

An hour later, she stepped out of the bank and into the bight winter sunshine with a very good feeling. It was cool but not *cold*. A brisk fifty degrees with an insistent wind. Mrs. T, as she'd insisted Kara call her, felt certain the loan application would be approved. Kara was going to have her day-care center.

She could hardly believe it!

She celebrated by allowing herself to indulge in her guilty pleasure of choice. Next door to the bank was Barlow's Jewelry, and her ring—the ring she'd always thought of as hers, anyway —was on display in the window. Oh, it wasn't huge. But it was the most romantic ring she'd ever seen. A pink diamond in a simple pear cut, accented by two tiny ruby chip, one on either side. She loved that ring.

Mr. Barlow saw her in the window, sent her a knowing smile. Her love of the ring was a secret they shared. She didn't worry about him telling anyone. He would keep her confidence as surely as her own doctor would. And one of these days, if all went well, maybe she would march into that store and buy that ring for herself!

She tore her eyes away from the dream ring and turned to head for her car, and home. Remembering her sister's words, she looked both ways before starting across the street. And then she looked again, because she thought she'd seen....

OhmyGod, she *did* see him. He was back in town.

Him. Jimmy Corona. The hottest hunk of Big Falls High, back in the day. He'd been the star quarterback of the football team. The most popular boy in school. And she'd been the biggest nerd. Too tall for her body, painfully shy, accident-prone and, some said, a jinx.

Klutzy Kara had been her nickname back then. Not that he'd ever called her that. She liked to think he was too nice to call her such a horrible name, but the truth was, she doubted he had ever so much as noticed she was alive.

Oh, God, he was looking at her!

She turned her head quickly so he wouldn't know she'd been staring, but the heel of her shoe caught in a crack in the pavement, jerking her off balance. Her arms shot out to her sides, wheeling crazily. A car was speeding toward her and she was going down fast.

And the next, thing she knew, a pair of strong arms scooped her right off her feet

THE CAR SLAMMED its brakes and skidded sideways as Jim himself half shoved, half carried the woman out of harm's way. He'd glimpsed her from a distance... and now he figured it was a good thing she was so stunningly beautiful, because he hadn't been able to tear his eyes away. Which was why he'd seen disaster about to strike. He was holding her with one arm under her legs, one supporting her back. Despite her height, she wasn't heavy, which was good because he had to keep moving to avoid the chain-reaction disaster unfolding around them.

The skidding car hit a lamppost and tipped it over. The lamppost hit the craft store's outdoor holiday display, bringing tangles of Christmas lights and tinsel down with it. A puppy tugged his leash from his owner's hand, raced into the mess and emerged with a length of silver garland in his teeth, growling and shaking it for all he was worth. People ran every which way. Displays and decorations were scattered over the sidewalk, and they tripped people, who fell down, tripping other people.

Jim saw it all in a single sweeping glance. And then he lowered his head to meet the eyes of the woman who was staring up at him and couldn't look anywhere else. He saw huge green eyes, wide-set and round.

"Jimmy Corona," she whispered.

He smiled at the breathless way she'd said his name and tried to place her face. It was familiar and yet not quite.

"Are you okay?" he asked, not wanting to admit he didn't know who she was. That tended to offend women. She wasn't one of the girls he'd dated in high school—or at least he didn't think so. He'd studied all those faces closely, memorized the names. He had six solid potentials he intended to visit before he left town.

She blinked at him. "Uh... yeah. I... I'm fine."

He set her carefully on her feet, and she stood facing him, close. Very close. Something stirred in his belly. Then she seemed to realize that her arms were still locked around his neck. She lowered them, though it was the last thing in the world he wanted her to do just then.

It was about that time recognition hit him—well, not specific recognition but better than none at all. He had the genus and species down, if not the name. "You're one of the Brand girls, aren't you?" he asked. As he spoke, he put a hand on the middle of her back to guide her the rest of the way across the street, away from the chaos she'd caused, back toward where he'd left the truck parked with Tyler safe and sound in the passenger seat and Colby keeping an eye on him.

He'd heard one of the Brand sisters had made it big as a model. No wonder her looks had taken his breath away like that. This had to be the one. She was tall, had legs up to her neck, and that kind of confident walk—or at least she had until she'd lost her footing in the road. "Edie, right?" he asked, recalling the model's name.

"No. I'm Kara."

They stepped up onto the sidewalk, and as they did he turned to look at her. "*Kara?*" No way, he thought as the name wormed its way into the crevices of his mind and wrenched open the pathways to musty old memories. Kara Brand. The name brought to mind a skinny girl who was taller than everyone and tended to slouch. The girl who kept her eyes downcast and shuffled her feet when she walked. The girl who used to let her untrimmed hair fall into a thick mass of nondescript brown that always looked messy. Who always seemed to be in a terrible hurry and was constantly tripping, falling, colliding with innocent bystanders. Who had, up until the tenth grade, worn thick tortoiseshell glasses so big he'd wondered if she meant to hide behind them. And her clothes had always been big, too. She had been a walking disaster. Klutzy Kara. No grace, confidence, social skill or self-esteem.

No way was this beautiful creature the shy and awkward wallflower he remembered from Big Falls High.

"Kara Brand?" he repeated.

"You probably wouldn't remember me." She smoothed her blouse. It was silky and wine-colored and brought out the vivid green of her eyes. "I was a year behind you in high school, but I—"

"I remember you. I just... don't remember you like *this*." He let his gaze slide down to her feet and up again, but then smacked himself upside the head with an unspoken *Knock it off, caveman.*

She almost looked as if she wished he didn't remember her at all. But there were other memories crowding into his mind now. Memories that made the gears in his brain start grinding and his pulse race a little faster. As he recalled, Kara Brand had been known as something of a pushover, mostly because she'd had the biggest, softest heart in the entire high school. He wondered if that had changed as drastically as the rest of her had. If not, then she was a real possibility.

He handed her the soft sided briefcase she'd dropped in the street. Several papers were sticking out the top. A couple of them fluttered to the sidewalk. He bent down to pick one up, taking a look at it as he did because he needed to look at something besides her. Man, he could barely take his eyes off her. The transformation was astounding.

"Brand-Name Day Care? That's cute." He handed it to her. "Sorry. I wasn't trying to snoop."

"It's okay."

God, she seemed uneasy. The cop in him wondered why. "So where is this day-care center of yours?"

"It's, um... nowhere. Not yet. I just applied for a loan to get started."

"You have a place in mind?"

She licked her lips, averted her eyes and shook her head. "What brings you back to town, Jimmy?"

"Wanted to show my boy where I grew up."

"Your... you have a son?"

He nodded. "You want to meet him?"

Her smile was quick and bright and her nervousness had vanished. "I'd *love* to meet him," she said. And she meant it, he could tell.

He took her arm gently, turning her toward his pickup truck parked by the curb. Tyler sat in the passenger side with his window rolled down, waving at them as they came closer. Colby stood outside the truck, leaning against the door and talking to Ty through the rolled-down window.

Jim walked up to the truck, met Colby's speculative glance and sent him a quelling one in return. Colby stepped aside to give the space to Jim and Kara. "Tyler, I'd like you to meet Kara Brand. She and I went to high school together. Kara, this is my son, Tyler."

"Hi!" Tyler said. He gave Kara a thorough looking over, from her toes to her head. "Can you make cookies?"

Colby tried to smother a chortle and failed. Then he stuck out a hand. "Colby Benton," he said. "Just along for the heck of it."

"Good to meet you, Colby."

Jim watched Kara's face as she turned her attention back to his son and then he got stuck there. The former tension, that frown of unease, was completely gone. She was relaxed now, open, and her smile was so sweet it melted his bones.

"Not only do I make cookies, I make the best cookies this side of heaven."

"Really?"

"Uh-huh. The only person in town who can make them better is my mom."

"Chocolate-chip?" Tyler asked.

"They're my specialty. If you're going to be in town long enough, I'll make a batch just for you."

"That would be great," Tyler said, his eyes wide. "Do you have a pony?"

"No. Why?"

Tyler pursed his lips in thought, then lifted his gaze to hers again. "Well, how 'bout a dog?"

"I don't have a dog of my own, but my sister has one. And it's as big as a pony, come to think of it."

Tyler grinned. He was leaning out the pickup window, and Kara bent closer to him. "Do *you* have a dog or a pony?" she asked.

"Not yet. That was cool the way my dad saved you, wasn't it?"

"It *was* cool," she agreed. She straightened away from the truck and turned to Jim again. "I didn't even thank you for that."

"Don't. It wasn't a big deal."

"No big deal," Tyler repeated. "My dad saves people all the time."

"Oh, does he now?" Kara's eyes sparkled with amusement. Amazing how relaxed and at ease she became as soon as she turned her focus to his son, Jim thought again.

Tyler nodded. "Uh-huh. He's a p'liceman. So's Uncle Colby."

Kara tipped her head to one side and looked at Jim as if seeing him for the first time. "Jimmy Corona, a cop? It fits."

"You think so?" he asked, and when she nodded he asked, "Why?"

She shrugged and a hint of nervousness returned to those huge eyes. She'd done something to her hair, something that made him want to touch it to see if it was as soft and thick as it looked. It was shiny and the curls bounced when she moved.

"So, um... where are you staying while you're in town?" she asked, not meeting his eyes.

"Boarding house. We checked in this morning."

"Mama would skin me if I didn't invite you to dinner," Kara said. "She and your father went way back, you know. Always stayed in touch, even after he moved away. I heard he'd passed. I'm sorry."

"He had a good life. I still miss him, though." Jim glanced at his son, wishing his father had lived to see his grandchild. Then he brushed that thought away. "To tell you the truth, it would be good to see Vidalia and catch up with the gang." The memories were flooding back now. The Brand girls, five of them as he recalled, all of them raised by a single mother. "How are your sisters doing?"

"Great. Edie quit modeling, came home and married Wade Armstrong. You remember him? He was a few years ahead of us in school. He owns a garage here in town and another over in Tucker Lake. They bought the big place out on the Falls Road. She opened a photography studio there."

"How about the others? I don't remember all the names, but"

"Half the time I don't remember all the names," she joked. "There's Melusine. She's married, to a private detective name of Alexander Stone, from the city. She's his partner now. They're in and out of town all the time, depending on what they're working on. Maya, she married Caleb Montgomery."

"The senator's son?"

She nodded. "They built a place up behind Mom's. Have three-year-old twins, a boy and a girl. Caleb has a law office just around the comer." She pointed as she spoke. The wind came careening around a corner, dry and cool with a wintry nip to it that didn't even resemble the bite of December in Chicago. It played with her hair, though, and pinkened her cheeks.

"Your mom used to own a bar, didn't she?"

"She prefers 'saloon,' and yes, the Ok Corral is still up and running, with a little help from the rest of us. Selene and I still live at the house with Mom."

"Wow. Unbelievable how things change. Mel settled down. Maya with twins." He shook his head.

"Dad, you said we could see the waterfall!"

Jim let his son tug his gaze away. "We're going, we're going."

"Go on," Kara said. "Dinner's around six, if that's not too early."

"It's just right," he said.

"You're welcome, too, of course," she added to Colby. "Any friend of Jimmy's... "

"Thanks. That's real sweet of you."

She nodded. "So, um, should I tell Mom to set four extra places at the table? Maybe five?"

Jim frowned, and she just looked at him with those big eyes, waiting. And he realized she was asking if he—or Colby—would be bringing a wife along. "Three, Kara. Only three."

"Oh," she said. "I thought maybe your wife..."

"I'm—we lost her four years ago."

He could have kicked himself for blurting it in a way that made it sound as if Angela had died, and he knew from the daggers he was hurling with his eyes that Colby wanted to kick him for it, as well. He was damned if he knew why he'd said it that way. Except that he'd be ashamed to admit to Kara Brand and her family—a family he remembered as being as wholesome as whole milk, if a little scandalous from time to time—that his ex-wife was a drug-addicted prostitute.

"I'm sorry," she said for the second time in their five-minute conversation. But this time she put a hand on his arm, and he thought the sadness in her eyes was genuine. Especially when she glanced again at his son.

"It's okay. It's...okay."

He was a slug. Now he had her feeling sorry for them when, in fact, Angela's absence was a blessing. He needed to change the subject. "So we'll see you at six then."

"Great. You remember where to find us?"

"I remember," he said.

"Till dinner, then. Nice meeting you, Colby." She turned to the truck again. "Bye, Tyler."

He held up his arms. Smiling, Kara leaned down and accepted the hug his little boy offered. Jim was close enough to see her notice the braces on Tyler's legs. He saw her frown at them and then hug Ty a little tighter.

"Bye, Kara."

She straightened, sent Jim a parting smile, then turned and started down the sidewalk. Jim leaned back against the passenger door of the pickup and watched her go. Damn. Who'd have believed little Kara Brand would turn out like that?

She hadn't gone ten steps when Tyler spoke in a very loud, slightly squeaky voice. "She's pretty, Dad. And she smells good and she can make cookies. She doesn't have a pony, but...well, that's okay. Can she be my new mom?"

He knew Kara had overhead because she tripped, careened sideways and just barely caught herself on the side of someone's car. Her touch set off a noisy car alarm. She straightened, smoothed her pants and never looked back as she walked the rest of the way to her car.

"Not that one, Jim," Colby said softly, in a voice not meant to carry to Ty. "Not that one, okay? She's too nice."

Jim shook his head. "No such thing as too nice."

"Come on, Jim, you can't. I got a bad feeling about this."

Jim shrugged, clapped a hand on his friend's shoulder. "We should bring something to dinner. It's good manners."

～

"WHAT HAPPENED?" SELENE asked the second Kara sank onto a bar stool at the OK Corral.

Kara looked down at herself in search of any evidence of the shock she'd just had. "What do you mean?" she asked. "What makes you think something happened?"

"I don't think it, I know it. Something big, too. Your aura's practically shooting off sparks. Did the bank turn you down?"

"Give the girl a chance to breathe, for heaven's sake," Vidalia said. But her eyes were raking Kara as if she saw something too.

"Could I have a drink?" Kara asked.

Vi blinked and shot a look at Selene, who only smiled knowingly as she grabbed a peach wine cooler, the strongest thing Kara ever drank, twisted off the cap and set it on a coaster in front of her.

"It's not even noon yet." Vidalia muttered. "And you never drink. What's going on? If that banker thinks she can brush you off and—"

"The banker was fine. Mom. I won't have an answer until the end of the day or so, but she thinks my application will be approved without a problem."

"Then what's going on?"

Kara sighed and took a big gulp from the bottle. The bar was empty. They didn't open for business until seven on weeknights. She loved the Corral when it was empty like this. It was such a wide, big space, with as much wood as a small forest. Polished red oak floors. Gleaming mahogany bar. Door made from a single slab of redwood. The round tables and ladder-back chairs were tiger maple, and the trim around the ceiling and windows was pine. She loved the blending of the woods, the colors, the scents, the giant wagon-wheel light fixtures hanging from the peaked ceiling. Green garland was draped from the barn beams that crossed it, the tablecloths were white with red poinsettias, and holiday music wafted non-stop from Thanksgiving to New Year's, when they were open.

Setting the bottle down on a coaster, Kara kept her gaze on it and said, "Jimmy Corona's back in town."

"Uh-oh," Vi said. "Does he know you're planning to buy his father's house?"

"No."

"You think he might intend to get the place back himself, child?"

Kara shook her head. "I don't think so. He said he came to show his son where he grew up. I didn't get the feeling he was planning to stay."

"He has a son?" Selene asked. "Damn, that implies a wife, huh?"

"No. No, he's alone. Just him and his son. The boy's adorable. I just wanted to hug the stuffing out of him."

"You'd best tell the man what your plans are, Kara," Vidalia said. "It's best to be up front with people right from the start. Don't go behind his back the way your sister Edie did with Wade. Why, they started out so far off track I'm surprised they got back on." She frowned at her daughter. "You look all out of sorts, girl. What did that man say to you?"

"Nothing. It's just..." Kara heaved a sigh. "I just caught a glimpse of him and it was like everything Edie taught me evaporated. I was tripping over my feet and babbling like an idiot and blushing." She rolled her eyes and took another sip of the wine cooler.

Vidalia looked at Selene, her eyebrows raised. Selene said, "You had a little crush on him in high school, didn't you?"

"*God*, no." It was a lie and she thought her sister probably knew it. "He was way out of my league. Most popular guy in school, don't you remember? Star quarterback, top scorer on the basketball team. Such an athletic guy, nothing but strength and grace. I always felt even clumsier than usual around him."

"But you're not clumsy, Kara."

Kara pressed her lips tight. "Not until I get nervous. Then I'm a walking insurance claim."

"So he makes you nervous. Why do you think that is?"

"Don't start with the pseudo-psychology, Selene." Kara took another drink from her bottle.

"Well, is he still good-looking?" her meddling sister asked with a twinkle in her eye.

"Better than ever," Kara whispered, then she bit her lip and wondered why she hadn't censored herself.

"What's he do for a living?"

"He's a cop." She got all tight in the pit of her belly when she said it. Why did knowing he was a police officer make him even more attractive to her? "I'm not sure where."

"Chicago," Vidalia said. "At least that's where he was the last time I spoke to his father, God rest his soul."

Might as well have been the moon, as far as Kara was concerned. "I invited him to dinner tonight. He's got a friend along, another cop named Colby... something. Seems like a nice enough guy."

"Good girl," Vidalia said. "And dinner will be as good a time as any to tell him your plans for his house." Then she sighed. "It'll be nice to see that boy again."

He was hardly a boy, Kara thought. He was all man. And she was probably going to spill something on him or dump soup into his lap at dinner.

❧

THE BOARDING HOUSE was not ideal for Tyler. The rooms were all upstairs, and Tyler detested being carried. But with the braces and the crutches, doing it himself was as risky as it was frustrating and time-consuming.

He convinced Ty that piggyback rides up and down the stairs were a lot of fun, but after the third trip the novelty of that wore off fast. Poor kid.

Clever kid, too.

He'd just about melted Kara Brand's heart with that hug he'd doled out this morning. And Jim knew his son too well to think it hadn't been deliberate.

Colby sat beside him. Tyler was having a snack and watching TV, and the two adults were out of his earshot, on the far side of the living area of their three-room suite at the only boarding house in town.

Jim had been avoiding Colby's questions all afternoon, but he knew he'd run out of time. Colby was his best friend and he knew him far too well.

"So what's the story on this Kara Brand?" he asked.

Jim sighed and knew there was no getting around it. "I've been thinking about that all day. Hell, Colby, you wouldn't believe how much she's changed. At least on the surface. Wait, I'll show you." He went to the bedroom he would be sharing with Ty and got the old high school yearbook he'd brought along, flipped it open to the page that showed Kara Brand and brought it back to shove it into Colby's hands.

Colby looked at the awkward-looking skinny girl in the photo. "No way is that the same girl."

"It is," Jim assured him. "I just hope the changes are only skin-deep."

"Why's that?"

He sighed as he sank into his seat, took the yearbook back and looked down at the ugly duckling who'd grown into a swan. "Because she had a heart as soft as a chocolate bar in the sun."

"Did she?"

Jim nodded, his eyes on the face in the photo, seeing now things he'd missed as a shallow high school jock. The Audrey Hepburn cheekbones, the delicate jaw and perfect nose. The wide set of her eyes and their exotic shape, thick lashes. So much natural beauty, but she'd kept it to herself.

"Whatever kid was having the worst time of it, that would be the one you'd see at her side. She'd latch onto them and protect them like a mother hen. Foster kids moving in and out of our district. Kids whose parents were going through a divorce. Kids so poor they came to school in secondhand clothes that didn't quite fit. Kids with disabilities."

"The outcasts," Colby observed with a nod.

"Yeah. She had this tendency to... I don't know... take care of people."

"I know the type. Rarely meet one, though."

"Yeah." Jim smiled, remembering. "She even tried to take care of me once."

"Since when were you an outcast?" Colby asked.

"Just once. Just once. Championship basketball game, tie score, seconds left on the clock. I had the ball and a choice to make—pass it to the benchwarmer who was wide open right under the basket or take a hot-dog shot from half court."

"What did you do?"

"I took the shot. Missed it. Blew the game." He lowered his head, shaking it slowly. "No one spoke to me after that game. The kids who usually flocked around me like groupies scattered. Teammates took off, cheerleaders. Even the coach. When I came out of the locker room, there was no one there. No one but Kara, who managed to overcome her shyness—no small feat —and come up to me and tell me nobody could be perfect all the time."

"That was sweet of her. 'Course, you already knew that."

"Yeah. What I didn't know was that the kid, the benchwarmer—damn, I wish I could remember his name—he was one of her causes. Poor kid, no confidence, no friends. Coach only put him in the game because the other three replacements had fouled out. Anyway, Kara told me he was standing there under that basket while the clock ticked down, praying I wouldn't pass to him."

"No kidding?" Colby asked.

"No kidding. She said he was scared to death. That if he'd taken that shot and missed, he'd have never lived it down. But because I did it, it would be forgiven and forgotten within a few days."

"Was she right?"

He nodded. "Yeah. I was back to being the most popular guy in school within a couple of days. And Kara faded back into the woodwork."

"So my gut feeling was right," Colby said. "She's too nice for you to play the way you're thinking of playing her."

"Playing her, hell. If she's the same girl she was back then, I'm not gonna play her at all. I'm gonna marry her."

CHAPTER THREE

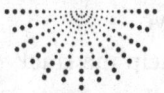

"YOU KNOW I'D do anything for you, Vinnie." Angela stood looking down at him, the man who was going to change her life, make it perfect. For so long she'd thought nothing ever could.

He sat in a leather chair in his office, wearing an expensive suit, the jacket unbuttoned. "So you say," he told her. "I don't believe anything without proof."

Sighing, she pushed her hair behind her ears, hiked up her short skirt, dropped to her knees in front of him.

"That's not what I meant, Angela," he said. "Just listen."

She sat back on her heels and listened.

"I told you what I needed you to do. I told you Corona's testimony could destroy me. But you didn't convince him to back down, did you?"

"Vinnie, I tried. I swear, I tried. He just wouldn't listen. I went back this morning, but his neighbor said he's left town."

"Then you're gonna figure out where he is," he told her. "You're gonna prove your loyalty to me, because I won't marry a woman who's disloyal. You understand?"

Lifting her gaze to his eyes, she nodded. He'd promised her so much. A good life. A big fancy house. Cars. Clothes. Money.

He reached into his pocket and pulled out a small plastic bag full of white powder. Angela reached for it, but he snatched it away.

"You'll do anything for me?"

"You know I will. I have."

"Then you're gonna help me track down this ex-husband of yours. And then you get all you want. Okay?"

"Okay, Vinnie. Okay."

IT BROKE KARA'S heart when she saw little Tyler making his way across the front porch with metal braces on both his legs, leaning on odd-looking crutches that snapped around his arms for support. He paused as she watched his approach, admiring the Christmas lights she and her sisters and brothers in law had strung from every possible part of the house. They lined the roof, following the peak up and down again. They bordered every window and door. And more trimmed the pine trees along the edge of the driveway. Their house looked like the North Pole. Christmas was huge in their family.

She felt a hand on her shoulder and turned to see Maya standing beside her, looking at her. "Ohhh, look at him. He's gorgeous."

"Yeah," Edie agreed, shouldering up to the kitchen window. "And his kid's cute, too."

Maya tried to scowl at her but wound up laughing. Then Vi shot the three of them a quelling look and opened the front door.

"Welcome, gentlemen," she said.

"Mrs. Brand," Jimmy said. "It's great to see you again."

34

"Don't you 'Mrs. Brand' me, boy. It's Vidalia. Now get in here and greet me like you mean it."

Grinning, Jimmy stepped inside and wrapped Vi in a bear hug.

Edie elbowed Kara. "Look at this. The woman's shameless."

"You blame her?" Maya asked.

A throat cleared, and Kara looked up to see that Colby had come in behind Jimmy and Tyler. Caleb and Wade, stood nearby, and each had a twin on his hip.

"Vidalia Brand, meet my good friend, Colby Benton," Jimmy said.

Vidalia took Colby's hand in a fervent grip. "Any friend of Jimmy's is welcome here."

"Thank you, Mrs. Brand. It's a pleasure."

"Please—Vidalia." She released his hand, then bent down to eye level with the little boy. "And you must be Tyler. Hello, there, young man. You can call me Gramma Vi, if that's okay with your dad."

Tyler tipped his head to one side. "Kara says you make good cookies."

"Cookies, cakes, pies, doughnuts—oh, you don't even know the half of it. You come on in here and I'll see if I can't find you a sample, all right?"

"Okay." He made his way through the kitchen, followed by the twins, who'd scrambled down and were following him closely.

"Tyler," Kara said, peeling herself away from her sisters. "This is Dahlia. And this is Cal."

The three-year-olds smiled shyly, Dahlia reaching out a hand to touch one of Tyler's crutches. "What's that for?"

"My legs are messed up. I need these to help me walk."

"Do they hurt?" Cal asked.

"Not much. And I'm gonna get better, anyway, pretty soon."

Vi nodded to Kara. "Introduce our guests to everyone,

daughter, while I get these kids set up with a pre-dinner cookie."

"Mom... " Maya began.

"Oh, don't start with me now. One cookie won't spoil their dinner. Good land, I raised five of you without losing a single one to malnutrition."

Maya bit her lip, closed her eyes, shook her head.

Kara saw Jimmy send her a sympathetic look. Then he offered a hand. "Hi, Maya."

"Good to see you again, Jim. This is my husband, Caleb."

"Jim." Caleb shook his hand.

Kara kicked in then to complete the introductions. "Wade Armstrong," she said, nodding toward Wade. Jimmy shook his hand. "And I know you remember Edie."

He smiled at Edie but spoke to Kara. "And how do you know that?"

"You thought I was Edie when you first saw me today."

"That's because I'd heard Edie Brand had become a supermodel."

"Model, yes. Super, never," Edie said. "So you took one look at my gorgeous little sister and thought she must be the one making a living as a model."

"Edie, don't—" Kara began.

Jimmy held up a hand. "No, she's right. That's exactly what I thought. I hardly recognized you, Kara."

She shrugged. "Thank Edie for that. Giving me makeovers is her favorite hobby."

"Thank your mother, Kara. I think it's got more to do with genetics than cosmetics." His eyes were on her as he said it and they were warm enough to raise her body temperature.

Selene popped into the room then. She'd been upstairs in her room, and Kara had noticed interesting aromas coming out of there for the past hour, while she'd been in her own room trying on everything she owned. She came in slowly, a tiny red drawstring pouch in her hand. "Sorry I'm late," she said.

"That's okay," Jimmy replied. "You have to be Selene. I think you were twelve or thirteen when I last saw you, but that blond hair is a dead giveaway."

"Hi, Jimmy. Long time, no see. I have something for you." She held out the little pouch.

He took it, frowning. "And this is...?"

"It's for protection."

Kara saw Jimmy's face change instantly. His brows drew together and his eyes narrowed. A quick look passed between him and Colby. "What makes you think I need protection?"

"Am I wrong?"

He watched her for a long moment, saying nothing. Selene just shrugged. "Keep it close to you. Better yet, close to your boy."

"You think Ty needs protection?"

Kara put a hand on his arm, drawing his gaze. "Selene... sometimes gets feelings about things."

"And she's usually right," Edie put in.

Jim shot a look at Caleb, then at Wade. They only nodded in agreement. "If she says you need protection, you probably better buy a guard dog."

"Speaking of dogs," Edie said, "anyone seen Sally?"

At the sound of her name Sally gave a loud woof, from the living room. The entire bunch of them trooped through the house into the living room, where the three children surrounded the dog, stroking her, feeding her bites of their cookies under the giant, Christmas tree with its flashing lights and glittering ornaments. The Great Dane, her tail wagging so hard that getting too close seemed risky, actually seemed to be smiling.

Tyler turned toward his father, his eyes wide. "Kara was right, Dad. This dog *is* as big as a pony!"

~

DINNER WAS TOO delicious and too plentiful to make moderation even possible. Jim only stopped on his third helping because his stomach would have exploded if he'd eaten any more.

It had been a pleasant evening. Tyler wore himself out playing with the other two kids and the Godzilla-size dog and then he ate more than Jim thought he'd ever seen him eat. He'd taken to calling Vidalia "Gramma Vi," so Jim figured those cookies of hers had passed muster. And if he didn't know for sure, he supposed he would find out, because she'd packed piles of them into a gallon sized zipper bag to go with him back to the boarding house.

After dinner he offered to help clear up, but Vi shooed him away. She and Selene handled cleanup. Maya and Caleb took the twins home, and Edie and Wade walked them to their house, on the hill behind this one so that Wade could listen to the noise Maya's car had been making. Colby had gone up with them to help walk off the dinner, he said. They said they'd stop on the way back out to pick up their monster-size pet.

Tyler curled up on the floor with his head pillowed by the big dog. Jim took a seat on the sofa, and Kara brought in coffee, a cup for each of them, then took a seat in a nearby chair.

"He had fun," she said.

"More fun than he's had in ages." He watched as his little boy's eyes fell closed. "And he didn't complain once."

Kara's heart twisted a little. "Is he in pain, Jimmy?"

"No, not usually. The braces chafe sometimes, and physical therapy is hell. One more surgery, though, and he'll be... well, if it goes the way it should."

Sally turned her head to watch over him, seemed almost protective of the child. "Look how much she loves him already,"

Kara said. "Jimmy, if it's rude of me to ask, say so. But, what happened to him?"

He sighed. "It was an accident. He fell down two flights of stairs when he was barely a month old."

"Dear God."

He understood the reaction. It twisted him into knots to think about it even after all this time. New subject. And a one he'd been thinking about all day. "Kara, have you been by my dad's house lately?" he asked.

She looked suddenly guilty, as if she had something to hide. Which was odd, because he couldn't think of a reason for it. "Yes, lots of times. Why?"

"Well, the stairs at the boarding house just aren't cutting it. We might be out here as long as three weeks, maybe longer."

She smiled suddenly. "You'll be here for Christmas?"

"Yeah, looks like." Her face lit up as brightly as the twinkling pine tree in the corner of the living room. "If that real-estate company I sold the place to, hasn't resold it yet and it's still habitable, I was thinking…"

"You and Ty and Colby could stay out there while you're here."

"Yeah."

She licked her lips. "You know, it's actually a great idea. There's a ground-floor bedroom and bath. He wouldn't have all those stairs to deal with. And it's a lot roomier there. I mean the boarding house is fine, but not for a whole month. And it's in pretty good shape, too. Betty Lou—your real-estate lady—has been renting it out to defray upkeep and taxes while waiting for a buyer. It's vacant at the moment, though. The furnace and central air unit have just been cleaned and checked over. Power's turned on. It has a great well and a brand-new pump."

He stared at her for a long moment. "You know an awful lot about it."

"Yeah. Well. That's because I'm buying it."

He was surprised.

She kept lowering her eyes, as if she felt guilty. "I mean, if it's all right with you, I am. The bank called tonight and the loan was approved. I should have told you that was the place I had in mind for my day-care center this morning, but I was just so stunned to see you back in town on the very day I was applying for the loan to buy your childhood home."

Again only a quick peek upward. He wanted to ease her mind. "I love the idea of a day-care center in that old house. I think Dad would have, too."

"There are lots of other places I could—"

"No. No way."

She lifted her head. "I don't need to start work right away, though. I think it would be good for Tyler to spend some time in the house where you grew up. And maybe... good for you, too. You know, before any drastic changes are made."

He shrugged. "I refuse to cause you to delay your plans."

"And I refuse to have Tyler dealing with the stairs in the boarding house when there's a perfectly good place sitting empty." She shuddered and rubbed her arms. "God, the very thought of him on stairs at all, given what happened... "

He wasn't sure, but he thought that her eyes got damp. "Maybe we could make some kind of deal, then?" he suggested.

She met his gaze, blinked that dampness away. "Such as?"

"I've got nothing to do for the next few weeks. Let me repay you by getting started on the work you need done on the place."

Tipping her head sideways, she blinked those big green eyes at him. Damn, she was something. "You're on vacation."

"Not by choice," he said.

"What does that mean?"

He waved a hand. "Doesn't matter. You'd be doing me a favor, Kara. I'll go stir-crazy before long."

She nodded slowly. "Okay, it's a deal. I'm supposed to meet

Betty Lou out there at ten tomorrow morning. Why don't you guys be there, too? We'll check it out together."

He nodded. "We'll be there. Thanks, Kara."

She hadn't changed a bit, he decided. She'd give the shirt off her back to the first person she met who needed it.

"Bring your gear," she told him. "You might as well move right in."

He wondered if Kara Brand ever did anything for herself. Was she as kind and giving as she seemed? As she had always been in the past? Time, he decided, would tell.

BETTY LOU JENNINGS was smiling when Kara walked up the sidewalk toward where she waited near the front door. The house was a large double-decker square with a roof. Nothing fancy. Not built in any particular style. It was white, with the front door smack center of its face between two bay windows, and its back door on the far right side in the rear. The place was backed by aspen trees, their leaves golden in the winter sun. No snow on the ground, of course. They didn't get much snow in Oklahoma as a rule, but Big Falls got more than most other places in the state. There had been a frost last night, though, and Kara could see her breath making little puffs in the air. At least the wind wasn't blowing this morning.

The round little woman held up a key ring with two keys and shook it to make it jingle. "I'm so pleased the bank approved your loan, Kara. All we have to do is sign the papers and this place is yours."

Betty Lou must adore the Brands, Kara thought. She'd sold the most expensive house in town a little more than a year ago to Edie. And now she was unloading what was probably its polar opposite on Edie's little sister. Betty Lou had bought the place from Jimmy Corona, through lawyers, after his father left it to him five years ago, and had been holding it and probably losing money on it ever since.

Kara turned at the sound of another vehicle. Jimmy Corona's white pickup truck pulled in. It was a Durango, tough-looking and big. Reminded her of a feisty white horse in some odd, obscure way. Something about the shape of its hood. Or maybe it only did because it had come galloping into town bearing a handsome hero.

He got out, smooth and easy, walked around to the passenger side and opened the door to lift Tyler down to the ground, then he handed the boy his crutches. A second later a red SUV pulled in behind him, and Colby Benton got out.

Tyler made his way over the smooth path to the door, his jacket making the crutches even more awkward than usual, Kara thought. His dad and Colby came along behind him. When Jim met Kara's eyes, his were warm, and he was smiling, and she had to remind herself he exuded that natural charm with everyone he met, not just with her.

"Mr. Corona!" Betty Lou shot worried looks from Jimmy to Kara and back again. "Oh, my, I hope this isn't going to be a problem."

"It's not," Jimmy told her. "Relax, Betty Lou. Kara and I have it all worked out Depending on what kind of shape the place is in, of course."

"This is it?" Tyler asked, looking at the place doubtfully.

"Yep," Jimmy said. "Hey, it doesn't look like much now, but—"

"Heck, it looks like heaven to me after being cooped up in the boarding house," Colby put in. "And with a fresh coat of paint—"

"And some Christmas decorations," Tyler said loudly.

"You've got that right, Tyler," Kara said. Then to Jimmy, "The inside's not bad at all. Betty Lou's kept it in great shape."

"That's right," Betty Lou said. "It's fully furnished. The last couple who rented it only moved out a month ago. And everything from the sofa to the carpeting has been cleaned. Heat and power are still on. You know letting a place get damp can cost you." As she spoke, she led the way up the two concrete steps to the front door.

"I think it needs a porch," Kara said. "A nice big front porch. Don't you think so, Tyler?"

Tyler looked up at her, frowning as if deep in thought. "If it had a porch, you could put a swing on it. And the dog could lay there sometimes. That would be good."

"But I don't have a dog, Tyler."

He tipped his head to one side. "But now that you have your own house, you'll prob'ly get one, won't you?"

She couldn't help but smile and she forgot to worry about tripping as she walked up the two steps with Tyler at her side. "You know, I might just do that." She kept one hand close to him but not touching. She didn't want to make him feel as if she were hovering, but she did want to be ready to help him should he stumble.

Jim stood behind them. "Ty, before we go in, come with me, huh? I want to show you the backyard."

Tyler turned. Kara glanced at the uneven ground the boy would have to walk over and frowned a little, wondering if it would be too much for him. "I'll come, too. Betty Lou, go ahead and unlock the place. You can leave the keys and the paperwork in the kitchen. Okay?"

"Well, sure, hon." Betty Lou tipped her head to one side. "I have two sets of keys. I take it you'll be needing them both?"

Kara pursed her lips. Betty Lou was fishing for information, wondering what was going on between her and the former high school hunk. "Well, it's that or keep a set for yourself, and you won't be needing them," Kara said with a smile. "When you go in, would you unlock the back door for us?"

Colby said, "I'll get our gear inside."

43

Kara nodded her thanks, then joined Tyler and Jimmy, and the three of them started around the house.

Jim mypaused, and Kara saw him notice that his son was having trouble negotiating the lawn on those crutches. He hunkered down. "How about a piggyback ride?"

"I can do it, Dad." Tyler seemed a little miffed at his dad for offering to help him. He continued moving over the grass, but it was clearly an effort. His little face was getting red.

"At least let me hold on to your arm, Ty."

"No, Dad." The boy sounded impatient now.

Kara moved a few steps ahead of him and then she deliberately tripped in a hole and fell.

"Kara!" Jimmy was beside her in an instant, leaning over her, his face full of concern. "You okay?"

"I don't know. I hurt my ankle. Darn." She looked up at him, and with her face hidden from Tyler's, she winked. "Maybe I'm the one who needs to hold someone's hand out here, before I really get hurt."

She let Jimmy help her to her feet. Then she turned to Tyler. "Would it be okay if I held on to you, Ty?"

Tyler smiled. Dimples appeared in his cheeks and his eyes twinkled. "Sure. But maybe you better hold my dad's hand, too. I'm not for sure if I could catch you all by myself if you fall again."

She reached down and closed a hand around his upper arm. "Thank you, Tyler. You're a real hero."

Her gaze was tugged away from the boy's, though, when she felt Jimmy take her free hand. He met her eyes, and there was something tender in his. He squeezed her hand, gave her a nearly imperceptible nod of thanks. She smiled, and together they moved across the back lawn.

"See that big apple tree right there, Ty?" he asked his son.

Tyler nodded.

"That's where I used to have my tire swing. And over there, in that maple, that's where I had my tree house."

"You had a tree house?"

"Mmm-hmm."

"Wow!"

"Come here, there's something else about this tree—let me see if it's still here... yep, there it is," he said, leading his son closer to the tree. He pointed and Tyler looked.

Kara looked, too.

"What's it say, Dad?"

Jimmy traced the heart-shaped carving with a forefinger. "It says J.C. plus question mark."

"Huh?"

"Your dad had so many girlfriends in high school," Kara said, "he probably didn't know whose initials to carve."

"Really?"

Jimmy sent Kara a smirk. And then Tyler said, "You went to school here, too, didn't you Kara? Were *you* ever my dad's girlfriend?"

Jimmy's eyes held hers for a long moment. She looked away first. "No, Tyler, I wasn't."

"How come?"

She smiled down at him. "Did you ever hear the story of the ugly duckling, Ty?"

"No."

"Well, I'm going to tell it to you one of these days and then you'll understand. But in the meantime, why don't we go inside, see how you like the place, okay?"

"Okay!" He turned and started hobbling over the ground again but soon mounted the fieldstone patio that led right up to the back door, so the going was a bit easier for him.

Kara started forward, but Jimmy stopped her with a hand on her arm, and she turned to look up at him, half smiling at Ty

45

and his silly questions. But her smile died when she saw the intensity in his eyes.

"You were never an ugly duckling, Kara Brand."

"Sure I was."

"No. No, I remember. You were shy. Painfully shy. A little unsure of yourself. Hiding behind all the hair your could grow and clothes you could disappear into."

"And too clumsy to make it down the hall without falling or crashing into somebody at least once a day."

He smiled. "I think it was more nervousness than clumsiness."

She shrugged. "Same result." She started to turn away.

He touched her cheek, turned her to face him again. "The only thing you have in common with that duckling from the story is that you grew into a swan."

She lowered her head quickly, heat flooding her face. "Jimmy, you don't have to say that. I know I'm—" She stopped speaking because she'd lifted her eyes to his and found them fixed on her lips. Almost as if he was thinking about kissing her.

Jimmy Corona, thinking about kissing *her*. Had the earth's magnetic poles reversed or what?

Her knees buckled a little and she lost her balance and had to grab on to his shoulders to keep from falling.

His hands closed on her waist and he steadied her. "Yep," he said. "Nervousness."

Then Tyler called to them to hurry up, and Jimmy turned her toward the house, keeping one hand on her arm as they walked onto the patio to join him.

"THIS IS IT, ANGELA. How do you like it?"

Angela tried to keep the tears from welling up in her eyes when she looked around the apartment. It was small, yeah, but it was light years better than the squalor in which she'd been living. It was a nice building in a nice neighborhood, a building her precious Vinnie owned lock, stock and barrel.

"Bedroom's through there," he said, pointing. And she peeked in. There were a bed, a dresser, and one window draped in a white curtain. "Bathroom's off the bedroom. Closet-size. No room for a tub, just a shower. And the kitchen's right here." He pushed open a swinging door and led her through. The fridge and range were half-size, and there was no room for a table, but two stools stood in front of the counter.

She didn't care. She turned to him and blinked through grateful tears. "I can't believe this. I can't believe you're doing this for me. God, Vinnie, I love you so much."

He shrugged. "There are rules, Ang. Don't think I won't throw you back into the gutter where I found you if you can't live with them."

She nodded. He might be known as a porn king, but he was a classy porn king. Wealthy. Well-dressed. "I know the rules," she promised. "This is a clean building."

"That's right. So you keep your dirt out of it. No drugs here, no Johns. And I mean it, Angie, it's important."

She nodded. "I promise." She didn't suppose the gram she'd jammed in the back of the useless watch she'd picked out of the trash and gutted really counted. She wouldn't keep a lot of coke here. Just what she needed for a day at a time.

He nodded toward the bedroom. "I picked you up a few things. They're in the closet."

Blinking in shock, she spun and ran into the bedroom, opened the tiny closet not much bigger than a high school locker and started yanking hangers out of it. Three blouses, three skirts and three jackets. And there were two pairs of new jeans stacked on the dresser nearby.

"Underthings are in the drawer. I'd have done shoes, but I

didn't know your size, so I figure you can buy your own." He tossed a wad of cash onto the bed. "Shoes, Angie. Not drugs."

She flung her arms around his neck and squeezed him hard. "You're like an angel, you know? You're like an angel to me."

"I'm far from an angel. Did you do what I asked?"

She nodded. "I went up the fire escape just like you said. Smacked out the window. No alarm there. I didn't find much in his apartment, though." She yanked her huge shoulder bag from her arm and tipped it upside down on the bed, then began pawing through the contents. "This is all the mail he left out, and the notepad that was next to the phone."

Vinnie reached down, yanked up the stack of mail, flipped through it, then picked up the notepad. "Ah, there's a phone number on here." Yanking his cell phone out of his pocket, he dialed, then sat on the edge of the bed.

Angela sat down beside him, close enough to hear. She heard ringing, then a woman's voice. "Peabody's Boarding House," she said. "Can I help you?"

"Yes, I hope so. My fiance and I have looked at so many places in trying to decide where to honeymoon." Vinnie glanced at Angela and her stomach turned soft as she smiled up at him. "Somehow I jotted down this number, but I neglected to write the location beside it. I know it was one of our favorites, though."

"Well, now, don't fret about it. We're in a little town called Big Falls in the great state of Oklahoma."

"Of course," he said. "Now I remember. Thank you so much."

"You're more than welcome."

He hung up, pocketed the phone and looked at her. "Why would your ex be in Big Falls, Oklahoma?"

"I should have known. It's where he grew up. He used to talk about it all the time, but he never went back before. At least not as far as I know. I always thought he had some unhappy memories from there."

"He may just get some more."

She frowned at him, but Vinnie ran a hand over her hair and sent her a wink. "You know I'm just teasing. You've done good for me, sweetie. You've done real good. And you can do even better."

"How?"

"Come with me to this Big Falls."

"Aw, Vinnie. I don't want Jim to think I'm harassing him. He's gonna get pissed and he's a cop, you know."

"I know. Believe me, I don't want to harass the police either. God knows I don't need to give them any more reasons to railroad me. But you always said Jim was a reasonable man. So maybe if I could just talk to him, reason with him, he'd understand what a terrible mistake is being made here."

She pursed her lips, lowered her head. "I don't know. I don't want...."

"What, Angie?"

"I don't want you to do anything to hurt him. He's... he's all my baby boy has."

"Come on, you know me better than that. There's not a violent bone in my body. I wouldn't hurt a fly. Just come down there with me, huh? Maybe you can help me talk to him. Make him see reason. This is my life on the line here. You know that."

Licking her lips, she nodded. What she really wanted was to settle into her new apartment, try on her new clothes, her new life. But she owed him. She had to help him if she could. "All right, Vinnie. I'll come with you."

CHAPTER FOUR

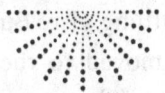

*J*IM WALKED INTO the kitchen and got hit between the eyes with the past. For just a second, he could almost hear his mother's voice.

Jimmy! Come on inside, dinner's ready!

He blinked back the rush of emotion and pressed a hand to the countertop for support

"Jimmy? Are you okay?" Kara asked, her eyes on him rather than on the old-fashioned kitchen.

He looked at her, realized she always called him Jimmy, just the way his mother had. No one else ever called him by his childhood name anymore. He'd missed it

He nodded, then focused on the room again. Tongue-and-groove boards normally reserved for floors had been used as cupboard doors and stained a pale oak hue that went nicely with the yellow walls and tile floor, a checkerboard of yellow and mint-green. "It's almost the same."

Kara nodded as she looked around the kitchen. "I doubt Betty Lou saw much need to change it."

He moved his head from side to side, looking the place over more thoroughly. "No, she did," Jim said. "She changed it a bunch. It's nothing like it was when Dad and I lived here alone. But it's *just* like it was before Mom... "

"I'm sorry. It didn't even occur to me how many painful memories this was going to bring flooding back for you."

He drew a breath as if it could steady him. "This was her color scheme." He said. "Dad couldn't be bothered. She'd been gone five years before he decided to repaint, and when he did, white was as easy as anything else. But Mom, she loved color. This sunny yellow." He moved to the windows, running one hand over the white casing. "She wanted the trim painted mint-green. Like those tiles in the floor. She used to talk about it all the time. If only she could get the casing painted mint-green and maybe find some ceramic knobs for the cupboard doors in that color, too, her life would just be perfect." He smiled at the memory.

"I remember her," Kara said.

"Do you?"

She nodded. "I don't think she and Mama were friends or anything. Different worlds, you know?"

"Yeah. Your mom and my dad only got to be friends after Mom was gone, I imagine, because Dad started spending inordinate amounts of time at the Corral."

She winced a little. He held up a hand. "It wasn't a problem. He was probably self-medicating, but he wasn't a drunk, didn't come home and smack the kid around, nothing like that."

She nodded, seeming relieved. "I remember your mom coming to school sometimes back in our elementary days. She was always so pretty. Always smelled great. Was always bringing things for our bake sales and whatnot and making sure to pack extra so we could sample them." She sighed. "I thought of her as the kind of woman I'd like to grow up to be."

"I think your mom would be disappointed to hear that," he said softly, studying her, touched by her memories of his mother and curious to hear more. To learn how his mom had seemed through the eyes of Kara Brand.

"Oh, don't get me wrong. My mother is the most incredible woman I've ever known. But I never deluded myself into thinking I could be like her. She's tough. Hard as nails, can take anything, get knocked down over and over again and always come back up swinging. Not me." She shook her head. "No, your mom, on the other hand, always seemed... I don't know... a little on the fragile side. Maybe not so strong and sure of herself, and yet somehow she managed to be beautiful and kind and graceful all the same. I think that's what struck me about her most. The way I could see myself in her, only a better version of myself. You know? She was like the me I wished I could someday be."

He studied her for a long moment "You have a way, you know that?"

"Do I?"

He nodded. "You say the most beautiful things. Touching things. Things that move me. I don't think my mother has ever been paid a higher compliment than what you just said."

She lowered her eyes, and her cheeks pinkened. "It's nothing but the truth."

"Yeah? Well, I think you got your wish, Kara. I don't know many women who could compare to my mother in my eyes, but you..."

She shook her head. "Don't Jimmy. I couldn't hold a candle to your mother."

"No, I mean it. You remind me of her. I hadn't even realized how much until this moment. Seeing you here in this kitchen." He shook his head. "It's a little surreal."

"Thank you. You, um... say some pretty nice things yourself."

He nodded and walked around the kitchen, absently opening cupboards and drawers, most of which were empty. "I miss her," he said idly. "I miss her a lot"

"I know. I can't imagine losing my mom even now, much less at the age of ten."

"Eleven," he told her.

"I don't know how an eleven-year-old could handle that. I don't know how you did."

He couldn't quite shake the feeling of *deja vu* that overtook him as he watched her. She was looking around the room now, just as he had, a little frown between her brows. And he was remembering again. Remembering the funeral, when he stood beside his mother's grave. Half the town had turned out. He'd been in sixth grade, just beginning to develop an interest in girls, but the fairer sex had been the farthest thing from his mind that day. He'd been drowning in grief, and wondering how it could possibly be true. How could he and his dad keep waking up every day, going to work and school, coming home and having dinner? How could they, when Mom was gone? He expected the entire world to just suddenly stop, and it would have been fine with him if it had.

And then this little girl had come walking up to the graveside. She'd been a fourth grader. Probably nine or so. And even then she'd been painfully shy, quiet. Somehow, though, she'd overcome that shyness to step forward, to lay her little bundle of wild-flowers, which she'd picked herself, onto his mother's casket. And then she'd come to him and she'd said, "I have a lot of sisters and a mom over there."

He'd followed her gaze to where a crowd of females stood. Some younger than him, some older, with their mother.

"So?" he'd asked.

"So you've only got your dad now. So if you need some extras—more family, you know—you can borrow mine."

He had been angry that day, angry at the world. But not so blinded by it that he didn't recognize the gesture as her way of trying to help him. He'd choked out a thank-you, and she'd run back to her family with tears rolling down her little cheeks.

As the memory faded, Kara turned, caught him staring at her. "That was you, wasn't it?" he asked.

She lifted her brows. "What was me?"

"The little girl at my mother's funeral. With the scraggly bouquet of forget-me-nots and black-eyed Susans and wild chicory. You offered to share your family with me."

She smiled softly and nodded. "That was me. I wanted to do something, but I just didn't know what. I couldn't imagine anything that would help."

"You cried for her," he said.

"No. Mama promised me she was fine, singing with the angels. I cried for you, Jimmy."

He shook his head slowly. "You've probably got the biggest, softest heart around."

"That's the rumor."

He reached out a hand, stroked a strand of hair behind her ear.

She trembled a little, but even as he thought she might lean closer, her eyes grew serious and she stepped away. "Where's Tyler?" she asked.

That snapped him out of his musings in short order. Since when did he get so lost in nostalgia for the past and admiration for a woman that he forgot to watch his son?

Already Kara was hurrying through the house looking for him. He heard her footsteps as she searched the ground floor, so he started up the stairs. Before he got to the top, she was calling to him. "It's okay, Jimmy. He's right here."

A lump came into his throat when he heard where that voice came from. He walked down the stairs and through the house to enter the bedroom that had been his mother's when she'd become too weak to negotiate the stairs.

He'd spent a lot of time with his mother there. Always believing she'd be well again someday. But that day had never come.

Tyler stood there now, near the window. Colby was nearby with Ty's duffel bag full of belongings, which he must have fetched from the car. The look on his face was accusing, and Jim knew he must have overheard at least some of his conversation with Kara Brand.

"Can this be my room, Dad?" Tyler asked.

Jim swallowed hard. "This is just the room I had in mind for you. It was your grandma's room, you know."

"Really?"

Jim nodded, then turned to Kara. "The place is in great shape, Kara. Better than I realized. You have to let us pay you rent for staying here."

"You're not paying me rent to stay in your own house, Jimmy. No way."

"It's not my own—"

"It's always been yours. Always will be, no matter whose name is on the deed."

"But you're paying a mortgage on it."

She shrugged. "I need a fence around the backyard, and that's just for starters. There'll be plenty to do. And..." She glanced down at Tyler. "Look, I just really want you guys to stay here. And to tell you the truth, I think you *need* to stay here. Tyler... he needs to touch his roots, Jimmy. And maybe you do, too. Please don't back out now."

He stared at her, studied her and thought she really meant it. Hell, he half thought she might be right. "Okay," he said. "We'll stay."

"That's great news," Colby said, joining them in the little room. He set the duffel bag on the bed. "I was getting tired of carrying that thing."

Tyler giggled at him, then made his way over to the bag to unzip it and begin unpacking his things all by himself, while Colby looked at Jim the way he'd look at an assassin.

JIM DIDN'T SLEEP that night. Colby had spent an hour after Tyler had gone to sleep, telling him that it was wrong, what he was doing to Kara Brand. That if he intended to go through with it, he wasn't going to be a part of it. He couldn't stand by and watch a woman like her get taken in by a damned con-artist who just wanted a mother for his son. And that yes, Tyler did deserve a woman like Kara. But Jim did not.

It ate away at him. Guilt. But it didn't matter. He'd do anything for his son. And he'd told Colby so.

In the morning he lay in the bed beside Tyler in what had been the last place he'd ever seen his mother alive. The place where he used to bring her hot tea and dry toast when the chemo got to be too much for her. The place where he used to sit for hours reading to her from her favorite books or watching her favorite TV shows or just talking.

God he'd missed that when she'd gone. He'd had his father, and they'd been close, but it just wasn't the same.

As he looked down at his precious little boy sleeping in that bed, he realized he was lucky. At least he'd had a mother for a little while. Hell, eleven years. Better than half his childhood. She'd been there and she'd been great, right up to the end. And the thing that had bothered her most about dying was that she wouldn't be there to keep doing things for him and for his dad.

Poor Tyler. He deserved to know that kind of love. And he wanted it. He wanted it so much.

He thought about that and he thought about Kara. And then he thought, why not? Hell, he'd have to be careful not to let Tyler get too attached until he was sure she was committed. Because there was always a chance she would tell him thanks but no, thanks. But really, why shouldn't he make a try for her? He liked her well enough. If he was going to trust any woman with Tyler, it would be her. She was gorgeous. He was pretty powerfully attracted to her and he had a feeling it was mutual. Those things would help.

And she was the farthest thing from a self-centered party girl that he could imagine. So why not? What did he have to lose?

He pursed his lips, paced through the living room and into the kitchen, thinking it through. There had to be a downside here. A solution this perfect couldn't be without pitfalls.

And as if that realization conjured them to mind, the pitfalls came floating up to make themselves known. He'd lied to Kara Brand. Well, he hadn't lied exactly, but he'd certainly twisted the truth. He'd told her he had lost his wife. But Angela was alive, if not exactly well. He was going to have to come clean about that at some point and hope Kara would forgive him.

And there was a second issue. If she were to sign on as Tyler's new mommy—*as my new wife*, a little voice whispered— she would have to relocate. She'd have to move to Chicago with him.

Jim sighed. He couldn't quite imagine Kara Brand thriving in the city. She was a wildflower, a long-limbed tiger lily, not a hothouse rose.

Hell, he doubted she would consider leaving her family anyway. Maybe, though. Maybe... for Tyler.

The sound of a motor drew his attention away from the subject at hand, and he looked up to see that the sun had risen some time while he'd been mulling, and the object of his thoughts was backing a red pickup truck into the driveway.

He watched her pull out into the road, straighten it and back in again. She cut the engine and got out, then tried to close the door softly. It made him smile as he opened the front door. "Don't worry about that. I'm already awake."

The way she looked at him, her eyes kind of landing on his chest and getting stuck there, reminded him what he was wearing. Jeans. No shirt. And it wasn't warm outside.

She stared at his chest hard enough to burn holes through his skin, then jerked her eyes away almost violently. She held up two big grocery bags. "I, uh, brought some essentials."

"Yeah?"

She nodded. "Can I come in?"

"It's your house." He held the door open and she came inside, started taking items out of the bags. There was a big box with the name of a local bakery on the cover, and he felt his stomach rumble in appreciation. Then a pint of half-and-half, a bag of sugar, a pack of paper filters and a pound of coffee. Finally she pulled out a drip coffeemaker, set it on the counter and plugged it in. "Mom had this one in the back closet. She bought a new one last year." She took the carafe from the burner, filled it with tap water and poured it into the coffeemaker's reservoir. He grabbed a filter, tucked it into the basket and added coffee, then slid it home.

She flicked on the power button.

He leaned back against the counter, crossed his arms over his chest and studied her. She wasn't dressed up today. She wore jeans and T-shirt. She was tall—he liked that. Tall and willowy. She had a denim jacket over the clothes, but it was unbuttoned. Her hair was loose and a little careless. He liked that, too.

"Where's Colby this morning?" she asked.

He frowned. "I assumed he was still sleeping. He took an upstairs bedroom."

"Nope. His car's gone."

Jeeze, he'd been serious last night, hadn't he? "I guess I must have dozed a little after all. I didn't hear him leave."

Kara took a few more items from the second bag—two boxes of cartoon-character cereal, a dozen eggs and a jug of milk. It was as she reached for the fridge that she paused, then yanked a sheet of paper off the door. "Note," she said. She handed it to him and put the milk away.

Jim scanned the paper. "I'm taking some time" was all it said.

Then he frowned. He'd really pissed his partner off, then, hadn't he?

"Maybe he met a pretty girl," Kara said.

"He hasn't had time to meet a pretty girl."

"Then maybe he's looking to meet one." She sent him a smile that somehow eased his mind.

He stopped worrying about Colby and got back to thinking about his plan of action with Kara Brand. "Actually," he said, "maybe he *has* had time to meet a pretty girl. I certainly managed to."

"No fair," she said. "You met me in grade school."

"I suppose that's true." He was glad she hadn't denied being pretty. "So what brings you around so early, Kara?" he asked.

"I didn't wake you, did I?"

"Hell, no. I told you you didn't. I've been up all night"

Instantly the teasing light left her eyes, and a flood of sympathy and concern replaced it. "It's this place, isn't it?" she asked. "I knew it got to you last night. Are you okay? I should have stayed here and let you guys use my room at the house."

He held her gaze and nodded firmly. "You ever worry about yourself the way you worry about everyone else, Kara?"

She seemed to consider the question. "There's no reason to. I have all I need."

"Do you?"

She averted her eyes, cleared her throat and changed the subject. "I've got the supplies for the fence out in the truck. Ordered everything yesterday, and it came in to the lumber yard this morning, so I went to pick it up. I thought I'd sneak in here and get it unloaded without waking you guys."

"Yeah? And what were you going to do with the groceries?"

"My plan was to slip in and leave them in the kitchen for you, along with a freshly brewed pot of coffee." She nodded toward the bag. "There's hot cocoa mix in there for Ty. With mini-marshmallows."

Her eyes met his, then traveled down to his chest again. He saw something in them. Attraction. Maybe a hint of desire. That *was* a good thing, wasn't it? Assuming he meant to go on with this insane notion. Now that he was face-to-face with it, standing at the threshold of it, it seemed a little crazy. And with Colby reacting as strongly as he was, Jim had to at least consider that he was doing the wrong thing here.

He glanced toward the bedroom, but Ty wasn't making a sound. Probably still out cold. He normally slept until at least eight-thirty. So it was safe to play with this thing a little, find out just how deeply her interest in him extended. He could at least do that much, couldn't he?

He moved a little closer to her. She backed up until the table blocked her and looked up at him with eyes so wide he thought he could fall into them.

She was nervous around him, though he couldn't imagine why. He put his hands on her arms, trailed an easy path from her shoulders to her wrists and back again, as he lowered his head a little closer.

She nearly hit him in the chin with the box of doughnuts when she snatched it off the table and lifted it between them. "I think the coffee's done," she blurted. "I'll just... " She shoved the doughnut box into his chest and let it go. He had to either take it from her or let it fall, so he took it and backed off a step. Kara darted out from between him and the table faster than a rabbit slipping from the jaws of a hunting dog, shot to the counter and started pouring coffee into the cups she'd brought along. She left his on the counter, took hers and sailed out the back door.

Jim stood there for a moment. Okay, something definitely went wrong here. He wasn't sure just what, but his approach apparently needed some honing.

He went to put on a shirt, located some shoes and checked on Tyler. Then he carried his coffee outside. Kara had slipped on a pair of calfskin gloves and was taking lumber out of the bed of the pickup and stacking it in the backyard.

"Hey, hey, hold on now. I'm the guy here. Shouldn't I be doing that?"

She glanced up at him. Wary. Skittish. "No such thing as man's work in my family." She shrugged. "Then again, that might be because there were no men. We did it all ourselves."

"Well, you're not doing it yourself today." He set his coffee cup on the stoop and came to the back of the truck, started unloading lumber. As he carried a stack of boards to the pile she'd started, he said, "I'm sorry if I got out of line in there, Kara. I wouldn't want to scare you for the world."

She shot him a look, maybe surprised he was being as direct as he was about what had just happened—or almost happened— inside the house.

"You didn't do anything out of line," she said.

He grabbed another armful of boards, carried them into the backyard, piled them and turned to face her. "Okay, in case you're not clear on this, I was about to kiss you in there. And I think you know it."

"Oh."

"It scared you."

"No, it—"

"You scurried away from me like a startled rabbit."

She shrugged, turning slightly away, apparently unable to look him in the eye. Her cheeks were pink again. "It's just that... I'm not used to... "

"What?" He came closer but not too close. He didn't want to scare her off again. "You're not used to men wanting to kiss you?"

She peeked at him, then lowered her eyes. "No."

"So the men of Big Falls have all been struck blind, have they?"

The color in her cheeks deepened to rose. "I'm not... this isn't... "

"I'm surprised they're not beating down your door, Kara."

She lifted her chin and met his eyes, a hint of boldness appearing in her own, though he thought she'd had to dig deep to find it. "It wouldn't matter if they were. It's not the same."

"Why not?"

She lifted one shoulder just a little, and he saw her throat move as she swallowed. "They're not you. They're not Jimmy Corona."

That took him by surprise. He hadn't been expecting it. And he wasn't entirely sure what it meant. Was being Jimmy Corona good or bad?

She turned and dragged a box of nails from the pickup bed, carried it to the pile of lumber and set it on top. "Take the tools, too," she said over her shoulder. "Should be just about everything you need in there to get started on the fence."

He took the toolbox out, set it in the backyard near the lumber pile and then returned to the truck for the long-handled posthole digger, pick and shovel, as well. "You thought of everything."

She nodded. "Yeah. I want to bring some wallpaper samples over later." She shot him a quick look. "Not for the kitchen. I don't want to change a thing in there. But that family room in the back? The big one? That's going to be the main part of the day-care center and I want it bright and cheerful and full of color. Is there a time when you and Ty wouldn't mind too much?"

"Have dinner with us."

She blinked and shot him a look of surprise.

"I owe you. Payback for dinner at your place. And for letting us stay here. And for... everything."

"I see."

Not enough. Okay then, he thought. A little more. Just not

enough to send her panicking. "Kara, I'd like to spend some time with you."

She lifted her head. And suddenly all her shyness was gone, all her uncertainty, all the color in her cheeks. She was dead serious now and she said, "Don't play with me, Jimmy. I couldn't handle it."

Her words shook him. Gave him the eerie feeling she knew exactly what he was up to with her. Had Colby ratted him out before taking off on him? "I'm not playing."

She studied his face for a long moment. He lifted a hand to cup her cheek and saw her catch her breath. But this time he leaned in before she could chicken out and brushed his lips very gently over hers.

When he lifted his head away she looked scared to death again. He stepped back, wondering how to ease her mind. But before he could think of a thing she said, "I... um... have to go." And she turned to start for the pickup truck, only to trip on the way. She caught herself on the truck, though, to keep from falling down and then yanked open the driver's door and got in. As she pulled away, she leaned out the window.

"Tell Tyler to enjoy the doughnuts. And that I'll see him later."

"Does that mean you're coming to dinner?"

She nodded, waved and pulled away.

Damn. The woman was not going to be an easy sell.

Maybe Colby was right. Maybe he ought to chuck this whole idea.

KARA WAS A basket case by the time she pulled up to the front of Edie and Wade's beautiful home on the hill above the falls. It was early enough that Wade hadn't yet left for work, but too early for Edie to have any customers in the studio. Her work kept her busy. She took plenty of nature shots, sold them to magazines and calendar companies. Did senior pics and family portraits in between. It wasn't the glamourous life she'd once led. But it had what that life hadn't. Happiness. Joy. Love.

Kara hurried along the stone walkway, hit the doorbell and heard Sally barking happily on the other side.

Wade had the dog by the collar when he pulled the door open. He greeted his sister-in-law with a broad, welcoming smile that quickly died as he studied her. "What's wrong?"

"Nothing. Everything."

He slid an arm around her shoulders and led her inside. "No, not everything. Nothing's ever as bad as you think it is, kid." He called toward the stairway, "Edie, Kara's here. We'll be in the sunroom."

"Be right down," Edie called.

Kara followed Wade through the house into the sunroom they'd added last year. It was octagonal, completely glass and had the best view of the falls of any room in the house.

"Sit," Wade said. "I'll get you coffee. Or would tea be better? Have you had breakfast?"

"I don't want anything." She lifted her eyes. "Thanks, though."

He took a seat beside her and studied her face. "So what's wrong? Is everyone okay?"

"Everyone but me."

"I knew it!" Edie all but shouted as she burst into the room.

Kara started so hard she almost came out of the chair, then she saw her sister in the doorway, wearing a beautiful silk kimono, purple with pink lilies.

"It's that man, isn't it? It's Jim Corona."

"What do you mean, you knew it? How could you know it? I didn't even know it. What are you, turning into Selene all of a sudden?"

"You knew what?" Wade asked.

Smiling, Edie came closer and leaned down to plant a kiss on his cheek. "You're so sweet when you're dense." Then she slid into a chair opposite Kara, beside her husband. The table was bamboo, round, surrounded by fan-backed chairs lined with thick floral-print cushions. "Mel and I spoke on the phone last night. She told me what a huge crush you used to have on Jim in high school."

"It wasn't a crush."

"No?"

"More like a case of idol worship. But he never so much as noticed me."

"Sure. That's what Wade thought about me, too. That I'd never so much as noticed him."

Kara blinked up at the handsome bad boy who'd married her sister. "You thought that?" He nodded. "God, she was nuts about you." Then she thinned her lips. "This isn't the same, though. I mean, I don't know what to think. Jimmy... he tried to kiss me."

Wade came out of his chair. "Do I need to take care of this? You want me to go over there, Kara?"

"No. God, no, Wade, he didn't get out of line. He just... sort of... well, it was nothing. It's not like... it's just that I don't understand it."

Edie tipped her head sideways. "You don't understand why a man would want to kiss you?"

"I don't understand why *Jimmy Corona* would want to kiss me."

"Oh. Now I get it," Wade said.

"Well, I don't."

He looked at his wife. "You *were* my Jimmy Corona, hon. You *wouldn't* get it."

"Oh, don't be ridiculous. Jimmy Corona is just a guy. He's in his hometown and he runs into a girl from high school who grew up to be a total knockout. Naturally he's interested. The thing you need to think about, Kara, isn't why he would give

66

you a second glance. You're a hottie now, you gotta just trust me on that. The thing you should be thinking about is, where can this thing go? He's in town for—what?—a couple of weeks?"

"Around three," Kara said.

"So then what? I mean, suppose you fall head over heels for the guy? What happens when he has to leave?"

"Good grief, Edie, you're worrying about long-term relationship decisions already?" Kara cried. "He's only been in town a day. It was one tiny little kiss."

"I thought you said he only *tried* to kiss you."

Kara averted her eyes. "Well, yeah. And then he tried again. And I sort of let him the second time."

"Aha! So you kissed him back."

"I didn't really do anything but stand there with my knees knocking."

Wade grinned and averted his face to try to hide it

"Look, Kara," Edie said. "You have to find out what he has in mind here. A vacation fling? Or...something else?"

"I can't ask him that. It's... it's too soon. I don't even know if it's anything more than... than just what it was. One kiss."

Edie looked at Wade as if for help. He shrugged, but Kara could see his mind working overtime.

"Don't, Wade. Don't do anything," Kara pled.

"What do you mean? What would I do?"

"I don't know, but whatever it is, don't. Just let me bungle my way through this, okay?"

"Okay."

She doubted he meant it. The man had a hero complex, liked to go charging in to save the day when he sensed trouble afoot. Usually she loved him for it, but not today. She pushed away from the table. "I gotta go."

"Remember who you are, Kara," Edie told her. "Remember that you don't have to hurry everywhere you go and that you can to hold your head up and look people in the eye. And don't forget the Perfectly Plum eye shadow. It's your best color."

Kara sighed. "I've got it, Edie. Thank you."

She started for the door and Edie raced after her, gave her a hug and whispered, "Don't give your heart away, Kara. Not until you're sure of him. I don't want to see you get hurt."

"Okay."

"Okay." Edie kissed her on the forehead and Kara headed home.

"HOW MUCH FARTHER, Vinnie?" Angela shifted in her seat, tugging at the dressy skirt that seemed entirely too fitted and snug. She'd taken off the jacket and tossed it over the back of the seat, heeled off the pumps and left them lying on the floor. She was restless. Itching for a hit—just one—but Vinnie wouldn't give her so much as a sniff. He said he wanted her to look respectable when they arrived in Big Falls, Oklahoma.

"You know, if they find out you left the state you could be in big trouble, Vinnie."

"So long as I show up for my trial, they won't do a damn thing."

"They might."

He shrugged. "We won't be gone long, sweetie. We'll get back just as soon as we've convinced your ex-hubby to cooperate, hmm?"

"I know." She looked lovingly at him. "It was so thoughtful of you to bring all those toys and games and things along for my little boy," she said. "I haven't sent him any Christmas presents since I left him."

"So this year you will."

She sighed. "I hope you don't mind so much that I... don't want to see him. I mean, it's not that I don't want to, just that... "

"It's too hard for you. I understand." He patted her thigh. "We can have the stuff shipped or give it to Corona to give to the kid after we're gone."

"I'm so glad you understand."

He nodded. "Lemme see that photo you have in your wallet again."

She opened her wallet, took out the photo of Tyler—the one she'd taken from Jim's apartment. It showed Tyler sitting on a rocking horse, wearing a cowboy hat smiling big. No braces on his legs in that shot. He looked like a normal little boy.

She handed the photo to Vinnie.

He glanced at it. "He's four, you say?"

"Almost five now."

"And he doesn't even know you?"

She pressed her lips tight "It's better that way."

He sighed. "Wouldn't you like to see him, Ang? I mean, not to tell him who you are or anything but just to look at him from a distance, you know? Wouldn't you like that?"

She blinked rapidly because tears welled. "It hurts too much to see him. He's better off without me messing up his life, Vinnie. And seeing him just makes it harder."

He shook his head. "I think you need to see him. I think you're going to." He nodded his head firmly. "Yeah. You're gonna see him. You're gonna do it for me."

She closed her eyes, knowing she would do whatever Vinnie told her to do, but even so, she knew it would be almost too painful to bear.

Vinnie glanced into the back seat, and Ang followed his gaze. She felt sorry for the man who lay back there. Vinnie had wrapped the duct tape awfully tight around his wrists and his ankles and his head so it covered his mouth. She didn't know how Vinnie got him to meet a hundred miles from Big Falls along a deserted stretch of road in the middle of the night, but as Vinnie was constantly telling her, she didn't *need* to know every little thing. He'd made a phone call, and two hours later the man was there and Vinnie was ordering him around at gunpoint.

He looked miserable back there, face red, hands turning almost blue, eyes watering. "It'll be all right," she told him. "We'll be there soon."

CHAPTER FIVE

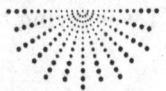

*K*ARA HAD CATALOGUES spread out on the dining room table and was trying very hard to focus on her excitement over her new business. Unfortunately she was failing. Despite the child-size furniture, swing sets, sandboxes and various educational toys and games lining the pages in full vivid color, she couldn't seem to focus on anything but her impending dinner with Jimmy Corona and his adorable son.

She'd been focused on that all day and was still no closer to knowing how she should approach the evening. As a date? It felt more like a nerve-jangling audition.

"I'd rule out that mini-trampoline, sis. Too dangerous." Kara looked up to see Selene looking over her shoulder at the catalogues. She smiled up at her and tried not to let her inner turmoil show too much, though hiding emotions from Selene was next to impossible. "There's this big room on the ground floor with double doors that open into the backyard," she said. "That's going to be the main focus. I want to make it almost magical for the kids. But educational and safe, too."

Selene nodded, pushing her silvery blond hair behind her

71

shoulders and crossing the kitchen to the large range. She flipped on a burner, set the teapot on. "I'm making tea. You want a cup?"

"Sure. What kind?"

"Chamomile. You're a nervous wreck." She said it with a quick glance over her shoulder and a wink. "I looked for you in your room. Looks like a fashion show exploded in there."

Kara rolled her eyes. "I was trying to decide what to wear to dinner tonight."

Selene took two china cups from the cupboard, dropped a pair of her homemade teabags into them, then turned to face Kara. "I guess that depends. Is it a date or just a casual thing?"

Kara thinned her lips. "I wish I knew. I mean, I guess it can't really be a *date* date, since Ty will be there."

"Oh, that doesn't mean much." Selene lowered her head. "Edie said Jimmy kissed you this morning."

Kara stood up, bumping her chair back so the legs scraped noisily over the floor.

"Relax, sis. You know you can't keep a secret in this family. So what kind of kiss was it?"

"What... what *kind* of kiss?"

"Yeah. You know, was it a peck or a slow, dreamy kiss? Or maybe a hot and hungry one? Was your mouth open a little? Any tongue involved?"

"Good grief, Selene, knock it off." Kara sank back into her chair and pressed her palms to her hot cheeks.

Selene giggled and turned to the now-steaming pot to pour water into their cups. "It sounds to me like tonight's a date."

"Maybe it is, but what I'd like to know is why."

Carrying a cup in each hand, Selene came to the table, set them down and took a seat. "You don't know why he would kiss you?"

"I mean why now? He never gave me a second look in high school."

"Well, you've changed since high school."

"That's just it. I haven't changed. Not at all."

Selene frowned at her. "You know that's not true."

"It is so. I'm the same girl. I look better, that's all. Edie taught me how to dress, gave me hair and makeup tips and endless lectures on posture and grace. But inside I'm the same."

Pressing her lips tight, Selene shook her head. "You are so wrong. You've changed in a dozen ways, Kara. On the inside, where it counts. You're not so painfully shy anymore. You're more confident, more sure of yourself, more comfortable in your body. You're starting your own business, you're stronger than ever before. You've stopped hiding your light under a bushel, as Mom would say."

Kara thought it over and finally nodded. "Okay, so maybe I've changed a little. But when I'm around him, I revert right back to that babbling, clumsy nerd I was before."

"And yet he likes you anyway."

"Yeah. Because of the changes that don't really matter. The surface stuff. So sue me if I'm a little wary of a guy who notices me just because I learned to embrace my inner Barbie."

"I think it's more than that. The inner changes show, you know, to anyone who cares to notice." Selene shrugged her shoulders. "But it's easy enough to make sure he sees beyond the glam."

"Yeah? How? I've been racking my brain all day and I haven't come up with the answer to that one."

Selene sipped her tea. "Don't do your hair or makeup. Don't dress for dinner. Wear old jeans and a sweatshirt and a ponytail. Maybe even your glasses from high school. You still have those?"

Kara had worn contacts since eleventh grade. But she still had the oval tortoiseshell glasses that had been the bane of her youth. She hated the idea of going back to them. And yet Selene's suggestion held a lot of appeal. Not so much because it would be a test of the true depth of Jimmy Corona's interest in her, but because it would no doubt end that interest faster than a pail of ice water over his head. He'd been shallow in high school, interested in the pretty girls, the shapely girls, the popular girls, regardless of what they had in their heads. Even if it was mostly air. No, the appeal of this idea was just exactly that. He'd cool toward her and she would no longer be burdened with this frightening new complication in her life.

It would ease things immensely.

"You're so smart, sometimes I can't believe you're the youngest," she told her kid sister.

"That's cause I got the benefit of all my big sisters' combined wisdom."

Selene picked a catalogue and began inspecting playground equipment.

∼

JIM DIALED COLBY'S cell phone a half dozen times, but only got his voice mail. He left messages, but he couldn't tell his friend what he wanted to hear. That he'd given up the notion of wooing and winning Kara Brand. If anything, he was more determined than ever. So he just asked Colby to call in, that he was willing to hear him out. Then he phoned Chief Wilcox to check in while Tyler crunched his Count Chocula.

"Good to hear from you, Corona," Wilcox said. "You settling in all right? Everything good?"

"Fine, Chief. Listen, does anyone besides you know where we are?"

"Not to my knowledge. Why? There a problem?"

Jim sighed. "No, I don't think so. Colby took off last night. But I pissed him off, so...?"

"It's still early. You have reason to think there's anything wrong?"

"No reason at all, Chief." And yet he had a niggling feeling all the same. "Anything up with Skinny Vinnie?"

"Nothing unusual. We're keeping tabs. I don't expect him to try anything now that you guys are out of town."

"Glad to hear it. Let me know if anything looks off, okay?"

"Sure. Call in when you hear from Benton." The chief paused. "Actually why don't we set up a schedule? Call me on the eights, huh?"

Jim told himself it wasn't necessary, but something in his belly disagreed. "Sure. On eights, beginning tonight."

"Great. I'll give you safe time of an hour. I don't hear from you by the nines, a.m. or p.m., I take action. All right?"

"Fine."

"Anything else?" the chief asked.

Jim paused, tipping his head to one side. Then nodded, his decision made. "I'd like a background check on one Kara Brand from here in Big Falls. Can you do it for me?"

"Sure. If you have a reason. Do you?"

"Suspicious behavior," he said.

"Very funny. You know, Corona, having a woman investigated probably isn't the best way to start off a romance."

"Who said anything about romance?"

"You want her checked out, check her out yourself. Talk to you tonight, Corona."

Jim spent the rest of the day wandering the town, admiring the fervor with wich Big Falls decked its proverbial halls for the holidays. Everything was tinsel and bells, reds and greens, silvers and golds. A tree had been erected in the very middle of the village square since he'd been here yesterday, and a sign proclaimed that Santa would be arriving in time for the official tree lighting. It was late, someone told him as they caught him admiring the giant blue spruce. Should've been up two weeks ago.

He spent his time renewing old acquaintances and visiting old haunts, asking casual questions about the Brands—one Brand in particular. Yeah, he felt guilty. What he was doing was dishonest, sneaky and not very nice. But if he was going to consider bringing another beautiful woman into his life—into his son's life—he was damn well going to know all there was to know about her. And while it seemed almost unbelievable, he was considering it.

It wasn't hard. And it wasn't his only area of interest today. He also dug into the reputation of the physical therapy facility where he had made an appointment for Tyler. It had come with glowing recommendations from his doctor back home, but there was nothing like hearing it from the locals—patients past and present. He couldn't be too careful where Tyler was concerned.

He and Ty picked up groceries and supplies for their stay, had a fast-food lunch and spent some time in the library. The air held a definite chill, but compared to what it was probably like in Chicago about then, it was downright balmy. It tasted like winter, though. Oklahoma winter. It was different from winter anywhere else. He had to argue to make Tyler keep his jacket on.

Everywhere they went, with everyone they met, Jim made sure to take time to engage in conversation, reminiscing about his childhood in this town, his parents, the PT center in Tucker Lake and his dear friends, the Brands. Gently, carefully, he extracted bits of information about Kara, never letting on that was what he was doing.

Or that was what he thought, anyway, until as he and Ty were heading back to their pickup late that afternoon, a man walked up beside him and slung a friendly arm around his shoulders. The sun was sinking, temperature already dropping.

He looked up to see Wade Armstrong, Edie's husband, walking beside him, and the look in his eyes gave the lie to his friendly smile. "Afternoon, Jim."

A MOMMY FOR CHRISTMAS

"Hello, Wade." He tightened his grip on Tyler's hand. "Something I can do for you?"

"Yep. Join me for a cup of coffee. Caleb and me, that is. Right, Cal?"

"That's right." The voice came from the right, and Jim realized that Caleb, Maya's husband, had come up on his other side, beyond Tyler. He smiled down at the little guy. "And maybe a slice of warm apple pie for you, huh, Ty?"

Tyler grinned and shot a look up at his dad. "Can we?"

"Sure we can." Jim knew what was going on. The two were playing protective big brothers to Kara He didn't blame them. "Where we headin', fellas?"

"Right over here." Wade nodded toward a festive-looking cafe on the corner, where red and green jalapeno peppers formed a Christmas conga line across the big glass window. It hadn't been there when Jim had left town. He followed the other men through the front door and saw that Julia's Place sported several small tables, a coffee bar, a sign that read Seat Yourself and a coin-operated racehorse that drew Tyler's attention.

He didn't even have to ask. Just shot Jim a look with his big blue eyes, and that was all it took. Jim scooped Tyler up and set him on the horse, inserted a quarter and took a seat at the table closest to it.

The other men sat, too, and came to the point as soon as a teenage waiter had taken their orders.

"So what's up with you and Kara?"

Wade was the one who asked the question. But Caleb was watching Jim's face as he thought about how to answer. He wasn't used to being on the receiving end of an interrogation, but he did know the drill. So he relaxed, didn't let himself tense up or become defensive. He leaned back in his chair, glad Tyler was out of earshot, and sighed. "I know what you're asking me,

77

guys. I'm just not sure how to answer. I mean, I hadn't seen her in years, until I got back into town."

"But you liked what you saw when you did," Caleb said.

"Sure. What's not to like?"

Caleb and Wade exchanged a look. Wade said, "You've been asking questions about her around town."

He lowered his head quickly, surprised at the speed of the Big Falls grapevine. "A few, yeah." He glanced sideways at his son. "Look, we've been through a lot, Tyler and I. You can't blame me for being... cautious."

Caleb nodded slowly. "I think maybe you've been a cop too long."

Jim allowed a self-deprecating smile. "You could be right."

"Kara's exactly what she seems, Jim," Wade said. "She's not hiding a thing. Been right here in Big Falls her whole life. And she's the most selfless person I've ever met."

"The most," Caleb confirmed with a firm nod. "She'd give her last dollar away if she thought someone needed it."

"That's the impression I always had of her. But she's changed. A lot."

"Not as much as you think," Wade said. "I mean, yeah, she's learned how to put herself together, largely thanks to coaching from my wife. But the rest was just genuine growing up. Growing into herself, I think."

Caleb nodded. "If it's Ty you're worried about let me put your mind at ease. Maya and I love all her sisters more than life itself, but we've agreed that should something awful happen to us, Kara would be named our kids' guardian."

"Really?" That surprised Jim and he didn't bother trying to hide it.

"Really," Caleb said. "I know Mel or Selene or Edie would be great with them, but Kara... Kara's special. She loves kids. She's a born nurturer and she's great with the twins."

If true, that would just about seal the deal as far as Jim was concerned. God, could she really be the one? The woman Tyler needed to make his life complete?

"But we didn't come here to ease your mind about Kara. We came here to ease ours about you," Caleb continued. "She's sensitive, Jim. Easily hurt. And just starting to come into her own. A heartbreak right now could set her back a whole bunch. Maybe send her crawling right back into her cocoon, you know?"

He nodded slowly. "I don't plan to hurt her. That's not my intent."

"Yeah, well, intentions don't count for a hell of a lot, my friend," Wade said. "Don't hurt her. Just don't."

He nodded. "Okay. I won't."

The men nodded, and the kid brought their coffee and delivered Tyler's hot apple pie with a scoop of ice cream melting over the top.

KARA WAS ABOUT to knock when Tyler yanked the door open, grabbed her hand, and tugged her inside, all the while holding one crutch under his arm. "Daddy's making lasagna! It's his best supper."

She took off her coat, hung it on a peg near the door and couldn't keep from smiling at Tyler's enthusiastic welcome. Then she closed the door behind her and followed Ty into the kitchen, where the smells made her mouth water almost as much as the sight of Jimmy Corona standing at the counter, tossing a huge salad, did. She couldn't take her eyes off him and suddenly she wished she hadn't taken her kid sister's advice to dress down. She wore jeans—nice jeans, but jeans all the same— and a little T-shirt with the Dixie Chicks across the front. She'd pulled on a milk chocolate-colored cable-knit sweater over it, in deference to the winter chill. Her hair was in a high ponytail, and she wore no makeup. She hadn't gone so far as to pull out the old tortoiseshell eyeglasses, thinking that would be too obvious. But to make up for it, she'd dressed her feet in ankle socks and running shoes.

She thought she must look pretty lame. Especially in comparison to Jimmy. He wore jeans, too, but on him they were delicious. She was staring at the way he filled them out in back when his voice startled her out of her state.

"I saw that," he said, looking over his shoulder at her.

She jerked her gaze up to eye level. "Saw what?" She was waiting for his face to change. For his shock at her appearance to show in his eyes. But it didn't.

"You were going to knock. I can't have you knocking at your own door, Kara."

"That's silly. Of course I'm going to knock."

He shrugged but didn't argue. "Lasagna will be ready in ten minutes. Table's set and ready. Get comfy. I get to be the server tonight."

Nothing. Not a word about her lack of makeup or the ponytail or the sneakers. As she followed Tyler into the dining room, she glimpsed her reflection in the tall windows and looked again. She hadn't completely reclaimed her former persona. She wasn't half running or tripping over her feet or slouching. She was standing up straight, looked almost poised. God, Edie was good. She should open a charm school for awkward girls.

Tyler was calling her. "Right here, Kara. That's where you'll sit," he said. She looked up to see a winter dandelion lying beside the place setting he indicated, and her heart melted into a warm puddle.

"My goodness," she said. "Somebody put a beautiful flower at my spot. Who could have done that?"

Tyler grinned wide. "Me!"

"You? Wow. That's just the nicest thing." She went to the

wilting yellow blossom, picked it up and brought it to her face as if to smell it. "Thank you, Tyler."

"You're welcome."

He made his way to his own chair and got into it then dropped the crutches on the floor beside it. Just in time, too. His father came in bearing a pan of lasagna large enough for to last them all a week. He set it on hot pad, eyed the dandelion and held up a finger. "Be right back."

He vanished and returned with a glass of water. "A vase for your bouquet," he said, holding it toward her.

She stood the flower in the water glass, and Jim placed it carefully in the center of the table. Tyler beamed, clearly proud of himself.

"I forgot the rolls. One sec," Jim said.

Kara leaned back in her chair. "So what did you do today, Tyler?"

"We had fun! We went shoppin' and we got some liberry books. And then we had pie and ice cream with... um... oh, you know. Them guys from your house."

She lifted her brows. "Guys from my house?"

"Uh-huh. And I rode the pony. Two times!" He held up his fingers. 'Course, it wasn't a real pony. It's the kind you have to put money in to make it go. But it was fun anyway."

Jim returned with a basketful of warm rolls and set them on the table. Then he sat down with them. "Dig in!"

Tyler reached for the rolls, took one and handed the bowl to Kara. His father cut into the lasagna and scooped a piece onto his son's plate. "We'll let this cool while we have our salad, okay, Ty?"

"Okay."

"So I hear you ran into Wade and Caleb today," Kara said. She put a piece of the luscious-looking lasagna onto her own plate to cool, then filled her salad bowl.

"They told you?"

"Not exactly." She slanted a look toward Tyler.

"Oh." Jim filled his own plate. "Yeah, we saw them in town. Stopped at that cute little place on the corner for coffee."

"And pie!" Tyler reminded him.

"Pie with ice cream," Jim corrected.

She watched Jimmy Corona's eyes, knew darn well he was keeping something from her—and she was sorely afraid she knew what it was. "They gave you a hard time, didn't they?"

He only smiled at her. "Now what would they have to give me a hard time about, Kara? We had a nice chat, and the coffee was great."

"So was the pie," Tyler said.

"Did they try to warn you away from me?"

He lowered his eyes. "They love you, Kara. They're worried I'm going to break your heart and they wanted to let me know they'd have something to say about it if I did. It was all perfectly civil."

She rolled her eyes, suddenly wondering where her appetite had gone.

"Is there somethin' wrong with your heart, Kara?" Tyler asked.

"No, honey. My heart's just fine."

He smiled. "That's good. You don't gotta worry. My dad hardly ever breaks anything. And I'll try hard not to break you either."

She looked at that child, at the genuine concern and the promise in his big blue eyes, and thought her heart was under siege and falling fast. Then she drew her gaze away and fixed it on Jimmy. "I'm a big girl. I can make my own decisions, take my own risks. I don't want anything those overprotective louts said to get to you."

"You get to me," he told her. He held her gaze for a long moment, until she had to look away, her cheeks flooding with heat

When she managed to look up again, he was focusing on his meal. But after he'd chewed and swallowed, he said, "And I told your brothers-in-law that I have no intention of doing anything that might hurt you."

"You shouldn't make promises you can't keep."

"Don't worry, Kara," Tyler said. "Dad always keeps his promises." He munched lasagna, his salad barely touched. Then he took a big gulp of milk. "Dad, can we go to that pie place again tomorrow? I wanna ride the pony again."

Kara saw Jim's face change. Saw a cloud come right over it. "Well, tomorrow we have... something else we have to do, son."

"What?" The little boy shoveled in more food. Chugged more milk. He'd already nearly cleaned his plate.

"Well, you remember I told you that just because we were going on vacation it didn't mean we could take a vacation from everything. Right?"

Tyler stopped with a bite halfway to his mouth. He looked up at his dad. his eyes wide and pleading. "Not PT, Dad."

"It's the only way you're gonna get better, Ty."

"But I don't wanna!"

"I'm sorry, son. But we have to. It's in the next town over, called Tucker Lake. It might be really nice there, Ty."

"No!" Tyler cried. "No, it's not fair!" He dropped his fork, and tears welled in his eyes. "I hate it. I hate it! I hate it!" He flung himself out of his chair but fell to his knees, off balance.

Kara jumped up, but Jim was beside his son in a heartbeat, gathering him up, trying to hug him even though Tyler wriggled. "Let me go! I can do it myself!"

"Ty, babe, I'm sorry. I know you hate physical therapy. I hate it, too."

"It's not fair."

"No. It's not fair."

The child was sobbing. Kara came around the table, put a

hand on Ty's shoulder. He immediately hid his face from her. "I wanna go to my room."

Jim met Kara's eyes over the boy's head. His were damp, and her heart tied itself into a hard knot. "Go on, Jimmy," she said. "Take as long as you need."

He nodded. "Don't leave, okay?"

"I won't."

Hugging his child tightly, he carried him to his bedroom.

Kara had completely lost her appetite, and doubtless Jimmy had, as well. Poor Tyler. No child should have to go through what he was going through. His entire day ruined by a single sentence from his father. She started to clear the table and she racked her brain for some way she could help ease the pain from little Tyler's eyes. If only she could think of something fun to do in Tucker Lake. Something to take his mind off the PT or even make it worthwhile. Something he would love so much that he would be willing to get through his therapy just to get to the reward on the other side.

She hit on something while loading the dishwasher.

She finished her task, then grabbed her phone from her purse and called the Corral. No one would be home at the house. Her mother answered on the third ring, the din of the evening just warming up around her.

KARA POKED HER head in the bedroom door just as Jim was finishing up one of Tyler's library books. Ty wasn't asleep yet. He'd brushed his teeth and put on his pajamas, been tucked in and read a story, but he was still agitated at the thought of the day to come. He would probably wake up crying tonight, Jim thought. It made him ache down deep to know there was nothing he could do about it

It wouldn't be the first time Tyler had lost sleep while

dreading another round of physical therapy. His eyes were red-rimmed, and Jim knew he was embarrassed to have cried in front of Kara. He almost waved her away, but Tyler glimpsed her in the doorway and gave her a halfhearted smile.

"I'm really a good boy most of the times," Tyler told her.

"I know you are, Ty," she said, coming inside. "Such a good boy that I wanted to do something nice for you. Something that would make physical therapy day into the most fun day you ever had. And I think I figured out just how."

His lower lip quivered. "Nothing could make it fun."

Jim almost told her to stop, not to get his son's hopes up, but she went on before he could form the words.

"Oh, I think *this* will. See I have a friend... well, she's a friend of my mom's, really. Her name is Barbara. She has a farm in Tucker Lake. That's the same town where you have to go for PT."

"A real farm? With animals and stuff?"

Kara nodded. "Uh-huh. And I'll bet you can't guess what kind of animals."

"I don't know," he said. His tone was sulky, his shoulders were slumped. "Cows, prob'ly. Or chickens."

"Ponies." Kara dropped the word into the middle of Tyler's dark mood as if she were dropping a glowing light into a dark cave.

Tyler's head came up off his pillows and his eyes widened. "*Ponies?*"

"Miniature horses if you want to be technical about it. I just spoke to her on the phone. And she said that after your physical therapy session tomorrow we can come over. And you can see the ponies. You can feed them and brush them, even ride one if it's okay with your dad."

Tyler sat up in the bed, his tears forgotten. "Can I, Dad? Can I ride a pony? Oh, please, can I?"

It was an effort for Jim to tear his eyes away from the face of the angel standing in the bedroom doorway, but he did. His son was transformed. Animated, excited, happy. "Of course you can ride the pony."

Tyler's smile lit up the room.

"So what do you think, Ty? Would that make PT day a better day for you?" Kara asked.

He nodded hard. "I still don't like it, but... I can't believe I'm gonna get to ride a real pony! I can hardly wait!"

Jim looked at Kara. She was blinking back tears. He thought the Almighty must have performed a miracle to put this woman into his path. Every doubt he had about whether he was doing the right thing for his son was obliterated tonight. She was the one. She was almost too good to be true.

My God, he was going to do this thing. He was going to marry this woman.

"It's settled then," Kara said. She focused on Jim. "What time should I tell her to expect us?"

"Around noon." His voice came out hoarse.

"Perfect. I'll call her back and let her know." She ducked out of the bedroom quickly, probably because those tears in her eyes were getting near to flood stage.

Jim watched her go, then turned to his son. "Think you'll be able to sleep now, Ty?"

"Uh-huh. I'm gonna dream about my pony."

"That's my boy. Night, Ty."

"Night, Dad." He hugged his father's neck, kissed his cheek and then sank into the pillows. Jim tucked him in nice and snug, ran a hand through his hair, kissed his forehead.

Then he got to his feet and returned to the dining room, where Kara was wiping off the spotless table as if she hadn't just performed a full-blown miracle. He went to her, put his hands on her shoulders. She straightened and turned to face him.

For a long moment he just searched her face, her still-damp eyes.

"I hope I didn't overstep," she said. "I wasn't trying to interfere, I just—"

He pressed a finger to her lips. "You're an angel," he said. "I
don't even know how to begin to thank you."

"There's no need."

"No need? You just did the impossible, Kara."

"It was nothing."

"It was everything."

She shrugged and lowered her eyes. He touched her chin,
drew her gaze back to his again and lowered his head until his
lips met hers, captured and held them. She didn't pull away.
Instead she twined her arms around his neck and held on, and
he deepened the kiss—but he was careful. Not too much, too
soon, he warned himself.

When he lifted his head away, her eyes were glistening again.
She whispered, "If that was just gratitude, Jimmy, I—"

He silenced her doubts by kissing her again. And this time
his body got involved, first when his hands moved to her hips to
urge her gently closer and then his arms when they tightened to
keep her pressed snug against him. He was aroused and he
considered that a bonus. This was going to work. This insane
plot of his was actually going to work. He was going to *make* it
work. When he moved his hips, she arched against him, and
when he slid his mouth over her jaw and down to her neck, the
frantic pulse there told him she was as turned on as he was.

But then her hands flattened to his chest and she pushed
gently, blinking up at him with eyes that were slightly glazed.
He could see passion and confusion and fear all roiling there in
those green depths. And she whispered, "I don't... this is
happening too fast for me."

He nodded and drew a deep, calming breath. "It's hitting me
like a ton of bricks, too," he told her. And it was—the very fact
that his plan seemed to be falling into place without a hitch.
That he'd not only found the perfect mother for his son, but that

marrying her wasn't even going to be the sacrifice he'd expected it to be—that he honest to God liked this woman. And even *wanted* this woman. And she wanted him, too. It was too good to be true.

God, don't let it be too good to be true.

"I don't know where this is going, Jimmy."

"Where do you want it to go?" he asked her.

She closed her eyes. "It's too soon. I can't—"

"Don't tell me you don't believe in love at first sight." He smiled a little. "Okay, first sight in way too many years."

Her eyes opened wider. "L-love? You *can't*... you don't even—"

His cell phone rang. He swore and let go of her just long enough to pick it up and glance at the screen. His first thought was that Colby was finally phoning home, but it was the chief's number on the screen. Dammit, he'd missed his eight-o'clock check-in.

A little chill whispered up his spine. "I'm sorry, Kara. I have to take this."

She nodded. He answered the call. Kara turned and headed for the door.

"Hold on," he said to the phone. "Kara, wait—"

She looked back at him, shook her head. "I need to go, Jimmy. I need to think. This is all... it's too much. But I'll see you in the morning, okay?"

He nodded, hoping to God he hadn't blown it. "We'll pick you up. Ten o'clock, okay?"

"Good night," she whispered. Then she took off as if a pack of demons were chasing her down.

Jim sighed and tried to focus on the phone call. "I'm back. Everything's fine. Sorry I didn't call, Chief, but—"

"Everything's not fine, Corona. Vinnie's dropped out of sight. Left a decoy in his penthouse apartment, so we can't be sure how long he's been gone. And Angela's missing, too."

"Hell. I don't like this."

"Neither do I, Corona. Have you heard from Benton yet?"

"Not a word. It's not like him not to call."

The chief drew a breath. "Vinnie Stefano has never been violent."

"That we know of," Jim put in.

"Listen, I still don't think this is a reason to panic. Is Angela likely to figure out where you are?"

"She knows I grew up here, but frankly her brain is so fried I'd be shocked if she could remember." God, he didn't want to blow this thing with Kara Brand now, especially if this Vinnie scare was all just bull. "I could kick Colby's ass for not calling in."

"He will. Wait for him. Meanwhile, I'm going to contact the local cop shop, Corona. That town have a police department?"

"Shares one with Tucker Lake. I think the headquarters is actually over there—used to be, anyway. The county sheriff's office is over in Ridgewater."

"All right. I'll let them know. And maybe have them keep an eye out for Colby's SUV just in case."

He didn't like the way his stomach clenched up when the chief said that.

"Go about your routine, Jim. There's probably nothing to any of this. Just keep your guard up, okay?"

"Okay, Chief. Talk to you in the morning."

CHAPTER SIX

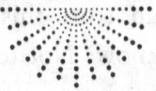

"*Y*OU DON'T HAVE a thing to worry about, you know," Vinnie told the cop.

He was standing behind the car with the trunk open, talking to the man inside. Angela thought it must have been cold in there overnight. Vinnie had found a motel twenty miles from Big Falls, and that was where they'd slept. The cop had spent the night in the trunk of Vinnie's car. Cruel, sure. But Vinnie couldn't very well have left him in the back seat, in plain sight.

Vinnie said he was going to let him go soon, though.

She was glad. It must have been cold in that trunk all night, and the poor guy was going to be lucky if his hands ever went back to normal, with the circulation cut off for so long. They were white now, his hands. Pale as fish bellies.

"Vin, why don't you loosen up his hands a little?" she asked.

Vinnie jerked his head up. It was dark outside, the parking lot devoid of any other movement. This was not a city, it was a motel situated in between a cluster of small towns. No one was around, and only a handful of cars were even in the parking lot.

"I thought I told you to stay in the room," he snapped.

She shrugged. "I wanted to see if he was okay."

He narrowed his eyes on her. "Hell, you know I wouldn't hurt anyone." He glanced at the cop, shaking his head. "Will you listen to this one? Where do they get it, huh?" He moved closer to Ang, put a hand on her shoulder. "I called a friend—an employee. Told him to go pick up the cop's SUV and bring it on down here. He should be here any minute."

She blinked. "You can trust this friend? 'Cause, Vinnie, kidnapping a cop—you know? Not to mention you ain't even s'posed to be out of Chicago."

"I trust the men who work for me, Ang. If I couldn't, I'd have been out of business long ago. But it's sweet, how you worry." He pushed her hair behind her ear.

She smiled, warming at his touch, at his soft words. "So... what are you gonna do? Just let him go? I mean, what was the point?"

He shook his head. "Don't worry your pretty head."

"Come on, Vinnie, don't treat me like I don't matter. I'm not stupid. And I don't know what good it's gonna do you anyway. You're committing more crimes to get these guys to drop the charges against you. What's to stop them from filing more as soon as you let 'em go?"

Just then, headlights came toward them. She squinted, shielded her eyes. Then she saw the red SUV pulling into the motel lot

It pulled right up behind Vinnie's car and a man got out. She'd seen him before once or twice, around Vinnie, but never in the office. He was a big guy, powerful build, crooked nose, and he was always wearing sunglasses. Even now, though it was still dark outside. And cold as hell. She could see her breath.

The guy got out, came over to them, took a quick look around and then in one swift and easy motion lifted the cop from the trunk and dropped him on the backseat of the SUV.

They were not going to loosen his hands. She thought it was kind of cruel.

"Watch him a second, Angie," Vinnie said, nodding at the backseat. "I gotta have a word with my friend, here."

She nodded, then got into the backseat beside the cop, because it was so freaking cold outside. She sat with her butt very close to the top of his head and looked down at his face. "Vinnie's not gonna hurt you. He promised."

The cop held her eyes, shook his head side to side. She felt bad, real bad. She glanced outside at the men, but they were involved in conversation. So she picked at an edge of the tape around his mouth and tugged it off in one swift yank.

The man didn't cry out, even though she thought the damn tape probably tore off several layers of tissue from his lips. "Man, you must be so uncomfortable."

"My... hands," he croaked. "Please."

"I really shouldn't." Then she shrugged. "Hell, they're gonna let you go anyway." Then she tugged a little blade from her jeans pocket and sliced the tape from his wrists. "You gotta fake it, though, or I'll be in big trouble."

He nodded, tried to speak, but his voice was just a croak.

She spotted a water bottle in the front seat and grabbed it, held it to his lips. He drank deeply. She put it back exactly where she'd found it.

"He's gonna kill me, you know."

"He won't. He wouldn't, he's not like that."

"He's exactly like that, Ang."

She blinked and stared down at him.

"Don't help him find Jim and Tyler. Don't do it, Angie. He'll hurt them, too."

"You talk too much." She reached out and smoothed the duct tape over his mouth again. Then she re-attached the two dangling pieces from his wrists, though she didn't make them as tight as before. "He's not gonna hurt anyone. He was falsely accused— framed and set up. You'll see."

Vinnie returned to the SUV, opened the door and scanned the cop with his eyes. "Everything okay?"

"Fine, Vinnie. Am I done here?"

"Yeah. You go on inside now."

She slid out of the SUV and Vinnie closed the door. Then the guy in the sunglasses walked around and got in the driver's side and drove away with the cop in the back.

She sighed. "You sure he'll be okay, Vin?"

"He'll be fine. My friend there is gonna stash him someplace safe until after my trial, Just in case he decides to testify against me after all. Someplace where he can lock him in so he won't need to be all trussed up like that. He'll be fed and warm and perfectly fine."

She studied him and pursed her lips.

"What? What's wrong?" He closed his trunk, took her arm and led her back into the motel.

"Well... is that what you're planning to do with Jim? Kidnap him and keep him locked up for the next three weeks so he can't testify?"

He shrugged. "I don't think anything that drastic is going to be necessary."

"I don't think anything that drastic is even possible," she muttered.

He lifted his brows. "You don't think I can handle your ex?"

"You don't know him. He's... tough. And stubborn."

Vinnie shrugged. "I think I'll be able to reason with him, Angie. I think once he hears what I have to say, he'll agree to do whatever I ask him to."

She looked at him for a long time.

He shrugged. "You're hurtin', aren't you, hon? You need to do a line, maybe two."

She closed her eyes. "God, yes."

"Okay. Anything you want, baby. Let's go inside."

~

KARA HAD A towel on her head when she answered the knock on the front door the next morning. Then she stood there blinking at the arrangement of yellow roses that greeted her.

The roses lowered, revealing Jimmy Corona's smile. "Morning, Kara," he said.

She frowned, puzzled, and looked from the clock on the wall to him again. "You're early."

"I know. I couldn't wait. And Ty was just about climbing the walls. I thought maybe you'd like to go out for breakfast. If you haven't already eaten."

"I want pancakes," Tyler said, standing close beside his father.

She nodded, wishing she'd had time to get ready first. She'd decided to do her hair and makeup today, since jeans and a T-shirt hadn't seemed to have any impact on Jimmy's inexplicable attraction to her anyway. She opened the door wider so they could come inside. Tyler entered first, looking around expectantly.

"The twins aren't here, Ty," Kara explained. "But when we come back, we can pay them a visit if you want."

"Okay." He sat down in a chair. His father came inside and placed the roses, which were already in a blue porcelain vase with cherubs painted on it, in the center of the table.

"That's really beautiful, Jimmy. You didn't have to do that."

"That doesn't even scratch the surface," he told her.

She smiled and looked down at herself. She was dressed much as she had been last night, in jeans and a T-shirt, her hair in a towel.

"Go on, go finish getting ready, Kara. I really should have called."

95

She nodded. "There's coffee made. And O.J. in the fridge, if you guys want a drink. Just help yourselves." She headed up the stairs, almost forgetting not to run. She didn't stop at the bathroom but instead tapped on Selene's door. "Hey, you in there?"

"Meditating," Selene called back.

"I'm sorry, honey. Jimmy and Ty are here and I'm nowhere near ready."

She heard movement, then the door opened. Selene smiled when she saw the towel on Kara's head. "Where'd you put 'em?"

"In the kitchen. Thanks, hon, you're a doll." She turned and started for the bathroom.

"Take your time, sis. They're not going anywhere."

Kara nodded but didn't slow her pace. She yanked the towel off her head, combed the snarls out of her hair, then put in a handful of mousse, scrunching the way Edie had shown her. She grabbed the hair dryer and wafted warm air over it. In five minutes her hair was done. Edie would be proud. As a former model, Edie had taught Kara more than the art of beauty—she'd also taught her how to achieve it with speed.

She flipped open her makeup case and gave herself the once over. When she finished and looked in the mirror, she was happy with the results. And for a moment she thought about what a change that was from the way she used to feel when she looked into a mirror. "Thanks, Edie," she whispered to the mirror. Then she smacked on some lip gloss and headed into her bedroom.

She picked out a pretty blouse—but not a fancy one—tossed her T-shirt into the hamper, grabbed socks, a pair of suede walking shoes and her denim jacket. Then she headed back down the stairs, where Tyler was telling Selene excitedly that he was going to get to ride a pony today.

Jimmy stood up when she entered the room, blinking at her as if he'd never seen her before. "Wow."

Kara lifted her brows, looked down at her clothes.

"How do you *do* that?" he asked.

"Do what?"

He shook his head slowly. "Never mind. You look great, Kara. Beautiful, as always."

"A far cry from last night, huh, Jimmy?" Selene asked.

Kara sent her a frown, but she only returned a wink.

"Last night?" He looked at Kara again. "I thought she looked great last night, too."

"Oh, yeah? Ponytail, no makeup, T-shirt and all?"

He looked at Selene a little oddly. Kara rolled her eyes. "Let's get going, huh? We've kept Ty waiting long enough for those pancakes."

~

THEY WERE SITTING at the unimaginatively named Big Falls Diner in the center of the village, when Tyler looked up, widened his eyes, and said, "Dad, look! It's Santa!"

Kara followed Ty's pointing finger. Santa Claus was straightening the big throne like chair on the round pavilion, a few yards from the giant Christmas Tree, just outside the diner.

"I've gotta talk to him. I've *got to!*" Tyler slid out of the booth, grabbing his crutches and hurrying toward the exit.

"Ty, wait! I don't think Santa's open for business yet."

"Duh, Dad. He's wearing the suit, isn't he?"

"Well, yeah, but–"

A woman opened the diner's big glass door to come in, and Tyler almost mowed her down hobbling out past her, belatedly calling, "'Scuse me," over his shoulder.

Jimmy grabbed the door, held it for the newcomer, and apologized. "I'm sorry, ma'am."

"Don't be silly!" she replied, smiling as she watched the little boy making his way across the street. "Some things are just too important to wait."

"Tyler, will you wait up!" Jimmy shouted, as he headed outside after his son.

Kara gripped his arm to slow him down. "It's okay. Let him be. It's Santa."

Jimmy looked at her, shook his head, then watched as Santa spotted the little boy hurrying toward him and smiled and ho-ho-hoed in the jolliest possible way.

"Oh, Santa! I'm so glad you're here!" Tyler said when he reached him.

The red-suited, full bearded fellow crouched down and said, "I'm glad you're here too, Tyler," with a glance over Ty's shoulder and a wink at Jimmy.

Ty said, "I wrote you a letter. But I want to make sure you got it, cause it's super important this year."

"I'll bet it is. Well, my boy, I get so many letters that I probably don't remember off the top of my head. Getting older, you know. And my list is home at the North Pole. So you'd better tell me now, just in case."

Tyler crooked a finger. Santa leaned closer, and Ty whispered into his ear. As he did, he pointed. He pointed right at Kara, and Santa looked her way too, and she could've sworn his lip quivered just a little bit behind his snowy white whiskers. Her heart melted, and her eyes met Jimmy's, tried to read what was there. But it was a mystery to her.

TYLER DIDN'T CRY or complain about going to PT once all morning. Not even when they were on their way to the clinic, though Jim had fully expected he would. Once there, Tyler refused to let Kara stay in the waiting room, insisting she come into the treatment area with them. And while he did his exercises, struggling through them without a whimper for the first time ever, Kara kept bringing up the ponies. "Only another half hour, Ty, and then we get to see the ponies," she'd say. "Just another fifteen minutes, Ty. I wonder if she has a brown one. I like brown ponies best. What color do you like?" And, "Maybe we'll have to get you a cowboy hat, Ty. If you're going to ride ponies, you really ought to have a cowboy hat, don't you think?"

Every time it got tough, every time it hurt, every time Tyler floundered, she was there. Kara Brand was reading his kid as well as he did, and jumping in to distract him or soothe him at all the right moments. And then, finally, it was over. Tyler was red-faced, sweating, but dry-eyed and smiling. He hurried ahead of them to the pickup, and Jim put a hand on Kara's arm to slow her down.

She turned to look up at him. He sighed, shook his head. "You can't possibly know what you did for him today, Kara. These sessions... they're usually hell. He's never managed to get through one without getting angry and frustrated, without crying and begging to stop. It's like a miracle."

She lowered her head. "I'm just glad it was easier on him this time," she said.

"I know you are." He stared at her, at a loss for words.

She put a hand on his arm. "Let's get him to the farm, Jimmy. He's really earned it."

He nodded, not sure how to make her understand the magic she'd performed today. And then they got to the farm and the magic multiplied tenfold. Tyler was in heaven when Barbara Jean Collins led the way to the pasture where a half dozen miniature horses grazed by the edge of a stream. She was a solidly built woman, dressed in bib overalls and a big flannel shirt.

She looked down at Tyler. "Do you know how to whistle?"

He nodded, puckered up his lips and blew. The resulting sound was faint and mostly air. Barbara Jean patted his shoulder. "Okay, pal, we're gonna have to work on that whistle. Meanwhile, let's try one together, huh?"

Tyler nodded. Barbara put two fingers to her lips, and when Ty whistled again, she did, too.

The little animals' heads came up, then they trotted right to her—and to Tyler since he was standing right beside her.

Jim watched, his heart swelling as his son's face lit up and the woman led him from one animal to the next, introducing them as Corky and Snuffy and Baby Jane and Rusty and... he lost track of the names after that. He watched Tyler point to the one he liked best, Rusty, and then Barbara nodded and took that horse by its halter, leading it into the nearby stable with Tyler right on her heels.

"You guys find a comfy spot and take a break," Barbara Jean called back to Jim and Kara. "Ty and I are gonna have a lesson in saddling a horse. We'll be back in a flash."

Jim nodded, even though it was against his instincts to let anyone, particularly a strange woman, take his son out of his sight

"It's okay," Kara whispered.

He looked down at her. And he knew when he met her eyes that she was seeing right through him. That uncanny empathy of hers again. She couldn't just read his son, he realized. She could read him, too.

"Mom's known Barbara for fifteen years. She's a good woman, Jimmy. Raised three sons of her own."

He nodded. Kara took his hand and led him to a bale of hay by the fence, and they sat down on it to wait.

A few minutes later the red-brown mini-horse with the shaggy cream-colored mane came plodding out of the stable with Tyler on his back, and Barbara Jean leading him. Tyler had never in his entire life looked the way he looked right then.

Jim stood up, not quite aware of doing so, and Kara stood beside him. And as Tyler rode past, laughing and waving, the sunshine gleaming in his hair, Jim put an arm around Kara's shoulders and pulled her close as he tried to swallow the lump in his throat.

"I'm riding, Dad! Look at me! I'm riding a real pony!" Jim waved again, unable to speak. And then he looked down at Kara. Her eyes were fixed on Tyler as he rode, and he thought she might have been as moved as he was. And he knew then that he needed this woman in his life. His son needed her. And he was going to do whatever it took to make her a part of their lives. Permanently. Kara wasn't just too good to be true. She was far too good to let slip away.

VINNIE HAD GONE out and he wasn't back yet. He'd been stingy this morning. Given her just a little sniff, and it hadn't been nearly enough. Angela was nervous, damned emotional, and that wasn't a way she enjoyed feeling. She'd been through every suitcase Vinnie had brought along, but she couldn't find a thing. And dammit, if she didn't do a couple of lines soon, she was going to pull her hair out.

She tried to go back to bed but was too restless to sleep. So she got up and hunted some more. By the time Vinnie came back, she'd torn the lining out of his suitcases, stripped the motel room's bed and shoved the mattress off.

He came in the door, looked at the mess around him and shot her a dangerous glare.

"I'll clean it up. Dammit, Vinnie, where's the stuff? You said you brought some, but you barely gave me enough for a buzz this morning. Where is it?"

Lips thin, he tugged a tiny bag from his pocket and slapped it down on the dresser. Angela lunged toward it, but he gripped her shoulder. "Not so fast. First, you listen, because you're working for me today. And if you don't do a good job, you won't be getting another sniff, baby. Understand?"

"I'll do whatever you want," she promised. She couldn't keep her eyes on him, though. She kept darting looks at the stuff on the dresser. "You know I will, Vin, I always do."

He nodded and let go of her. "You're going to clean this mess up, fast. Then I want you to take a shower. Put on some of the clothes I bought you. Something nice, so you don't look like a ten-dollar whore. Fix up your hair. Slap some makeup over the circles under your eyes. I want you to look respectable. You got it?"

By then she'd already had a hit. She straightened, sniffing and rubbing a knuckle over her nostrils. "Got it." She bent again, but he grabbed her straw out of her hand before she could do anymore.

"You've had enough."

"Can I just put it in my purse for later?"

He shook his head firmly. "No way. I say when and I say how much. Get used to it, Ang."

"Okay, Vinnie." She watched him pocket the cocaine.

"I'm gonna get us some lunch. Have this mess cleaned up by the time I get back."

"I will."

"Don't answer the phone and don't go out. Don't talk to anybody, you got that?"

She nodded and leaned back against the dresser. "You gonna tell me where you were this morning?"

"Doin' some research, sugar. You're gonna get to see your boy today. So you make sure you do yourself up extra pretty for him." He glanced at his watch. "I'll be back in a half hour. Lock up behind me."

She nodded and he left. When he opened the door, she noticed the Do Not Disturb sign hanging from the knob on the outside. He must have put it there before he left. She locked the door as he'd told her. She didn't think about the rest of the day, about seeing her son for the first time in more than four years.

Part of her sort of hoped things would get in the way, that it would never happen. Something would come up, and Vinnie would get called back to Chicago. Or maybe Jim would pack Tyler up and head somewhere else.

She kind of hoped so. She'd gotten used to being without her son. It stopped hurting after a while. At least, it stopped hurting when she was high, and she was high most of the time. Her life was just fine without a kid cluttering it up. She didn't need that kind of responsibility again.

VIDALIA WAS ADDING mulch to the more delicate plants in her flower bed to protect them during the winter months, when they would lie dormant. Selene had taken one of her so-called weed walks through the meadows out back. She would no doubt return with a basket of stalks, roots and snips. She would know all their folk names and medicinal uses and she would brew teas that tasted remarkably good and actually seemed to work.

Vi didn't mind Selene using nature's gifts for easing bouts of sinus or nervous energy or a bad stomach. But the other things the girl did with those weeds didn't sit well with her. In fact, she was downright worried about her youngest daughter. She had stuffed a pair of pillows with some wild herb or other and given them to the twins to keep away nightmares and ensure they had only sweet, happy dreams. Then there was the time she'd stuffed flowers into a tiny drawstring bag and told Mel it was for protection.

And there was more. Tarot cards, crystals all over her bedroom and all those books she was always reading about folk magic and shamanism.

It was worrisome, that's what it was. The girl was meddling in places she ought not to be, and Vidalia felt more and more certain she needed to step in and do something about it. Lordy, while the rest of them talked about Christmas, Selene referred to the holiday as the Winter Solstice and insisted doing so wasn't the least bit disrespectful to the Lord.

She was worried about Kara, too, what with Jimmy Corona back in town with that precious boy of his. Oh, that child could tug every one of Kara's heartstrings. The girl was a pushover for any child, much less one with troubles of the kind that boy had. A motherless baby with braces on his legs. Wouldn't have mattered if his daddy had looked like a billy goat, much less the handsome devil he was. Lord God Himself couldn't have sent anyone more likely to make her Kara fall head over heels.

The question was, was this Corona fellow worthy of her? Would he treat her the way she needed to be treated? Or would he break her heart? Of all the girls, Kara was the most sensitive, the most tender-hearted, the most easily wounded. She was also the most selfless, giving and caring of the bunch. It would take a special man to make her happy, and Vidalia Brand intended to see to it she got one.

And if this Jimmy Corona jerked her girl around, he was going to find out he'd woken up a sleeping mama tiger. With big, sharp claws.

She yanked a weed harder than she'd intended, pulling up a good-size hunk of topsoil with it, and told herself to calm down.

"Excuse me?"

Vidalia looked over her shoulder, irritated at the intrusion, and saw a woman's head perched atop a broomstick body. Hell, even that yellow, lifeless hair kept the broomstick image intact. Her face looked older than Vi's own, dry, drawn, unsmiling. The woman needed twenty pounds to qualify as skinny.

Vi stood slowly, brushing the soil from her hands and forcing a friendly smile. "Can I help you with something?"

"I'm... looking for Mrs. Brand," the woman said.

"Well, you've found her." Vi extended a hand. "You can call me Vidalia."

The woman shook her hand, her grip cold, damp and weak.

Vi had to resist the urge to wipe her hand on her jeans when the girl released it.

"I'm Angela Corona," the stranger said. "They told me in town you might know where I can find my husband, Jim, and our son. Tyler."

CHAPTER SEVEN

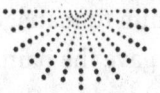

COLBY DIDN'T KNOW how long he'd been lying there. And as for how badly he was hurt, it wasn't possible to assess. The pain was an all-encompassing orb that contained him within it. Pulsing, blood-red, blinding pain.

But he was alive. The pain proved it, and for that he loved it. Dammit, he wouldn't have been if it hadn't been for Corona's drugged-out ex. Thanks to her, he'd been able to get free.

Vinnie's thug had parked the Blazer near the edge of a steeper-than-hell drop-off, gotten out long enough to drive a screwdriver blade through the gas tank. Then he'd put it in Neutral and given it a push.

Colby had had to work fast and even then he almost hadn't made it. He'd jerked his wrists free and wrenched the door open, flinging himself out of the car just before it had gone over the edge. He'd hit hard, and he'd tumbled, unsure whether his would-be killer had seen his escape. And then his head had crashed against something hard and he'd come to rest, barely clinging to consciousness. He'd managed to open his eyes, to look around him, but all he had seen was thorny brush. And then he'd heard the Blazer explode when it hit bottom.

No wonder the bastard hadn't been worried about removing the duct tape. Hell, there wouldn't be a body left to examine in a wreck like that.

Thank God for the little drug addict, he thought. At least he was alive.

And then he'd sunk into oblivion.

Now he was awake and fighting through the pain. It took a long time, it seemed, for him to manage to move. First one limb, then another. Movement gave the pain a focus, it seemed. When he moved his hands, it screamed in them. His legs, too. His back. His head. Everything.

It didn't matter. He had to get up, get moving. Get the hell out of here, wherever here was. He struggled to his feet, hands on a boulder to help him, probably the one his head had struck. Damn.

Looking around, he saw no one. But his vision was far from dependable. The ground seemed to swell and rise toward him, then recede again like an uneasy sea. Dizziness sickened him. Hell. There were trees in one direction, a steep drop in another, open space in a third. Probably the road.

He headed for the trees. Best to stay concealed in case Skinny Vinnie or his drone decided to check on the job they thought they'd done. Almost as an afterthought, he checked his pocket for his cell phone, was relieved to find it still there. And getting a signal—not a strong one—but maybe enough. He began punching the keys...but before he finished, his vision blurred and he had to start over.

He figured he got about a hundred yards and accurately entered six digits before he collapsed again.

BARBARA JEAN SEEMED moved by Tyler's reaction to the miniature horses. Kara thought it must be clear to her, as it would be clear to anyone with a pair of working eyes, how important this was, what a major event this was in Tyler's life.

They all trooped into the barn, standing by while Tyler helped Barbara remove Rusty's saddle, blanket and bridle, then brush him down. Barbara turned to Jimmy and Kara. "How long you gonna be in Big Falls, Mr. Corona?"

"Jim." He glanced down at Kara, seemed to be considering before he answered. "I don't know. It depends. But I do know it'll be three weeks at the very least."

"And Ty here has PT—what?—once a week?"

"Twice a week," Jim told her.

She nodded. "Well, you can consider this a standing date, then."

"Oh, Barbara, we'd be taking advantage," Jim said.

Barbara shrugged and nodded toward Ty. He was singing to the pony as he brushed him. "Frankly I don't see how you can *not* do it. But if it makes you feel any better, I can charge you for the time. Tell you the truth, I've been considering doing something like this for a while now."

"I didn't know that," Kara said.

Barbara nodded. "Been reading about programs where these miniatures are brought right into hospitals for sick kids—kids with cancer, burn victims, all sorts of different problems. And so far it looks as if it makes a heck of a difference in those kids' lives. So I'd been playing with the notion, kind of mulling it all over, and then you called." Barbara smiled. "Now that I've seen the results firsthand, I can't come up with a single reason not to pursue this."

"You're an angel, Barbara."

"Seems this state's full of angels," Jim muttered. Then he called to his son. "Hey, Ty, what do you think about us doing this after every PT session while we're in Big Falls?"

"Really?" He hugged Rusty's neck. "Oh, Dad! That would be so cool!"

Jim sighed and his hand closed around Kara's.

She swallowed the lump that came into her throat. "Let's get Ty home," she said. "Look at him, he's tired out. You can see it in his eyes."

"I can. I guess I shouldn't be surprised you can, too." He crossed to his son, whose head now rested against the pony's side. "Time to go, Ty. But we'll be back. Day after tomorrow, okay?"

"Okay, Dad." He stroked the pony's nose, then reached for his crutches, which were leaning against the side of the stall.

"You did a good job today, Ty," Barbara told him. "I think Rusty really likes you."

He smiled tiredly and Jim scooped him up. Kara scrambled to gather up the crutches, noting that Tyler didn't even argue with his dad about being carried. When Jim slid his son into the truck, Kara climbed in beside him.

Tyler leaned up and wrapped his arms around her neck just as Jim was getting in the driver's side. "I love you, Kara," Tyler said softly.

Kara's eyes filled and she looked into Jimmy's. He'd frozen behind the wheel, keys halfway to the ignition switch. She knew he could see the tears brimming in her eyes, but there was nothing she could do to prevent them.

"I love you, too, Ty," she whispered.

He released her neck but snuggled close beside her for the ride back to Big Falls and fell asleep before they'd gone a mile.

Jimmy looked over at Kara. "What do you say we go on a real date tonight? Just you and me."

She blinked at him. "What about Tyler?"

"Can we get one of your sisters to watch him?"

Kara nodded. "I did tell him he could play with the twins later on. And I think Maya would love to have him." She shrugged. "Okay."

Jimmy didn't come inside when he dropped Kara off at

home. She wouldn't let him walk her to the door, not with Tyler sleeping soundly in the pickup by then. She promised to ask Maya about babysitting and call him only if it was a problem. Otherwise, she would expect him at seven.

She watched him drive out of sight, then went to the door and walked inside. Maya, Selene and Edie were at the kitchen table waiting for her.

Probably waiting to grill her about her day with Jimmy, she guessed, and then painted a smile on her face and reminded herself that her family loved her and only meant well.

"Looks like someone called a family meeting," she said, half joking. "Maya, would it be terrible of me to ask you to watch Tyler tonight while Jimmy and I go out for dinner?"

Maya looked at the others, who shrugged as if helpless. Then she said, "It's not terrible of you to ask at all, hon. I'd love to have Ty. He can sleep over if he wants." She shrugged. "I mean, unless your plans change."

"Which they might," Edie put in.

"We don't have the whole story," Selene said. "There's more going on here than meets the eye."

"What are you guys talking about?" Kara asked. "Where's Mom?"

At that moment her mother came into the kitchen, met Kara's eyes and immediately lowered her own. Something was wrong, Kara realized. Something big. "What's going on?"

"Sit down, daughter."

She didn't even consider arguing with her mother. She pulled out a chair and sat, then waited, knowing that whatever it was, it was going to be bad. There was nothing wrong with Caleb or the twins or with Wade. Edie and Maya wouldn't be sitting there, grim-faced but calm, if there was. "God," Kara said, rapidly ticking off possibilities in her mind. "Has something happened to Mel? Or Alex?"

Her mother shook her head. "It's about Jimmy and Tyler."

She drew a deep breath before plunging on. "A woman came by here today, Kara. Claimed she was Tyler's mother and asked if I could tell her where to find her husband and her son."

Kara felt as if she'd been punched in the belly. "He told me Ty's mother was dead. He... why would he lie to me about something like that?"

"Kara, don't think the worst," Selene said, getting to her feet. "We don't have his side of the story yet."

Kara got up slowly and moved past them all, needing the solitude of her room before she let the tears flow. "I knew all along he was too good to be true. God, I was so stupid to let myself think... to hope... "

She ran then, tripped halfway up the stairs and almost fell on her face. Then she got her footing again and hurried the rest of the way to her room. She closed the door, turned the lock, and sank onto her bed to hug her pillows and cry. She couldn't think, couldn't reason, couldn't even begin to plan how she was going to handle this. Not yet. Right then all she could do was cry her heart out.

~

"IS KARA READY?"

Jim stood just inside the door in the kitchen and wondered what he'd done to make Vidalia Brand look as if she would like to skin him alive. Come to think of it, Maya had been acting oddly, too, when he'd dropped Tyler off a few minutes ago.

Vi opened her mouth to reply, but before she got a word out, Kara came into the room, and he took a moment to drink in the sight of her. She looked great, as she always did. Her hair was curly again tonight and it bounced when she moved. She wore a skirt that was long and loose and flowed like a floral-print breeze around her long legs, with a pale green sweater that only hinted at what hid beneath it. He thought she was wearing more makeup than usual. Especially around her eyes.

Her mother gaped at her, apparently too distracted by her to remember what she'd been about to say. "Don't tell me you're still going," she blurted.

Kara squeezed her mother's arm, met her eyes and passed some silent message to the woman. Vidalia pursed her lips, shook her head and spared Jim one last glare before she stomped to the door. "I've got to get back to the Corral," she said. "We'll talk in the morning, daughter."

"Good night, Mom."

Vi moved past him without a word and left the house.

Jim looked again at Kara, his eyebrows raised. "Is she angry with me for some reason?"

Kara lowered her head, not meeting his eyes. "Is it okay with you if we skip dinner tonight?"

He frowned at her. Something was wrong. "Whatever you want to do is okay with me, Kara. Did you have something else in mind?"

"Yeah. Something else." She swallowed hard. "We need to talk, Jimmy."

He bit his lip and moved closer to her. "Kara, what's wrong? Clearly your mother is angry with me. And you... " He frowned and touched her chin, lifting her face so he could verify what he thought he saw there. "You've been crying?"

She closed her eyes. "I thought I got rid of the evidence."

"Tell me why."

She met his eyes now. "Not here," she said. "Too many people running in and out all the time."

She was working up to something. Something big. Hell, he'd screwed up somewhere along the line and he'd better figure out how. And soon, so he could fix it.

"Come on, then." He took her arm, led her out of the house.

"To where?"

"To dinner. Just as planned."

"But I—"

"Trust me on this, Kara, okay?"

She sighed but nodded and let him help her into the pickup. He saw her noticing the picnic basket on the seat between them, the mini cooler in the back. But she remained silent—maybe brooding?—for the entire ten-minute drive.

When he pulled to a stop by the falls, she shot him a look.

"I'd planned a... special evening." He got out of the truck and took the picnic basket with him. He noticed she didn't get out right away, but he decided to give her a minute to gather her thoughts. He took the blanket and the ice chest from the back, spread the blanket on the ground. Then he took the bottle of wine from the picnic basket and stuck it into the ice he'd brought along. He hoped it wasn't too chilly out here for her.

He heard the pickup door, looked up to see her coming toward him. She stood for a moment, staring out at the falls. So he walked up beside her, slid an arm around her shoulders and took in the view, as well.

"I never get enough of this spot," she said. "There's something about the sheer power of a waterfall. You can feel it thrumming right in the middle of your chest."

"Can you?'

"Mmm. Close your eyes and try."

He closed his eyes but only briefly. He was more interested in her than in the falls, beautiful though they were. She stood there, eyes closed, face turned toward the thundering cascade. Some of the mist gathered on her cheeks, dampening them as she seemed to inhale the scent and sound and feel of the place.

Then she opened them again and turned to look at him. "Mom had a visitor at the house today." She drew a breath, seemed to square her shoulders before she went on. "A woman named Angela. Said she was your wife, Tyler's mother."

Jim drew back in reaction to that blow. His gut clenched tight, as did his fists. "Was she alone?"

Kara blinked, apparently surprised by the question. "I tell you a woman shows up claiming to be your wife and all you can think of to ask is if she was alone? Jimmy, you told me she was dead."

"I told you we'd lost her," he said. He turned quickly and strode to the area he'd set up for what he'd intended to be a romantic evening. "You assumed she was dead and I let you. And I've been kicking myself for it ever since. But for the record, Kara, she's my ex-wife." He yanked the wine out of the ice chest, crammed it back into the picnic basket and picked up both of them. "Grab the blanket."

Kara did so, then ran to keep up with him as he carried the other items into the truck. "Jimmy, don't you think you owe me an explanation?"

"I owe you more than that. Hell, a lot more." He took the blanket from her and crammed it into the truck, then held the door open. "Get in."

She got in. He went around to his side and started the vehicle moving.

"Jimmy, please tell me what's going on."

He glanced sideways at her, pushed a hand through his hair. "I'm sorry. Kara, dammit, I'm so sorry I wasn't honest with you from the beginning. It's just... my marriage to that woman is not something I'm proud of."

"But why?"

He closed his eyes. "It's a long story. She's trouble, Kara. She hasn't seen Tyler since she left us four years ago. She hasn't wanted to see him. He doesn't even know who she is."

Kara lowered her head. "I don't understand. If she doesn't want him, then why is she here?"

"That's what I'd like to know." He pressed harder on the accelerator and soon was turning into the driveway that curved uphill from Vidalia's farmhouse to Maya and Caleb's recently built one, higher up the hill. He jumped out of the truck and ran to the door, knocked once before flinging it open.

Maya and Caleb looked up fast, and Maya frowned. "Back so soon?"

"Where's Tyler?" he asked, scanning the living room.

"In the playroom with the twins," Maya said, pointing.

"Is something wrong, Jim?" Caleb asked.

But Jim was already striding through the house in the direction Maya had pointed. He didn't think he drew a breath again until he burst into the playroom and saw Tyler on the floor, making motor noises as he drove a toy truck along the floor. Ty looked up with a smile. "Hi, Dad."

Jim scooped his son up and hugged him hard.

"I thought you was goin' on a picnic with Kara," Tyler said.

"I missed you."

"Already?" Tyler's face fell. "I don't have to go yet, do I, Dad? We were gonna have popcorn and watch Rudolf."

He kissed Tyler's cheek, ruffled his hair and set him back down. "You go ahead. I'll be right outside if you need me, all right?"

"Okay, Dad."

Jim turned to see Kara standing in the doorway staring at him. He nodded at her inquisitive look. "Yeah. We can have that talk now. Just one more thing first." He pulled out his cell phone and dialed his chief. When Chief Wilcox picked up, he said, "Ang is in Big Falls."

THEY SAT ON the porch swing as the sun went down. Jimmy still seemed nervous, watchful. Kara had lost her grip on her righteous indignation and her anger at having been lied to. Now all she felt was fear, because if he was this upset over his wife—

ex-wife, she corrected herself—appearing in town, then there must be a good reason. Jimmy Corona was not a stupid man. He was a cop, for God's sake. And he'd been afraid when she'd told him about Angela's visit. No cop got that scared without a reason.

He took her hand in his and she looked into his eyes. "Marrying Angela was a huge mistake," he told her. "But she gave me Tyler, so it's a mistake I'd make all over again. Except this time... I'd keep him safe."

Kara frowned. "Safe? From his own mother?"

He nodded, leaned back in the swing, closed his eyes. "She liked to party, liked to have fun, never wanted kids. She resented getting pregnant. Resented having to give up her fun to carry a baby to term. But she did it. And I thought... I thought she would keep on doing it. I thought once she held our child in her arms, she'd see what was really important in life."

"You thought a baby would change her."

He nodded. "God knows nothing else did."

"But it didn't work."

"No. She was worse than ever after Tyler was born. And one day while I was at work, she got high and tried to take him out for a walk. He was a month old. We lived in a fifth-floor apartment and the elevator wasn't working that day. She fell, crashed down two flights of stairs, took him down with her."

"Oh my precious little Ty," she whispered, her hand going involuntarily to her heart.

He drew a breath, an unsteady, stuttering breath, as if just the memory was more than he could bear. "He was all busted up. We almost lost him. But the lasting damage was to his spine. That's why he's wearing the braces, suffering through PT twice a week, and waiting for yet another operation."

"I'm so sorry, Jimmy."

"I divorced her, naturally. Gave her the option of surrendering parental rights to Tyler or going up on charges for possession and neglect. She signed him away like he was noth-ing. She never wanted him to begin with. And we didn't see her again. Oh, I knew, though. She was still using, sliding further into the gutter with every month that passed. Last I knew, she was selling herself on the streets for drug money." He looked at Kara intently. "I didn't know she was using. I never would've left her alone with my son if I'd known." Then he shook his head slow. "Maybe I just didn't want to know."

She stroked the back of his lowered head. "Why is she here?"

"I busted a man in Chicago for dealing in child pornography. He's a wealthy pig, made his fortune in legitimate porn. We got a tip and raided his home. Found the evidence and made the arrest. But this guy has money and apparently powerful connec-tions. The evidence vanished. Just disappeared from the evidence room."

She frowned, searching his face, her heart in her throat

"Angela showed up at my door before I left Chicago, begging me to change my testimony against this guy. Says he's the love of her life. He's got her convinced he's going to scrape her out of the gutter and make her fantasies come true. Fact is, I'm convinced he only took up with her to get to me. After the evidence vanished, the only thing left to put this guy away is my testimony. Mine and Colby's, that is. Our chief thought it best we both get out of town until the trial."

"You think this man is with her? That he's come down here after you?"

He nodded. "Last night I learned that both he and Angela had fallen off the radar. Today she shows up here." He shook his head. "No way is it a coincidence."

She nodded slowly.

"And Colby's missing." He shook his head hard. "I thought he'd just taken off. He was a little pissed at me over... something. But now that I know they're in town... "

She blinked and sucked in a sharp breath. "Do you think they've done something to him?"

Jim closed his eyes. "God, I hope not."

He turned to face her, took her hands in his. "I know none of this gives me a reason for misleading you before, Kara. I just—hell, it's just easier to say she's gone and let people draw their own conclusions than to admit the truth. That I left my son in the care of a drug addict who damn near killed him."

"She was his mother, Jimmy. You can't take responsibility for what she did. No one can, no one but her."

"I don't agree with that. But that's beside the point, Kara. I shouldn't have lied to you."

"You didn't exactly—"

"I did. I knew what you assumed and I didn't correct you. I'm sorry. I can't tell you how sorry I am that I hurt you like that. You don't deserve it."

"Given the circumstances, I think I can forgive you."

He smiled a little, but then his eyes turned solemn again. "Not that it matters at this point. I can't risk them catching up to us. I've got to take Tyler and leave town."

She put a hand on his shoulder. "I'm not sure that's the best thing here."

He lowered his head. "It makes no sense to think all Skinny Vinnie wants is for me to pull my testimony against him. What would stop me from changing it again as soon as conditions changed? No, he's up to more than that. I don't want to leave Big Falls—or you—but I have to put Ty first."

"So do I," she told him. "Come on. Jimmy, you know me well enough to know I wouldn't suggest anything that would put you or Tyler at risk. What I want doesn't even enter into it. Just hear me out, okay?"

After a moment he nodded. "You're right. I do know you well enough to know that. Okay, so what are you thinking?"

"Just this. If you take Tyler anywhere else, what's to stop

these two from tracking you down again? And then there would be no one but you to watch over him. What if they get to you? What if they do something to you, make you disappear the way they maybe did to Colby? What happens to Tyler then? He'd be all alone."

Jim lowered his head. "I won't let that happen."

"You might not have a choice. But here—here there are tons of us. I can call Mel. She and Alex will drop whatever they're doing to get back here to help, I know they will. Alex is one of the top P.I.s in the country, Jimmy. He's good at what he does. And Mel is no slouch. Besides that, here you've got Caleb and his father, Cain. A lawyer and a retired senator, with all the power and influence that go along with that. You've got Wade, the toughest guy I know. You've got Mom and Maya and Edie and Selene."

"I can't ask you all to—"

"You don't have to ask." She shook her head. "Hell, you won't be able to stop them from getting involved in this once I tell them. And I *am* going to tell them. And you've got me, too. I'd do anything for Tyler. I... I love him, Jimmy."

He stared at her as if considering what she said. Thank God, she thought.

"If this goon is out on bail, awaiting trial—" she said.

"He is."

"Then he isn't supposed to leave the state, is he?"

"No."

"The authorities know he's here somewhere. They'll be hunting for him here. Let us help keep Tyler safe while they do. If you go elsewhere, they won't know where to look for the guy. But if you stay here and he's really around looking for you, then he'll stay, too. And they can get him back behind bars where he belongs."

"I don't know..."

"We can have people watching Ty twenty-four, seven,

Jimmy. If you go off alone, who's with him when you're sleep-ing? Or in the shower? You can't do this alone. Not the way we can do it here."

"I just... I can't believe your family would really do all that."

She smiled a little. "It's a Brand family tradition. When one's in trouble, we all come running. Hell, if things get scary, I can call in the Texas branch of the family."

He smiled, and she saw some of the tension leave his eyes. "And how many of those are there?"

"Eighteen, not counting the kids. Let's see, there's a sheriff, a martial-arts expert, a Comanche shaman—"

"Okay, I get it." He lowered his head. "You've convinced me. If your family really is willing, then..."

"Her family is more than willing," Maya said from some-where behind them.

Jimmy swung his head around. So did Kara. Maya was standing near an open window, her husband close beside her.

"Did I mention," Kara asked, "that my family is also terribly nosy, snoopy, rude and intrusive?"

Maya nodded hard. "We are, Jim," she said.

"They really are," Caleb agreed.

"Because we love each other." Maya slid the window closed and came out through the door, Caleb at her side.

Caleb said, "Jim, everything Kara told you about the Brands is dead-on accurate. No one's gonna get within ten miles of your boy with us on the job. I guarantee it."

"Come on, Kara," Maya said. "Let's call Mel, then we'll fill in the others."

Kara looked back at Jimmy.

Caleb said, "Go ahead, sis. I need a minute with Jim anyway."

Jimmy nodded, telling her with his eyes he would be fine. She had no doubt he would, but she also knew Caleb wasn't going to pull any punches. And nothing she could say would be likely to dissuade him.

Sighing, she went inside with her sister. As the door swung closed behind them, Kara heard Caleb's voice, speaking low. "If there's anything else you're keeping from her, pal—"

"There's not."

"There had better not be."

~

ONLY THERE WAS, Jim thought. There was one very big thing he was still keeping from Kara Brand.

He'd been forced to say goodnight to Kara with most of her family watching, and though the entire situation had been explained to them and they had wholeheartedly embraced Kara's plan, Vidalia still looked at him as if she'd like to take him out to the woodshed with a switch. Maya seemed undecided. Edie, blatantly suspicious. Wade and Caleb watched him like bulldogs watching a steak. Only Selene and Kara looked at him with complete understanding and concern. And even Selene seemed to wax uncertain every now and then.

They all seemed to adore Tyler, though. And hell, Jim couldn't blame them for being protective of Kara. If they knew what he was really doing with her, they'd probably run him out of town without thinking twice.

By the time the family was through questioning him and offering opinions and making plans, Tyler had climbed into his lap and fallen asleep.

Jim had been watching Kara, paying close attention all evening to try to assess the extent of the damage he'd done. But he was damned if he could see any sign of any in her eyes.

He'd been craving a moment alone with her, but in the end he gave up on it. He said his goodnights with the entire clan watching him and then carried his sleeping son out to the pickup. He would just have to try to get some private time with Kara tomorrow. He'd made too much progress with her to risk screwing it up now, especially if he was sticking around here in Big Falls after all.

He shifted Tyler onto his shoulder so he could reach for the pickup door, only to see a hand grip it before he could.

Kara had come out behind him, and he hadn't even heard her. Hell, he'd better snap out of this habit of being lost in his thoughts.

She opened the door, and he laid his son gently on the seat, then fastened the seat belt around him, stepped back and closed the door softly.

He turned and leaned against the truck. "You never got any dinner, Kara."

"You didn't, either." She shrugged. "Anyway, it's not like I could think about eating with all this."

Jim wanted to know where things stood with her, how bad a setback this had been. He could happily strangle Angela for showing up now of all times. Ruining his plan when it had been going so damn well. God, he hoped Colby was all right. He'd had phone calls from the Oklahoma state police, the county sheriff's office and the Tucker Lake-Big Falls PD. They were coordinating with Chief Wilcox in Chicago and conducting an all-out search for the missing cop. There wasn't a hell of a lot more that could be done on that score.

Kara looked tired. There were faint circles under her eyes that hadn't been there before. He decided to touch her just to see if she would still allow it. He put his hands on her shoulders, then slid one inward, to move over the curve of her neck.

She surprised him by stepping closer, wrapping her arms around his waist, leaning her body into his. She rested her head on his shoulder and she whispered, "I'm so sorry you're going through all this, Jimmy."

He held her, one hand cupping her neck, his fingers just starting to thread into her hair. "You're sorry? Kara, you don't have anything to be sorry about."

"You could have told me, you know. From the beginning, I mean. You didn't have to keep all this from me."

"I know that. I know. I'm the one who owes you the apology. I just hope... I haven't messed this up."

"Messed what up?"

She was still in his arms, still resting against him, so he couldn't see her face. He wished he could, so he could try to read whatever might be in her eyes and be sure she was asking what he thought she was asking.

He had nothing to go by except the feel of her in his arms, her warm breaths on his neck, the stars twinkling overhead. Hell, no, the stars had nothing to do with this. "Kara, I... I think there's something special between us. I think you feel it, too, don't you?"

She raised her head, stepped back slightly, looked into his eyes just the way he'd been wishing she would. Only, she was the one doing the searching, the probing, trying to read what was in his. He hoped she saw what he was trying to show her and nothing more.

"I feel—" She dipped her head suddenly. He thought he saw color flooding into her face.

"Don't be afraid to tell me what you feel," he said softly.

She raised her eyes to his. "I'm not afraid. Not really. It's just... I'm not sure what I feel. It's too soon for it to be... as big as it seems." She drew a breath. "And I don't want you worrying about my feelings anyway. Not right now, when you've got so much else to contend with."

"I want to worry about your feelings, Kara."

She shook her head. "Tyler comes first."

His heart knocked against his rib cage. He hooked a finger under her chin, tipped it up and pressed his mouth to hers. She kissed like an angel. Like a fragile, timid angel, hungry for something she couldn't begin to understand.

When he lifted his head, he said, "I'm feeling things, too, Kara. The same things you are."

"It's hard for me to believe that."

"Why?"

She shrugged, turned in his arms and leaned back against his chest, tipping her head up as if to search the stars for an answer. "You were always the guy I fantasized about. The one I knew I could never have. Way out of my league."

"I was too shallow back then to know a good woman from a bad one, Kara. Believe me, I know the difference now."

"That doesn't matter so much, though. I mean, you can't decide who you're attracted to. It just happens." She swallowed hard. "Handsome men aren't usually attracted to me. I keep thinking this is just too good to be true. And then when Mom said your... your wife was in town, I thought that was it. I was right, it *was* too good to be true. You were married."

He shook his head slowly. She wasn't looking at him, but at the stars. He was looking down at her, though. She had no idea just how beautiful she was, did she? "That hurt you. I hurt you. I'm sorry, Kara. I swear, I'm going to do my best not to let that happen again."

She closed her eyes.

"I want you in my life. In Tyler's life."

Her eyes popped open, and she turned her head, staring at him in what looked like shock.

"I know it's too soon for that, but it doesn't seem like it is. It makes perfect sense to me. You and me and Tyler—we make sense, Kara. Don't you think?"

She licked her lips nervously. "I... it doesn't feel like it's too soon to me either," she said. She spoke slowly, haltingly, thinking her words through before speaking them. "But it is. We both know it is, Jimmy. I mean... there are so many things to think about, to talk about."

There were, he knew that. But Tyler adored this woman, and

she would do anything for him. Nothing else mattered. Nothing. He'd work through whatever problems there were. "I know."

"No," she said. "I don't think you do." She met his eyes. "I don't want to leave Big Falls, Jimmy. I love it here. It's my home. My family is here, my new business. I'm just starting to make my own way here. To find my footing. And you, your life is in Chicago. Your career, your home, your friends. It might as well be on Mars. A big city. God, I could never—"

"Okay, okay. I'm moving too fast and I've got your head spinning. I'm sorry, Kara. I'm sorry." He ran a hand through her hair, saw the panic taking hold in her eyes. "Take a breath."

She did. Then released it in another rush of words. "And then there's your ex-wife. A drug addict, for God's sake, involved with a criminal. I mean, I don't know if I could handle having a person like that in our lives."

He smiled. "I like when you say 'our lives.'" She didn't smile, though, so he wiped the smile off his own face. "I'm not dismissing your concerns. They're real and they're valid. But Angela is one thing you don't have to worry about. She's not a part of my life or Tyler's."

"But, Jimmy, she's his *mother*." She drew another deep breath. "Maybe she just needs help. Maybe she could get clean, go to rehab, change her ways."

"She doesn't want to change."

"A child needs a mother, Jimmy."

He met her eyes. "I know that." Which was precisely why he was here, he thought. But he didn't say it aloud and he hoped to God it didn't show in his eyes. "I've dumped too much on you," he said. "After the scare of learning Skinny Vinnie might be in town and then all this..." He shook his head. "You know, chances are Vinnie isn't any threat at all to Tyler. Hell, I can't even be sure he's a threat to me. Maybe Colby met a girl and took off for a fling. It wouldn't be the first time. Vinnie and Ang might have just come down here to try talking me into changing my testimony again. Maybe even offering me a bribe this time."

Kara nodded. "But you don't really believe that, do you?"

His lips thinned. Damn, she was a little too insightful. "It's possible."

"But not likely. If he wanted to offer you a bribe, Jimmy, he could have done it over the phone."

He nodded. "I hate that this is happening now. That it's having a negative impact on what's been growing between us."

"It's not," she said. "Nothing's going to have any impact on you and me but you and me. I won't let it."

"But you just said–"

"I changed my mind."

He pulled her close and kissed her again. "You're one special woman, Kara Brand."

"I never thought so. But you're starting to make me feel like one."

Hell, he thought as he hugged her close. He was a real bastard. Because she *was* special and she deserved a hell of a lot more than this. A man who wanted her only because she'd be the perfect mother for his son. A man who didn't really love her. Who wasn't capable of loving her.

She deserved so much more.

But Tyler deserved a woman like Kara. And even Kara agreed with him—Tyler came first. He'd be good to her, he promised himself. He'd treat her like gold, give her everything she could ever want.

Except love, a little voice inside whispered.

Hell, love wasn't all that important anyway. He'd loved Angela. If that wasn't proof that love didn't matter, he didn't know what was. Tyler mattered. Tyler was the *only* thing that mattered.

CHAPTER EIGHT

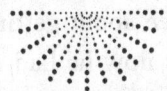

*J*IM WAS PREPARED to spend the night sitting up, watching the house. It wasn't like he was going to be able to sleep anyway, with Ang in town up to God only knew what and that slimebag Vinnie more than likely with her. And Colby missing. Damn, he wished he knew where his friend was. He'd tried calling his cell phone again, just as he'd tried every hour or so since Colby had left. But it was no good.

He should be out there. He should be searching for Colby himself. But dammit, he couldn't leave Tyler and he couldn't drag his son along. Not while there was any risk at all. So he had to settle for phoning the chief for an update.

"Stay put, Corona," Chief Wilcox told him. "We've got officers combing three counties for Benton. His photo and a the tag number and description of the Blazer are with every law-enforcement agency in the area, and tonight they made TV news, as well."

"Still—"

"Still nothing. We've circulated photos and information on Vinnie and Ang as well. Not for the press, though. We don't want to tip them off too fast. But trust me, Corona, we've got this covered. We're gonna find Benton one way or another. And you leaving your kid alone and putting yourself at risk isn't going to change the outcome anyway. So sit tight."

He nodded, hating that his chief was right. "Okay."

"You secure there?"

Yeah, as long as I don't sleep, he thought. Aloud he said, "Yeah, we're good." He would see about getting some better locks on this place tomorrow. For now he had every door and window closed and locked. The bedroom where Tyler slept had only one window, and he'd moved a two-hundred-pound hardwood armoire in front of it for added security.

He'd left Tyler's light on, the bedroom door open. He never moved far enough away to break his line of sight to his son. They'd be all right.

"I'll talk to you in the morning then," the chief said.

Jim said good-night and disconnected. Then he kept his lonely vigil over his son for another hour and a half without incident, sitting in a hard-back chair he'd dragged in from the kitchen so he wouldn't get too comfortable and nod off. The chair was tipped back on two legs, propped by his feet on a coffee table. His side-arm was in his lap. He thought he probably looked like an over-reactive drama king, but he'd rather look like an idiot than risk an unexpected visit from Vinnie Stefano.

Around ten a knock on the door startled him into sitting up straight, feet and chair legs hitting the floor at once. A key scraped in the lock. He came to his feet, gun in his hand, barrel down. His forefinger moved without conscious command, nudging the safety off.

The door swung open and Kara Brand stepped inside. She stopped and eyed him, then his gun, then him again. She'd changed clothes, was dressed more casually now in jeans and a sweater, a warm coat. She nodded at him as she dropped her house keys back into her coat pocket. "Good," she said, eyeing the gun in his hand. "I was afraid you'd think I was overreacting." Then she reached outside the door, retrieving a shotgun from where she'd leaned it.

He felt his eyes widen but said nothing as she hefted a satchel in her other hand and dropped it just inside the door. Then she closed the door and locked it

"I didn't expect to see you again until tomorrow," he told her, not quite sure what to say. This was not a side of Kara Brand he'd seen or even suspected might lurk underneath her tender surface.

She shrugged and brought the shotgun across the room, took a seat on the sofa and leaned it nearby. "You probably aren't going to like this any better than Mom did, but I'm here to stay."

He tilted his head to one side. "So what's not to like?" He crossed the room and picked up the satchel she'd dropped, then carried it up the stairs and put it in the second bedroom. Colby's stuff was still in the first one, and Colby was coming back.

He paused to look into Colby's room, bit his lip, then forced the worry away and headed down the stairs again.

"I take it you didn't bring the shotgun to keep me in line."

She smiled just a little. "Not likely."

He met her eyes, and a spark passed between them. She was frisky tonight. He liked that. But then she broke the contact, hefted the gun and tossed it to him. He caught it easily, knowing even before he checked that it wasn't loaded. Kara was too intelligent to toss a loaded shotgun.

It was a nice old gun, a classic twenty-gauge Ithaca, pump action. Held five shells. Black barrel, rich glossy hardwood stock. It had been freshly cleaned, still smelled of gun oil. He nodded his approval and tossed it back to her. "What did you bring for ammo?"

"Slugs. Hollow-points. Someone comes sniffing around you or Tyler, I don't plan to play games with birdshot."

There was a hint of ferocity in her eyes that he had never seen before. "You're full of surprises, you know that?"

"You didn't think I had a mean bone in my body, did you?" She shrugged. "Most people don't."

"You know how to use that thing?"

Her smile spread wider. "My mama made sure her girls could take care of themselves, Jimmy. Every one of us learned to shoot by the age of ten. And Brands never miss." She gave the gun a half pump, which opened the chamber, and leaned it against the arm of he couch. Then she set a slug in front of her on the coffee table. With the gun in that position, she could slam the slug directly into the chamber, jerk the action upward again and fire. It would save a step. She knew what she was doing.

He pursed his lips as he thought about the possibility that Vinnie might actually show up here. The nightmare image of a shoot-out with Tyler and Kara Brand—sweet, shy, giving Kara Brand—in the middle of it, flashed through his mind. The thought made his stomach convulse.

"Kara, um, I'm not real sure I'm comfortable with this."

"No, I didn't think you would be once you gave it some thought." She looked toward the stairway. "Which bedroom are you using?"

"I'm staying in Ty's room or on the sofa, close enough to hear him."

"That's a good idea. I was going to if you weren't."

"I put your things in the second bedroom. Colby's been using the first."

"Good, I wouldn't want to put Colby out," she said as if there was no question about whether he was coming back. "But maybe after tonight I can stick a cot down here."

"No."

She met his eyes, didn't argue. Didn't ask why not. Maybe

she knew deep down that he'd be too damn distracted if she was sleeping that close to him.

"I was thinking... tomorrow we should put some better locks on this place. And maybe we can start looking for a dog."

"A dog?" He'd just been marveling at how much her thoughts mirrored his own—right up to the part about the dog, which he hadn't even considered.

"We need a good dog," she said. "I know Ty wants a puppy, but I'm hoping we can take him to the pound and convince him to fall for an adult dog. One that will bark if anyone comes around."

"I thought I told you the chances they're going to try anything are slim."

"Which is why you're sitting in the dark with a forty-five in your lap, right?"

He shrugged.

"So chances are slim," she said. "We do whatever we can to make them even slimmer." She nodded toward the window. "Caleb's parked outside, just so you know. He'll be there for three hours, then Wade comes and takes over from one until four. Edie's taking the four-to-seven shift."

"They don't have to do all that"

"They want to do all that. The shifts will get shorter once Mel and Alex get back. They're due in tomorrow morning, by the way. So have you called someone back in Chicago to find out where things stand?"

He glanced at the clock. "Did that as soon as I got Ty settled into bed. My chief says they've got every cop in three counties on this. They all have photos of Colby, as well as Ang and Vinnie's mugshots. Colby's face showed up on the TV news tonight."

"Maya told me. She saw it."

He nodded, still uneasy. "Kara, if this guy is dangerous, I'd really feel better keeping you out of the line of fire."

"I know that. But Tyler's more important, don't you think? And the more of us here watching him, the better."

"Still... " He sighed and tried another tack. For some reason he just wanted her safe in her own home, away from him—far enough away that Angela's sickness and Vinnie's filth couldn't touch her. "There's more than just that to consider, Kara."

She was walking up the stairs now, so he followed. She stood just inside the bedroom door, eyeing the place. It was a usable room, clean, freshly painted. It had been his own room as a kid. It made him feel odd to see her standing there in what had been his bedroom. She moved to where he'd put her bag on the bed, bent to unzip it and yanked out a bundle that included fresh sheets.

"What else is there to consider?" she asked him as she tossed the bag aside and began to make the bed.

He got on the other side to help her. "Tyler. He's...he's getting attached to you, Kara. If you seem to be moving in with us... "

She lifted her eyes to his. God, they were pretty. "I'll make sure he knows from the beginning that it's only temporary, Jimmy. I promise, I won't let him get his hopes up for anything more."

"It's probably already too late for that," he told her. He swallowed, his throat suddenly dry. "God knows, I've already built my hopes pretty high that there will be something more. How can I expect him to do any different?"

She looked at him, her eyes wide with surprise. Then he swallowed hard, lowered his head and told himself that was the wrong thing to say to get rid of her. But hell, he didn't want to get rid of her. Not really, not down deep.

They got the sheets on the bed and he straightened. "This was my room. My entire childhood, this was my haven."

"Really?" She looked around.

He nodded toward the closet. "I used to pretend that was a fort. Sometimes I slept in there, but only with the door open."

She went to the closet, opened it and looked inside. "I don't blame you. It's not very big." Jim moved to stand beside her, laid his hand over hers on the door. She lifted her eyes to his.

"It means a lot, you coming over here like this. Your family... " He stopped there, shook his head. It really did mean a lot. He didn't have to pretend at all, he realized, his throat getting tight.

"We care about Tyler. And about you, Jimmy. We wouldn't want to be anywhere else."

He couldn't take his eyes off her face. She was sincere, right to her soul. She meant every word she said. He couldn't think otherwise.

"I, um... have blankets and pillows in the car," she said. "And another bag, just a small one."

"I'll get them for you."

She nodded and they walked downstairs together. The phone was ringing before they reached the bottom. Jim hurried across the room to where he'd left his cell phone on the coffee table and yanked it up, knowing it had to be something important for anyone to call at this time of the night. And when he looked at the panel and saw the chief's number on it, he was even more certain.

"Corona," he said into the phone. "What's up, Chief?"

"They found the Blazer, Jim. We were able to trace his cell phone's ping to narrow down the search and an eagle eyed deputy spotted it."

It was bad. He knew it was bad. The chief never called him by his first name. "Colby?" he asked, standing motionless.

"We don't know yet. The Blazer took a plunge into a deep ravine. It burned. They only identified it by a license plate that got knocked free on the way down. There's a crew out there now trying to find any sign of anyone inside, but with a fire that bad... "

"Where?" Jim asked. Kara was beside him, her hand on his shoulder, her face searching his as the chief told him where Colby's Blazer had been located.

When he hung up the phone and related what the chief had told him, he thought Kara was going to burst into tears. Instead she set her jaw. "Colby wasn't inside," she said. And she said it firmly. "He wasn't or they'd have found something, some sign."

"I hope you're right."

"You have to go," she told him.

He closed his eyes, feeling as if his heart was being torn right in half. "I can't leave Tyler."

"Jimmy, Caleb is here. I'm here. Nobody is going to get near that boy with me around. I swear you can trust me to keep him safe."

He frowned as her words wormed their way deep inside him.

"I'm not Angela, Jimmy. I'd step in front of a freight train for that child."

More amazing than the power of her words was the fact that he believed them, he thought. He believed her, trusted her, in a way he had thought he would never trust any woman ever again. He trusted her with his son.

Amazing.

He took enough time to jot his cell phone number on a pad by the phone and then went out to find his best friend.

KARA WASN'T SURE how she was going to sleep in the room that had been Jimmy's, much less live under the same roof with him, without giving in to what she was feeling.

She'd never been with a man. Not... intimately. And she was afraid to admit that to him, even a little bit ashamed of it. It seemed so backward in this day and age to be a virgin at twenty-three. She wanted to be with Jimmy. And she thought he wanted to be with her, too. But she was afraid—so afraid of him. He was making her believe things she had always thought were impossible. Making her think there was suddenly a chance she could win the heart of the boy of her high school dreams. The man of her grown-up dreams, now. She was scared half to death, because if it wasn't real, it would kill her.

Maybe it was already too late to worry about that. Maybe she'd already let herself fall. She looked out the window and saw Jimmy talking to Caleb on his way out to join the search for his friend. And just how could she be thinking about her own problems, her own hopes and fears and silly little-girl dreams, when hell was breaking loose all around Jimmy and Ty? It was selfish of her. She needed to focus on what was important. Keeping Tyler safe, praying for Colby's well-being. That was all. Whatever happened—or didn't happen—between her and Jimmy Corona wasn't important. Not now.

She walked through the house, checking every window to be sure the locks were in place, checking the back door to make sure it was locked, as well. Then she went to Tyler's bedroom and stood looking in on him for a long moment. Her heart swelled. Jimmy was worried about Tyler getting attached to her. She wondered if he realized just how attached she was becoming to Tyler. To both of them.

JIM FOUND THE spot, off a side road surrounded by forest, within a half hour. It wasn't hard to find. The entire area was packed with emergency vehicles, police cars and a giant crane with its nose out over a drop-off. As he got out of his pickup, the crane growled and strained, and slowly the burned wreckage of the Blazer rose from the depths. Spotlights followed its progress. He winced when he saw the thing, almost doubled over from the pain that clutched his belly. Hell, no one could have survived a crash like that, much less the inferno that had followed.

A hand clapped his shoulder. "You Corona?"

He turned to face the man with the county sheriff badge pinned to his chest and nodded because he didn't trust himself to speak.

"We don't think he was inside," the sheriff said. "No sign of a body. And there should have been something. Some trace. Of course, we'll have forensics go over it to be sure. And we can't be sure he wasn't thrown from the vehicle on the way down, but we've got dogs working the slope. If he's there, we'll find him."

Jim swallowed hard. "Suppose he got out before it went over?"

"Slim chance, but I suppose it's possible."

Nodding, Jim looked around. "I'd like to start searching these woods."

"I'll get you some men. It would be easier by daylight"

"I don't want to wait. If he's injured... "

The sheriff nodded. Jim got the feeling the man presumed Colby was a goner and was just humoring him, but he didn't care. Within ten minutes searchers were fanning into the woods. Jim searched using a borrowed flashlight. He strained his eyes until they watered and walked until he had no idea where the hell he was. He searched every clump of deadfall, every pile of brush, every shrub and weed patch and fallen log.

He searched until the tiny flicker of hope he'd felt began to fade away. And then he got an idea. Maybe a stupid idea, but hell, it couldn't hurt to try. He'd have tried anything by then.

He pulled out his cell phone, dialed Colby's. The techies couldn't locate it any more narrowly than they had by its ping, because Colby didn't have his location services activated on his damn phone, the paranoid shit. But still, this was a low tech idea.

He hit send, then lowered the phone from his ear and listened to the woods around him.

And he heard it. Small, faint, distant, but there. Colby's cell phone, playing the old cavalry bugle charge. He followed the sound until it stopped, then he hung up and dialed again. And again, working his way closer every time.

Then his flashlight beam found a lump on the ground, and he ran closer, dropped to his knees, fear like an ice-cold weight in his chest as his fingers fumbled around Colby's neck in search of a pulse. When he found one, he damn near cried. He shouted instead. "I found him! He's alive. Get some paramedics out here!"

CHAPTER NINE

*J*T WAS NEARLY three in the morning when Jimmy
returned home. Kara surged to her feet when she
heard the car in the driveway, saw the headlights painting the
house walls before they went dark.

"Easy," Caleb said. He'd come inside to sit with her after
Jimmy had left, and when Wade showed up to relieve him, he'd
decided not to go home. Wade had been brewing coffee nonstop
—in fact, he was putting on a fresh pot when the car pulled in,
but he heard the vehicle, too, and quickly joined them at the
front door. "It's Jim," Caleb said.

"God, I hope... " Kara bit her lip. She didn't need to finish the
thought. All three of them were dreading the news Jimmy might
bring, the devastation he might have encountered when he'd
gone out there tonight.

Kara unlocked the door and pulled it open as he came up the
front steps, shoulders slumped, head low. He looked exhausted.

"Jimmy?"

He lifted his head, met her eyes, then glanced past her at the
two men who stood behind her in the doorway. He had to see
the questions in their eyes.

"He's alive," he said.

"Oh, thank God." Kara put her arms around him. It wasn't planned—it was instinctive. She hugged his neck and he hugged her waist, right there in the open doorway.

She felt the looks Wade and Caleb exchanged behind her, and a rush of self-consciousness slid through her. She released her hold on Jimmy, but he didn't reciprocate. Instead he shifted to the side, keeping one arm around her waist, holding her close beside him as he walked into the house.

"You look wrung-out," Wade said. "You want coffee?"

"Thanks, Wade. That would be great."

Nodding, Wade went to the kitchen. Jim walked through the living room to the open bedroom door and peeked inside at Tyler, who slept soundly. He sighed, then turned to move back to the sofa, still holding Kara beside him as he sank onto its cushions. Caleb took a seat in the chair across from them, and Wade returned, handed a hot mug to Jim, then sat in the rocker.

Jim sipped. Then he talked. "They found Colby's Blazer in a deep ravine, up on a side road north of town." He wrinkled his brow. "Devil's... something or other."

"Devil's Drop," Wade said. "How the hell did he survive the plunge?"

"He got out before it went over. I don't know how—he was unconscious when we found him in the woods, and by the time the E.R. docs finished with him, he'd had enough drugs to keep him incoherent for a while." He lifted his head. "He'll probably have to stay in the hospital for a couple of days. It could have been a lot worse. The Blazer exploded on impact. It's burned black, completely gutted. They wouldn't have even known it was the vehicle we were looking for, except that one of the tags came loose on the way down."

"Thank God he got out," Kara whispered.

"Do they know what happened? How he wound up over that drop?" Caleb asked.

Jim shook his head. "No skid marks. It's a dirt road, so the tire tracks are good. It's too dark to be certain of anything, but we had spotlights. It looks to me as if the Blazer drove straight ahead, then turned right to veer off the road, through the grass and over the drop-off. No signs of veering out of control or fishtailing or sudden braking."

"How badly is Colby hurt?" Kara asked.

"Aside from a solid blow to the head and a couple of broken ribs, not too badly. The doctors say he's gonna be fine. He's got a concussion but no sign of anything more serious. They said we should be able to talk to him in the morning."

"That's good news," Wade said.

Jim nodded. "For now, we're not saying anything about finding Colby. The press is going to get that the vehicle was found and that it will take forensics teams a week or more to try to determine whether any human remains burned with it."

Caleb nodded. "If this was an attempt on his life, there's no point giving his attacker a reason to try again."

"Exactly. We booked him into the hospital under a false name." He sighed, shaking his head. "It's not gonna stay quiet long. Too many cops know, the paramedics at the scene know. People tend to talk. They'll tell their wives, best friends, and it'll get around."

"Yeah," Caleb said. "But out-of-towners aren't going to be as tuned in to the local grapevine. They won't hear for a while."

"I'm counting on it. Meanwhile, now that every cop in three counties is involved, they aren't going to get far."

"Even though he hasn't been conscious long enough to identify his assailants?" Wade asked.

Jim nodded. "There was a sticky residue around his wrists, ankles and face. One piece of duct tape still on his sleeve. He was definitely held against his will. This accident was either an escape or attempted murder. Colby's a cop—Chicago cop, but it doesn't matter. Cops don't like people messing with their own.

Stuff like this goes down, they close ranks. They're on this." Jim drew a breath, sighed. "Frankly I feel better about things than I have in a long while."

"That's saying something," Wade said.

Jim nodded, then lifted his head. "Thanks, you guys. This was above and beyond, coming out here like this. I don't know how I'll ever repay you."

Wade sent him a smile. "Don't worry. We'll think of something."

"You don't need to stay. There's a State Police unit outside for the night," Jim said. Wade got to his feet and Jim did, too. The two shook hands, and then Caleb repeated the gesture. When they left, Jim followed them to the door to thank them again, then remained there and watched as they drove away.

He locked the door, then he turned to Kara. She was standing close to him. He pulled her into his arms and held her so tight she felt truly cherished. "I really think everything's going to be okay," he told her. "I really do."

"I know it will," she said, resting her head on his shoulder. There was so much on her mind. A thousand questions whirled around inside her, eager to escape and have their answers. But this was no time for any of that. He'd been through enough today. "You should get some sleep, Jimmy."

"So should you," he told her. "I'll climb in with Ty. I need him close tonight. So rest easy. Don't lie awake worrying or listening for things to go bump, okay?"

"Okay."

He stroked her hair and looked into her eyes. "I'm really, *really* glad you were here tonight."

She smiled a little. "I'm glad I was here, too. I like being here." She leaned up and pressed a kiss to his cheek. "Good night, Jimmy."

"Night, Kara."

She went up the stairs and felt his eyes on her all the way.

~

KARA SLEPT FOR five hours, then bounded out of bed wide awake and incredibly upbeat. And maybe that was because Colby had been found and Jimmy was sure things were going to be okay now. Or maybe it was because she was finally letting herself be convinced that his attention to her, his tenderness toward her, came from more than just a casual interest.

She showered, dressed, fussed a little with her hair and barely-there makeup. Then she headed downstairs and felt joyously domestic as she cooked pancakes and sausages in the functional kitchen, brewed fragrant coffee. And she felt pretty— and suspected that had to do with Jimmy Corona's constant, convincing attention over the past few days.

When she felt eyes on her and turned from the frying pan to see him leaning in the doorway, arms crossed, watching her, she knew he liked what he saw.

She let her smile come, though it was a little self-conscious, a little nervous. "Good morning."

"Morning," he said. "The whole house smells so good my mouth is watering. Sausage?"

"And pancakes."

"Tyler loves pancakes." .

"I know. That's why I made them." She turned her attention back to the pan, rolling the sausage links with a fork. The burner beside it held a griddle, pancakes bubbling on one side, ready to flip. "Is he up yet?"

"Not yet. Won't be long." He crossed the room to stand beside her, looking over her shoulder at the food. Then he reached around her to pick up a spatula, used it to flip the pancakes. The action brought him very close, his body rubbing against hers, his face close and bristly, his arm encircling her.

She could have easily closed her eyes and leaned back against him. But she managed not to.

"I could get used to this, Kara."

She lowered her head a little, then started when first his breath and then his lips whispered across her neck.

"I like having you here when I wake up."

"I... I like it, too."

"Yeah?"

She turned to face him. His body was still very close, touching hers. She brought her gaze to his and asked, "Did you love your wife, Jimmy?"

He blinked. Clearly those had not been the words he'd been expecting to hear. "I did. I loved her a lot. She lied to me, cheated on me and damn near killed my son."

She nodded. "I didn't think you were the kind of man who'd marry a woman he didn't love."

He lowered his gaze a little too quickly, and a flutter of alarm came to life in her chest. She pushed it down and swallowed her fears. "And what about since then? Have you... dated a lot of women?"

His frown told her he wondered why she was asking so many questions. "No. Hardly any, as a matter of fact. I'd pretty much decided I didn't need anyone again. But then I came back here and saw you again, Kara. And everything changed."

"Did it?"

He nodded firmly. "What's wrong?"

Hell, she didn't know what was wrong—aside from the fact that she was falling and falling hard. For him, for Tyler, for this whole dream he'd planted in her mind. It was growing too fast, unfurling skyward like Jack's bean stalk and carrying her hopes into the clouds as it grew. She was afraid to climb to the top, afraid she would find one giant heartbreak, instead of a dream come true.

But she couldn't very well tell him all that.

"Nothing's wrong," she said. "I was just curious."

He nodded but seemed to be studying her. "I think you're worried. Maybe a little unsure of me. You shouldn't be, Kara. Maybe... maybe if I tell you my plans for the day, you'd feel better."

"You have plans?"

He nodded. "Our dinner by the falls got ruined last night. And I had such big hopes for that. I'll make it up to you tonight, I promise."

"You don't have to apologize for that. You were worried about Tyler. And I'm not going to feel save leaving him with anyone but us. Even my family. I just... want him within reach at all times until we're sure that creep who hurt Colby is behind bars." She looked up at him, saw something like admiration in his eyes. "So if you're planning to try again with that picnic by the falls, I think we should bring him with us."

"I agree completely," he said. "I was thinking of something else entirely. Later in the day. My first errand today is going to be to see your local police chief, Earl Wheatly."

"I thought your first stop would be to visit Colby in the hospital."

He nodded. "You're right. That's where I'm meeting Wheatly."

"To talk about the case," she surmised.

"Among other things."

She blinked and searched his face. "What other things, Jimmy?"

"Last night, while we were in the hospital waiting room, Chief Wheatly told me how impressed he'd been with my work out there. My observations about the tire marks, the duct tape residue, all of that." He shrugged. "He offered me a spot on the Tucker Lake-Big Falls Police Department."

The fork she'd been holding fell to the floor. "Are you serious?"

"I'm very serious." He drew a breath, sighed deeply, slid his arms around her waist. "To be honest I've been thinking about getting Tyler out of Chicago for a while now. My job there is too demanding. I'm away from him too much of the time, and there's always a fair chance I might not make it home to him." He looked toward the bedroom. "The change in him since we've been here in Big Falls is amazing. He's happy, Kara. It's the first time I've been able to look at my son and see that he's truly, honest-to-God happy. I can't take that away from him."

She nodded slowly. "You'd do anything for him, wouldn't you?" She asked the question softly, already knowing the answer.

"Of course I would. Wouldn't you if he were yours?"

A smile tugged at her lips. "I would, even though he's not mine."

His eyes moved over her face, and she wasn't sure if they were searching or caressing. It felt like a little of both. Out of the blue, he leaned down and pressed his lips to hers for a long, slow, wonderful kiss that left her head spinning and her heart pounding.

She lowered her eyes, wishing to heaven she could ease her doubts. But she felt as if she had more of them than she'd had before.

He reached past her to flick off the burners, and she realized she'd been so distracted the food had been in danger of burning.

"And as an added bonus, I'm going to get that fence put up for you today." He said it quickly, releasing her and turning to a cupboard to take down a handful of plates.

She arched her brows. "All in one day?"

"I thought I'd see if Wade wanted to come over and help out. Our State Police guard is only going to be outside by night, so the more sets of eyes on Ty by day, the better." He set the table while she scooped the last of the pancakes onto the platter nearby. She brought the platter and a smaller one holding the golden-brown sausage links to the table while Jimmy opened the fridge for margarine, maple syrup and orange juice.

"Maybe Tyler should spend the day with me," Kara said.

She saw the way Jimmy stiffened just a little bit, halfway through filling a juice glass. He didn't look at her, just seemed to shake himself before finishing the task. "He won't be a problem with me this morning."

"You're going to take him with you to the hospital, to your meeting with Chief Wheatly?" she asked, watching him carefully now. "Have you even talked to him about this mother of his, Jimmy?"

"No. He... he only knows she left us. Nothing more."

"Then you don't really want him around, maybe overhearing your conversation do you?" She shrugged. "Besides, I'm going to be at the Corral most of the day. We're doing inventory. Maya and the twins will be there. And Edie and Sally. Ty can ride the mechanical bull and play with the kids and the dog. The place will be closed to the public. He'll have a blast."

Jim drew a breath, lifted his head.

"You do trust me to take care of him, don't you?" she said.

"Sure I do." He turned and met her eyes. "I really do, Kara."

"It's okay to be honest with me, you know I understand. After what a woman you loved and trusted did to your baby, it's no wonder you have a few scars. But Jimmy, I'm not a drug addict. And I don't lie. Especially not to you. And besides all that, there's nothing I wouldn't do to protect that little angel."

"I know that. I know. And any other woman would have been insulted and angry at me for even hesitating." He ran a hand through her hair. "It's been a long time since I've trusted anyone with Tyler's well-being."

"You trusted him with Maya the other night."

"That was before I knew Vinnie and Ang were in town." He gave his head a shake. "But even with that, it's different with you. I do trust you. It's just a little tough to get used to the idea, you know? My knee jerk reactions need revising. I'll get there."

"I know."

"Okay, how about this?" he said. "Take him with you to the Corral this morning while I go into town. I'll meet you there around lunch-time. I'll bring pizza, enough for everyone. Then I'll head back here to work on that fence and bring him with me."

"Sounds great," she said.

"Good. Thank you for understanding." He reached for her, and she thought he was going to kiss her again. But just before he pulled her close, a little voice interrupted them.

"Hey, you guys didn't have breakfast without me, didja?"

Kara smiled and stepped easily away from Jimmy to bend down to Tyler. He wasn't wearing his leg braces, had scooted out to the kitchen on his backside instead.

She scooped him up and rubbed noses while tickling him until he giggled. "I made pancakes. And after that you and I are going to spend the morning together while your dad takes care of some business. How does that sound?"

"Are we going to see the ponies?"

"Nope. Ponies are tomorrow. After PT. Today we've got other fun things to do. And my mother will be there and—"

"Gramma Vi?"

"Did she tell you to call her that, Ty?" He nodded. "Well, she only asks people she really likes to call her Gramma Vi."

"I never had no gramma before. I think it's cool."

She set him in his chair and pushed it up close to the table. "The twins are going to be there, too. And your dad's bringing pizza later."

"Alllll *right!*"

Kara took a chair and felt Jimmy's gaze. She turned to see him standing there, looking from her to Tyler and back again, pensive and deep in thought for a long moment. Then he saw her watching him and seemed to snap out of it. He took a seat and dug into the stack of pancakes.

～

JIM CAME OUT of the hospital feeling very good about things. Colby was awake, still hurting and a little groggy but much more himself than he had been before. Enough to ID Vinnie as his abductor and the man who gave the order to have him killed. He also gave a good description of the thug who'd shoved his Blazer over Devil's Drop with him still inside.

What surprised Jim was Colby's insistence that he would have been killed if not for Ang. She'd felt sorry for him and sliced through the tape on his wrists. It was enough to save his life. He also insisted she was unaware of Vinnie's plan to have him killed.

Vinnie and Ang were being hunted by every cop in Oklahoma. They'd have to keep their heads down. Any attempt they made to get to him or to Tyler would get them nailed. Colby was under police guard in the hospital, even though as far as anyone knew, he'd died in that fiery crash at Devil's Drop. It was a load off Jim's mind. He'd feel better once Vinnie was caught and locked up, but this was a good start.

After he'd seen Colby, he'd spent some time with Wheatly. The chief promised him a job as soon as he was ready, provided it was within the month. He had a slot opening up that would need filling. Jim didn't intend for it to take that long. Hell, when this notion of accepting the chief's offer had first occurred to him, he hadn't intended for the new job to last more than a year. In a year, he'd thought, he would have convinced Kara to leave this town and he could get back to his life in Chicago.

But something had changed inside him when he'd seen Kara with Tyler this morning. It had been changing right along. He loved her. And he loved her family too. It would be wrong for him to expect Kara to leave her mother, her sisters. That was no way to treat a woman who was everything his little guy could ever want or need in mother. A woman who was, even now, making Tyler's fondest dreams come true. Hell, everything inside him was changing. And when he'd told Kara how happy Tyler was here, happier than he'd ever been, he'd realized it was the truth. And now he didn't know what the hell his long-term plan was anymore.

Except for one thing. He was going marry Kara Brand. And that plan, he thought, was going well. He didn't think she would turn him down.

He drove back to downtown Big Falls, and parked the pickup in a public lot that took up space behind the local businesses, hoping it wouldn't be spotted there. This had to be a surprise, and it wouldn't take long. He locked the pickup and hurried into the local jewelry store. It was dim and smelled of pine and cinnamon. Glass cases lined three sides, all of them filled with glittering, sparkling things.

"Well, well. This *is* a pleasant surprise," said a slender salt-and-pepper-haired man with a neat beard and a suit with a bow tie. He came from behind the counter and extended a hand. "Mr. Corona, isn't it?"

Jim took the hand he offered, surprised. "I'm sorry, do I know you?"

"No, no, we haven't met. But you know how small towns are. Everyone knows everything. You've been pointed out to me once or twice. I'm Barlow, by the way. Milton Barlow."

"Well, Mr. Barlow, I hope the small-town gossip mill isn't going to get wind of the purchase I'm going to make here today. Because it's a surprise."

"For Miss Brand?"

Jim lifted his brows. "Wow, everyone around here really *does* know everything, don't they?"

"Rest easy, Mr. Corona. No one will hear about this from

me. So what are you in the market for? A tennis bracelet, perhaps? We just got in some earrings that are absolutely—"

"A ring," Jim told the man. "An engagement ring."

Milton Barlow's jaw dropped. He quickly snapped it shut again, clapped his hands together and blinked fast, like he had a rush of tears to blink away. Then he turned and hurried toward the back of the shop, calling, "Follow me."

Amused and a little puzzled, Jim followed. The man opened a door and ushered him through it into a cozy office. "Now, you just sit here. That way folks who pass on the streets won't glimpse you through the windows. God knows, that would get the speculation started. When do you plan to ask her?"

"Tonight," Jim said.

"Good. Good. Any longer and I can't guarantee she won't hear about it before you do."

"Well, all due respect, Mr. Barlow, but how am I going to pick out a ring from in here?"

Barlow smiled. It was a big, wonderful smile, accompanied by him clasping his hands under his chin, hunching his shoulders and closing his eyes. "Trust me," he said. "I know that girl. Kara comes in here, oh, once every three or four months. Makes up some excuse, you know. Buys a gift for one of her sisters or her mother, that dear woman. But she always spends time looking at the diamond rings."

Jim lifted his brows. "She does? Any particular ring?"

Barlow's eyes popped open and he nodded hard and fast. "Oh, yes. One particular ring. I'll show you!" Then he spun around and all but skipped out of the office.

THE DOOR OPENED and Jimmy came in, pizza boxes stacked in his arms. His eyes, when they met Kara's, were warm and kind. Then they slid to where his son sat on the floor, braces off,

Selene held her hands over his legs, palms down, moving them every now and then.

"It's okay," Kara said, moving close to him and keeping her voice low. "He said his legs were hurting him. Selene's into all sorts of alternative healing."

He lifted his brows. "What exactly is she doing?"

"Reiki." She shrugged. "I figured it couldn't hurt."

He lifted his brows, tipped his head to one side.

"Hi, kiddo. What do you think? Is it working?"

"It really is! This magic stuff is for real!"

He smiled and Kara read his face. "I know what you're thinking," she told him. "Placebo effect."

He shrugged.

"A few years ago I might have agreed with you, but not now. I've seen too much. Selene—she has something."

"I believe you. To tell you the truth, I don't care what it is. I'm all for anything that makes him feel better."

"That's good," Selene called. "'Cause I have a few suggestions I want to run by you. But we'll save those for another time."

From the back Vidalia called, "I smell pizza!"

Then she and Maya came out of the store room, Maya wiping her hands on a dish towel, Vi heading straight for a table to begin taking the upturned chairs off it. Jim carried the boxes to the table and set them in the center. Then Selene came over, carrying Tyler in her arms.

Ty sent his father a look and said, "I should put my braces back on."

"Oh, it can wait until after pizza," Selene said. "Can't it, Jim?"

Jim nodded. "Sure. A few minutes longer won't hurt."

Selene put Tyler in a chair, and the twins clambered up into the seats on either side of him. Kara went behind the bar to retrieve paper plates and napkins, then turned to find Jim standing behind her.

"Any problems?"

"Not a one," she said. "Ty's a doll."

"Yeah, he's a con man, too. I can see he's got the whole crew eating out of his hand."

"Hey, he did that his first day in town."

He smiled at her. "And how did your morning go?"

"Fine. Enjoyed it immensely. How about you? How did your morning go?"

"Terrible," he said.

She had opened the cooler to take out soft drinks, but she paused there. "Why? What happened?"

He lifted a hand to her face, caught a wisp of hair between his fingers and smoothed it slowly. "I missed you."

She felt the blood rush to her face. "Jimmy, be serious."

"I am serious." He held her eyes for a long moment, until she turned away, unable to bear the intensity in them. "Other than that, it wasn't too bad," he went on. "But I'll tell you more about that tonight." He reached past her to grab colas from the cooler and carried them back with him to the table.

Kara joined him there and tried to eat. The man was sweeping her off her feet, and she had no doubt it was exactly what he intended.

"Hey, you guys having pizza without us?"

Everyone looked up at the shout from the doorway. Melusine stood there, arm in arm with Alex. Kara hadn't seen her sister in weeks and she jumped up and ran to hug her hard.

"Oh, Mel, it's so good to see you!"

Mel hugged her back. "Same here, kid." She moved to the table to hug her mother and each sister in turn, then she turned to stare down at Jim. "You haven't changed much," she said.

"More than you would even believe," he replied, rising. "Hello, Melusine."

"Jim, this is my husband, Alex Stone. Alex, this is Jim Corona, former high school hunk and current cop with the Chicago PD."

"Not exactly current," he said, turning to shake Alex's hand.

"No? What, you turn in your badge or something?"

"I'm on leave. Thinking about making it permanent."

Kara blinked up at him, her questions in her eyes. Jim sighed. "I was going to tell you later, Kara. But I can't wait. I spoke to Chief Wheatly this morning. I told him to hold that job on the local PD for me. I'm planning to take it."

She couldn't believe what she was hearing. "Jimmy, I.... I mean, just like that? Shouldn't you give it some time before making such a drastic decision?"

"The decision is made."

He was serious. About her. About them. He wasn't playing around. He'd mentioned the job offer this morning, but she'd never thought he'd just up and accept it this fast. Suddenly everything turned upside down. Her head spun as she recalled telling him she would never leave Big Falls. My God, had he done this because of her?

"I... excuse me, I need to—" She got to her feet but knocked the chair over in the process. Then she hurried to the ladies' room.

Kara leaned on the sink and stared at her reflection in the mirror. Her eyes were wider than normal, her face perhaps a little pinker.

The bathroom door swung open, and she looked without turning, using the mirror to ascertain whether Jimmy had followed her in.

He hadn't. It was Mel. She stood just inside the doorway, hands on her hips. "So you want me to kick his ass or what?"

"Right. The first guy to look more than twice in my direction since I don't know when, and all I want is for my big sis to chase him away."

Mel lifted her brows. "You're exaggerating. Lots of guys have looked in your direction."

She rolled her eyes. "Until they get hurt, at least."

"You're not a klutz anymore, Kara. Stop thinking like one." Mel came closer, nodding slowly. "So you want this thing to work out with him?"

"Yeah. I do. It's just... hard to believe it's real."

"Maybe for you it is." Mel put a hand on her sister's shoulder, holding her gaze in the mirror. "I gotta tell you, sis, it's not all that surprising to anyone else."

"Isn't it?"

Mel shook her head. "Why would it be? You're gorgeous, smart, single, hardworking, kind. What's been tough for us to swallow is that men haven't been swarming the place trying to steal you away from us for years now."

Kara made a face, knowing full well why. She'd been clumsy, self-conscious, shy, hiding inside a shell where she felt safe from the world.

"Jimmy probably thinks I've lost it."

Mel smiled. "He wanted to come in after you. I asked him to let me do it. Told him we had a lot of catching up to do anyway."

Kara nodded. "He'll come in before long if I don't come out. Probably thinks he did something wrong."

"You think?" Mel looked toward the door. "So what's the deal with him anyway?"

"I wish I knew." Kara turned and leaned back against the sink, facing her sister full-on. "He shows up back in town and starts paying attention to me."

"Normal behavior."

"He seems to be getting awfully serious awfully fast."

"And that's a problem because...?"

Kara thought about that for a long moment and couldn't come up with an answer. Then the door opened again and the man himself stood there. "My turn yet?" he asked.

Kara drew a breath, squared her shoulders, faced him and nodded. Mel sent her a questioning look, but she said, "It's okay, Mel. Give us a minute."

"All right."

Mel left the room, patting Jimmy's shoulder on the way out as if to offer encouragement. Kara pushed off the sink and walked to where he stood. She expected him to talk to her, to ask her what he'd said wrong, to question whether she was all right. But he didn't do any of those things. Instead he slid his arms around her waist and pulled her to him and kissed her as if he'd been starving for her.

Everything inside her turned molten. Her nervousness, her questions, everything just burned away at his touch, his taste. Nothing remained but sensation, desire, a wanting and yearning she had never felt before. Knots tied themselves in her stomach while butterflies rioted in her chest. She was breathless and overwhelmed. He held her tighter than he ever had.

When he lifted his head away, her legs were shaking so hard she didn't think they would hold her. His arms around her loosened and she whispered, "Don't let go, Jimmy. If you do, I might fall."

She glimpsed a relieved smile just before he folded her into his arms again. He held her gently, as if she was cherished and fragile. "I'll never let you go if you don't want me to."

"Really? And we'll just live out our lives in a ladies' room?"

He laughed softly. It rumbled in his chest, beneath her head. "I've been dying to kiss you all day. Sorry I let it get the best of me." His hand stroked her hair. "You okay?"

"Okay? I wouldn't exactly describe it as okay, no. I'm... " She lifted her head, met his eyes, then lowered hers quickly.

"Turned on?" he asked with a waggle of his eyebrows. She felt the blood rush into her cheeks. Jim caught her face in his hands and tipped it up so he could meet her eyes. "Don't be embarrassed, Kara. I need to hear that you want me as badly as I want you."

Her self-consciousness was quickly replaced by amazement

"I... I do," she admitted. "But it's new to me, Jimmy. I'm not... I mean, I've never... "

He blinked three times and then his face changed. He didn't release her, but she sensed him pulling back in some other way. "Kara?" When his prompting didn't result in a reply, he went on. "Kara, you have... you've been with other men, right? That's not what you meant just now."

She forced herself to look him in the eye. "I'm a virgin, Jimmy."

He stared at her, shaking his head slowly.

"That doesn't mean I don't want to. I mean, I do." She paused, then said, "You're disappointed." He was probably used to experienced women. She'd probably be terrible in bed, nowhere near able to satisfy a man like him.

"Disappointed?" He seemed to shake out of his state of wonder and he folded her into his arms once more. "No, Kara. Feeling a little guilty, wondering why your family hasn't run me out of town on a rail for the impure thoughts I've been having about you. Hell, if they knew, they probably would."

"Don't feel guilty. I've been having the same thoughts."

"Oh, I seriously doubt that." There was heat in his eyes as they skimmed her head to toe. "Mine are pretty detailed."

She tried not to blush, felt her face heating anyway and kept her eyes averted. He was searching her face, reading her eyes, she was sure of it. Then he pulled her close and kissed her softly, deeply, on and on and on. Then he hugged her, burying his face against her neck.

Kissing her neck again, he whispered, "I'll never push you, Kara."

God help me, she thought. *I kinda wish you would.*

He released her as if reluctant to do so. "I should go. I have to get to that fence before our special evening."

"Splash some cold water on your face, beautiful. Your family will lynch me if they see you looking like you've just been ravished."

She smiled. "Okay."

"I'm going. Taking Ty back to the house. See you later?"

"Soon," she said.

"Not soon enough."

He leaned close and kissed her gently, then he turned and left the room.

CHAPTER TEN

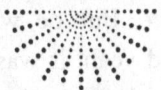

*H*E PUT TYLER in the truck and drove back to the house—*her* house, where she was kind enough to let him stay free of charge while he did his best to seduce her, deceive her and use her for his own ends. He wondered if she'd intended to live in the second story, while having her daycare facility on the ground floor, and he thought that wouldn't really be enough room for a family of three. They'd probably have to buy another place, either for her center or for their home.

He sure was starting to think as if this was a done deal, wasn't he?

Tyler was completely involved in the coloring book he'd brought from the bar with him. He had a giant box of crayons between his knees, and was concentrating so hard on his picture that he had a little furrow between his brows.

Sighing deeply, Jim told himself he was not a *complete* bastard. He was giving Tyler the mother of his dreams. And giving Kara a son she already adored. And, hell, he intended to do his best to make her happy for the rest of her life.

Okay, not the rest of her life. The next fifteen years or so. Just until Tyler grew up. Still, that was a lot to offer, right?

Wrong, idiot. It might be a lot to offer if she knew that was all she was being offered. But what you're pretending to be offering is a lot more. You're making her believe in a big fat lie.

Why the hell did she have to be so damn *good?* It made it tough not to feel guilty. Pretending to love her, pretending to want her so badly he could barely keep his hands to himself...

He shifted in his seat. Okay, so maybe the wanting part wasn't *quite* make-believe. But he was human and she was gorgeous. And good. And yeah, it was a shame to play such a nice, decent girl the way he was playing her. And yet if she wasn't a nice, decent girl, he wouldn't want her, anyway. She wouldn't be good enough to be a mother to his son, and that was what this was all about

So he had to play her. Sweep her off her feet, convince her he had fallen madly in love. He thought he'd accomplished a major part of that. Clearly she wanted him. Wanted him badly. He'd been amazed at the instant and powerful responses he'd managed to elicit in her. She responded so easily when he touched her. A fine sheen of sweat broke out on her smooth skin, and her heart pattered rapid-fire against her chest. And her breathing quickened and her eyes... Hell, he had to break this train of thought and break it now. He was having enough trouble focusing without...

She was a virgin. She'd never been with another man. He would be the first to show her how good it could be. And yet he knew he would have to be careful, gentle, take it slow. Because he didn't want to hurt her or frighten her or...

Damn, he was doing it again.

He pulled into the driveway of the house and shut off the engine, then carried Ty straight to the backyard and got to work on the fence. He needed physical labor and lots of it.

∼

BY THE TIME they finished inventory, Kara was wrung out, coated in a layer of sweat and dust and sure she looked hideous.

"Good grief," she said, "I don't even want to pass close to Jimmy and Tyler looking like this." She sniffed herself. "Do I smell?"

"You can always come home and shower there, daughter," Vidalia said as she pulled the bar's door shut and turned the lock. Then she hung a sign on the hook, eye level on the door. It read Closed for Inventory.

"Maybe I will."

"Up to you. You want to be deceptive, that's your call."

"Deceptive?" Kara shot a look at her mother, then sought help from Selene. Alex and Mel had already gone home—they'd be using Mel's old bedroom while they were here in town. Maya had taken the twins and gone home, as well. They'd been cranky and tired and needed a nap.

Only Selene, Vidalia and Kara remained. And Selene's helpless shrug was no help at all.

"In case you haven't seen it for yourself, Kara, that man is falling fast and hard. It's not fair that he never sees you with dirt under your nails until it's too late."

Kara rolled her eyes. "You think it might put the brakes on him a little?"

"Nope. He's got the bit in his teeth, that one. Still, it might make you a little more sure of him if he likes you just as much dirty and tired as he does bright-eyed and fresh-faced."

"What makes you think I'm not sure of him?"

Her mother just looked at her as if she had said something utterly stupid.

"I swear, Mom," Selene said. "Sometimes I think you're as psychic as I am."

"Psychic schmychic. I know my daughters. If that's not doubt I see in her eyes, then it's the best imitation I've ever seen. So what is it, Kara? You think he's just playing games?"

"No. I think he's dead serious. I'm just not convinced it's for the reasons he wants me to believe."

"Such as?" her mother asked. She was keeping pace beside her as Kara left the saloon to the parking lot in front.

Kara shrugged and unlocked her car. In her mind she heard her doubts, but she wouldn't voice them now to her mother. "Never mind, Mom. It's just that I'm not used to this kind of attention."

"High time you got used to it, child. And don't go thinking you have to settle for the first man bright enough to pay you any, either. There will be others."

Not for me.

The thought whispered through her mind so firmly it startled her. She gasped at the power of it, the trueness of it. It resonated with such validity that she didn't doubt for one moment that it was absolutely correct. And it was a revelation for which she'd been unprepared.

"I'd better go."

"Coming to the house to shower?"

"Nah. I have a house of my own now. I'll use it."

Vidalia nodded in approval.

She got into the car and drove. It was only five minutes to her home, and when she pulled into the driveway and got out of the car, she heard the sound of a hammer falling repeatedly, coming from the backyard. Wade's pickup was parked along the roadside, so she knew he was out there helping. The sounds of work never stopped as she walked to the front door of the house and went inside. She moved past the living room, into the big playroom with the huge doors, and looked out its large windows. Wade was out back. So was Jimmy.

Jimmy.

It wasn't a cold day. The temperature hovered around fifty-nine and the sun was beaming down from the western horizon. It would get a lot cooler once it set, but right now it was warm enough that Jimmy had stripped down to a tank-style undershirt and his jeans. His skin was damp and she watched for a few minutes as he swung a hammer.

Then she glanced at the clock and raced upstairs. Twenty minutes later she was clean, dressed in fresh clothes, sporting a still-damp pony tail and stirring a pitcher of sweet tea. She poured two tall glasses full and carried them out the back door and into the yard.

When he heard the creak of the door, Jimmy turned from his work, met her eyes and smiled. "You're back."

"Uh-huh. You've been busy." She crossed the backyard, handed him the iced tea and forced her eyes to leave his long enough to look at the fence that surrounded the backyard. "It looks great."

"Just about done," he said. He put the glass to his lips and drank, tipped his head back to drain the glass. His neck was corded and moist, and his Adam's apple moved with every swallow. She thought about putting her fingers there. Or her lips. He lowered the glass and caught her looking. His eyes held hers, dark and intense.

Wade cleared his throat and she turned. "That for me?" he asked, nodding toward the glass she still held.

"Oh. Sorry, Wade. Here." She handed it to him and then felt someone tugging on her blouse.

Tyler stood there smiling up at her. "I helped," he said. "It's a cool fence, isn't it, Kara?"

"It's a beautiful fence, Tyler. You did a great job."

He beamed, clearly proud. Jim patted his shoulder. "I don't know that we could have got it done without him. You, Wade?"

"No way. We'd have been another two days at least."

Tyler lifted his chin.

"I would have brought you a drink, too, Tyler," Kara said. "But I only had two hands. You want to come inside and get one?"

He looked up at his father.

Jim said, "Go ahead, Ty. I've just got one more board to put up and we're done anyway. I'll be right behind you."

"Okay." Tyler took up his crutches and walked beside Kara back into the house.

She felt Jim's eyes on her all the way inside, then she heard him say to Wade, "Let's get this last board nailed on, pal. I've got things I'd rather be doing."

A little shiver whispered up her spine, and she wondered what surprises the night would hold.

TWO HOURS LATER she held the front door open while Jimmy dragged a huge Douglass fir tree into the living room. Tyler was so excited he was bouncing up and down. He'd looked at just about every tree in the lot before finally settling on this one. This was the special evening Jimmy had planned.

He couldn't have come up with anything better.

"Okay," Jimmy said. "Where are we standing this bad boy?"

Kara shrugged. "What do you think, Ty?" Tyler was standing in the center of the room. "How 'bout right here? In the middle?"

"We can do that," Kara said. "Unless you think it would be better near the windows. So the lights show from outside. Hmm. I don't know. Which is better?"

"By the windows!" Tyler said.

"By the windows it is." Jimmy took the tree stand he'd purchased on the way home and started to fix it to the bottom of the tree, while I moved a chair and end table away from the big window to the left of the front door. And minutes later, he had the tree standing there, straight and majestic.

"It's the best tree ever," Kara said, and then realized Jimmy had said it at the same time. He looked her way, smiling in a way that made her heart flutter.

Tyler was sitting on the floor now, digging through one of the boxes of decorations his "Gramma Vi" had sent over. She'd said there were still more in the attic if they needed them. He pulled out a glitter coated reindeer, and held it up by its string. "Which one is it, Dad?"

"Prancer," Jimmy said. Then he leaned closer and took another look. "Nope, sorry. That's Dancer. Dancer for sure."

"Hello Dancer. Wanna hang on our tree?"

"Ah-ah, lights first. Then ornaments," Jimmy told him. And he began unwrapping the strings of lights they'd picked up in town. Once they were unwound, he said, "Let the decking of the halls begin!"

Kara found a radio station playing holiday music, and joined in the fun. But every now and then, she got a huge lump in her throat and just stood still and watched as Jimmy lifted Tyler up to hang ornaments in the glow of the lights. The smell of pine was so heady, and the tears in her eyes, nothing but joyful.

CHAPTER ELEVEN

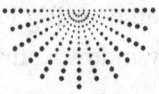

"*Y*OU'RE SO BEAUTIFUL tonight, in the lights from the Christmas tree," Jimmy said.

Tyler had fallen asleep admiring the tree, and he'd carried him in to bed. Now they were dancing together in the tree-lit living room to the country Christmas music wafting softly from the radio.

She lifted her head from his shoulder, let her cheek brush his on the way up, then met his eyes. "This is the most beautiful evening, Jimmuy. It's like a dream. It's almost... it's hard to believe it could be real." She threaded her fingers into his hair. "Tell me it's real, Jimmy."

"It's real." He kissed her lips, then her cheek, snuggling her head down onto his shoulder again. When she brushed her lips over his neck, she felt him shudder.

"I've loved you since I was sixteen, Jimmy Corona. Do you realize that?"

He stopped moving, pulled his head back and blinked down into her eyes. For a moment she didn't think he could find words—and she wondered if she'd said too much, gone too far.

But then he ran a hand through her hair and said, "You're so special, Kara. So honest and open. No pretense, no games."

"I don't have any reason for pretense or games," she told him. "Do you?"

He stared into her eyes for a long moment, then blinked as he noticed something beyond her. "Wow," he whispered, and he turned her so she could see what he did.

The full moon had risen over Big Falls, and spilled its silvery light in through the windows, drenching them both in moonglow.

"Have you ever seen anything so beautiful?" she whispered.

"Never." The tone of his voice made her look at him. His eyes were focused on her, not on the moon. "Never in my entire life. Probably never will."

And then suddenly, he dropped down to one knee in front of her. He took her hands in his and looked into her eyes. "Kara, I know it's only been a few days, but I don't need any longer than that to know you're the only one for me. And Tyler knows it, too. We want you to be in our lives. I want you to be my son's mother. I want you to be my wife."

Her heart seemed to jump into her throat and flutter there. "I don't... I can't believe this."

"Marry me, Kara." He held something up—a box. He opened it and the moonlight spilled down on the pear-shaped pink diamond she'd been admiring for the past several years. She couldn't believe her eyes.

"How... how did you know?"

"The jeweler was very helpful. Even knew your size." He took the ring from the box. "Will you wear it, Kara? I swear to God I'll do my damnedest to make you happy. I'll never ask you to leave Big Falls if you don't want to. Be my wife. Be Tyler's mom."

She felt as if her world was spinning out of control, and

could hardly breathe. And yet she heard herself saying, "Yes, Jimmy. Yes. Of course I'll marry you."

His fingers deftly slid the ring onto one of hers. Then he bent over her hand and pressed his lips to it. He lifted his head, looked into her eyes. "Thank you, Kara. Thank you." And he kissed her.

But he hadn't said he loved her.

HE HAD AN odd feeling with her. The uncharacteristic urge to cradle her, to protect her. As if she was fragile or weak or in danger. After he'd popped the question, he held her in his arms for a long time. They danced, and stared out at the moon climbing ever higher in the sky. "I hope you won't make me wait too long to marry you," he said. Because it was essential he move on to this part. More than essential.

"I'd marry you tonight," she whispered.

That was exactly what he needed to hear. "I don't think your family would forgive me for that one. But do you think we could get away with Saturday?"

She looked up quickly, her eyes widening. "That's only three days from now."

"Yeah." He smiled at her. "If I can stand it that long." He sighed and dug deep for the gumption to tell her the truth. All of it. "But wanting you to the point of distraction isn't the only reason I'm in a hurry, Kara. I have to be honest with you."

She tipped her head to one side. "I didn't say we had to wait until we were married to... "

"You're a virgin. That's an amazing thing. Sacred. I'm waiting."

"Wow. You're... you're a special man, Jimmy. You know that?"

He shook his head. "I know Vinnie and Ang are probably running for cover about now. And they aren't likely to try anything. But they think they killed Colby. That means I'm the only thing standing between Vinnie and a prison sentence. There's still a chance Vinnie will try to make sure I can't testify against him in court."

She blinked, lowering her head. "And if something happens to you, Tyler would have no one left."

"No one but his birth mother. I want you in our lives. I want you there legally, on paper, with my wishes recorded somewhere. There's no one else I would want Tyler to be with."

She nodded. "That means the world to me, Jimmy." Pursing her lips, she nodded. "Okay," she told him. "I'll marry you on Saturday."

CHAPTER TWELVE

"*S*ATURDAY?" VIDALIA BRAND sat at the head of the table and looked at Kara as if she'd suddenly announced she was running for president. "You want to get *married* on *Saturday?*"

"Isn't it cool, Gramma Vi?" Tyler said, practically bouncing in his chair.

"Yes, it's very cool, Tyler. Are you through with your breakfast?"

"Uh-huh. It was real good. Does this mean you'll be my *real* gramma?"

Vidalia's tight expression eased into a smile. "Son, you can consider me your real gramma now. How's that?"

"Cool!"

"Now why don't you take the twins to play in the toy room, hmm?"

"Okay!" He got out of the chair, put his crutches under his arms, then made his way through the house to the giant play room off the living room, calling the twins to come with him on the way.

"I'll go keep an eye on them," Caleb said, taking each of the twins by the hand and leading them after Tyler. He paused beside Kara, gave her a "hang tough" kind of a look, then nodded to Jimmy. "Welcome to the family, Jim."

"Thanks, Caleb."

Vidalia drew a deep breath and pressed her palms to the table. "All right then, let's dispense with the nonsense and get to the truth here. What's the big hurry?"

"Mom—" Kara began.

"No, no," Jim said. "It's a legitimate question. Vidalia, I promise you, there's nothing shady or sneaky going on."

"No?" She shot a look at Kara. "You can't be pregnant. He hasn't been in town long enough so you'd even know if you were."

"Mother!" It was Maya this time, reprimanding her mother in a tone usually only heard from Vidalia herself.

"I'm not pregnant. We haven't even—" Kara bit her lip, shook her head. "It's nothing like that. Mom, Tyler needs me. We're living in the same house anyway, and he's facing surgery in a couple of weeks. We don't want anything big or fancy. A simple ceremony on the back lawn is fine. I don't need anyone here other than my family. We can call the justice of the peace—that's still Hugh Matthews, isn't it?"

"We will call Reverend Jackson, young lady. Not the justice of the peace. And you'll be married in the church, assuming it's not already booked for Saturday. You're a foot too tall to wear my wedding gown—"

"She can wear mine," Edie said, jumping to her feet. "Oh, we'll play with it a little, make it different enough so it's your own. Maybe run into town and pick you up a new veil and tiara."

"I've still got my tux in the closet," Wade put in. "God knows I'll never find another use for it."

Vidalia sighed. "Are you absolutely sure this is what you want?" she asked, her eyes probing Kara's.

Kara felt as if her mother could see things no one else could. And she was not comfortable with the probing, searching stare. "I am. I'm sure, Mom."

Vi held her gaze for a long moment, then finally lowered her head. "All right," she said. "If it's what you want, we'll make it happen!" She lifted her head again, and this time she pinned Jimmy with a steely stare. "You'd better make my daughter happy, young man. Or you'll have me to answer to."

"I promise to do my best," he said. Then he pushed away from the table. "We should get cracking. We need to get the license before we take Ty in for his PT today."

"Once that's done, bring Kara to our place, Jim," Edie said. "We'll get to work on the dress tonight."

"I'll phone Reverend Jackson," Vi said. "My goodness. You girls are going to be the death of me."

～

THE TIME FLEW past. Kara made time to spend with Tyler but found herself so busy there was almost no time for her to spend with Jimmy. Especially *alone* with Jimmy. And there was just as little time for her to wallow in her doubts and worries. Thankfully other worries faded rapidly, as well.

There had been no further trouble from Vinnie or Ang, no sign of them still being anywhere near Big Falls. Colby improved, but not fast enough. He'd be spending the weekend in the hospital, but might be out by Monday. She could tell Jimmy was relieved that things were going as well as they were —he was relaxing more and more. And the more relaxed he became, the more attentive he grew.

He smiled whenever he looked at her. He treated her as if she was made of rare and fragile crystal. He was thoughtful and kind and seemed to love spending time with her. Why was she looking for trouble where there was none?

But dammit, why hadn't he said he loved her?

She spent Friday night at her mother's to keep to the custom of the groom not seeing the bride on the day of the wedding. And she awoke Saturday morning with such a nervous stomach that even the smell of breakfast made her ill.

"Lookin' a little green around the gills, sunshine," Vidalia said. "Perk up, girl, it's your wedding day."

Kara smiled in response to her mother's teasing. Vi had set her worries aside, determined, it seemed, to embrace events and celebrate them rather than fighting the inevitable. If Jimmy screwed up, that would be soon enough for Vi to wreak vengeance. Until then, Kara thought he was safe from his mother-in-law's wrath.

Selene turned from the kitchen range with a steaming mug in her hands and brought it to the table, setting it in front of her sister. "Here, hon. Special blend. Mint for the tummy ache, chamomile and valerian for the nervousness and some honey to make it taste good."

Kara didn't for one minute doubt her sister's tea would help. Selene had a knack for things like this.

She'd no sooner finished her tea than Edie and Maya were bustling through the front door with Edie's recently remodeled wedding gown in their arms. They'd added a bowlike bustle to the back, with a trailing train that hadn't been there before. It glittered with hidden sparklies.

"Ready to get ready?" Edie asked.

"Not even close. The ceremony isn't until ten."

"That only gives us two and a half hours!" Maya clapped her hands together. "Let's go, chop-chop!"

"I'll go run your bath," Selene said, smiling in that mysterious way she had. "I've got special wedding-day bath salts ready to go. You're gonna smell so good, Jimmy's eyes will pop." With that Selene trotted up the stairs.

The morning wore on—slowly, unlike the past two days had.

Kara bore up well. Several more cups of Selene's calming brew helped. Her sisters did her hair, her nails, her face. They fussed over her and sang love songs in perfect harmony as they did.

And finally she slid into the gown. The girls wouldn't let her near a mirror until they'd declared her finished.

Then Mel marched her up to the mirror.

Kara looked at her reflection. A princess looked back at her. Beautiful, graceful and glowing. Ringlets tumbled from the up-do and fell to frame her face. Tears welled up in her eyes as she looked at the other faces around her—Mel and Maya crowding over one shoulder, Edie and Selene leaning in over the other.

"You're beautiful."

"Perfect."

"Oh, God, I think I'm going to cry already!"

"Someone get the camera."

A throat cleared and they all turned. Vidalia stood in the doorway. "You girls have kept me at bay long enough. Let's see how you've done."

The four stepped away, and Kara turned slowly to face her mother. Vidalia took an openmouthed breath, blinking rapidly. "Oh, my," she whispered. One hand fluttered to her chest, and she repeated herself. "Oh, *my*. You look like an angel come down from heaven, Kara Brand."

Kara smiled and tried to keep her eyes dry. "My makeup's gonna smear, Mom."

"If these girls didn't use waterproof makeup, they haven't learned a thing from the last three Brand weddings."

"We did, Mom," Maya told her.

Vidalia wrapped her in a gentle hug and sniffled before she stepped away. "Well, that's enough of this nonsense. Let's get ourselves over to the church." Then she snapped her fingers. "Oh, wait. One more thing." She stepped out of the room and returned with a box, wrapped in white and silver paper with a red velvet bow.

"Mom, what did you do?" Kara asked.

She smiled. "Open it and find out."

Kara opened the package, letting the paper and box fall to the floor as she pulled out a fur trimmed white velvet cloak. "Oh, Mom... "

Edie took it and moved behind her to drape it around her. She arranged the loosely fitting hood, and everyone oohed and ahhed.

"Thank you, Mom."

Vidalia looked pleased and proud. "Now you're a proper Christmastime bride," she said.

Kara took one last look in the mirror and met her own eyes. They were still filled with doubts, still lacking conviction. She thought maybe that look would fade later. Once she was married and she saw for herself that everything was all right. Once Jimmy told her how he truly felt about her. He would, she thought. He would say the words she'd been longing to hear. Today, of all days, he would say them.

JIM STOOD IN front of the mirror, straightening his borrowed black bow tie over and over again. Then he noticed his son standing right beside him, staring at his reflection with the same intense, impatient look on his face, trying to straighten his own.

A mirror image, only smaller.

His heart swelled and any doubts still plaguing him about the wisdom of what he was about to do melted away. Kara Brand would make Tyler happy. She would be the mother his son had never known, fill the terrible void in his young life. That was all that mattered. All that would ever matter.

There was a knock at the door. He knelt to tug Tyler's tie straight for him. "Now run a comb through that hair, pal. I'll go get the door."

"Okay, Dad."

Jim smiled at Tyler's serious expression as he began taming his wavy hair and went to the front door. He turned the locks, opened the door, fully expecting to see his future brothers-in-law, who'd planned to meet him here so they could all head over to the church together.

But it wasn't Wade or Caleb or Alex who stood there on the step. It was Angela. His blood chilled and his skin went cold. What the hell was she doing here today of all days?

"Hi, Jim." Her eyes skimmed down him and her brows drew together. "Why all dressed up?"

"I'm not doing this with you, Ang. Not today."

"Doing what with me? You don't even know what I came for."

"I don't *care* what you came for. You need to leave. Now."

"No. I want to see Tyler. Is he here?" As she spoke, she leaned to one side, trying to get a look around him.

Jim stepped out onto the front step, pulling the door closed behind him. "You surrendered all your rights to Tyler. You're under court order to stay away from him for his own protection, Angela. Beyond all that, you're wanted by every cop in the state right now."

"Wanted? Why would I be wanted? I haven't done anything."

"No?" He narrowed his eyes on her. "You're running with a fugitive. That's aiding and abetting, Ang. And don't think you're going to shirk your share of the blame for what your boyfriend did to Colby."

She blinked rapidly. "Your... partner?' Averting her head, she said, "Why, what happened to him?"

"Like you don't know? Someone shoved his car off a cliff with him in it. It hit the bottom and burst into flames. That's what happened to my partner."

He watched her face go dead white, felt a little guilty for dumping it on her like that. Colby had insisted she'd had no idea what Vinnie's plans were for him. But Jim hadn't really believed that. As for letting her believe Colby was dead, well, he didn't have a hell of a lot of choice in that. "You've got no business being here."

"But—"

"No buts. Get out of here. Go back to Chicago before a cop comes along and slaps a pair of handcuffs on you."

She sighed, lowering her head. "Walk me to the car and I'll go."

He frowned, not liking the suggestion. His police protection was only here by night. His instincts kicked in, and he scanned the area, the car that sat in the driveway—a late-model Ford, mid-size, dark blue, nothing fancy but out of her price range. He didn't see anyone else around. "Where did you get the car, Ang?"

"Vinnie bought it for me. I drove it all the way here from Chicago just to talk to you. That's all I want, Jim. Just to talk to you. Two minutes."

"I thought all you wanted was to see Tyler."

"I want that, too, but if you won't let me... " She sighed. "Jim, I have a chance to start my life over. And I'm trying hard to change, I swear I am." She sniffled. "I tried to help your friend. I did. And I left Vinnie. I left him, Jim. You were right."

He softened just a little. Hell, he'd loved this woman once. She was the first and last woman he'd ever loved. But God, he didn't want her complicating his life just when things were going so well. Especially for Tyler. He took her arm and started walking her toward the car.

"I'm going to do this on my own, Jim. Get clean, get a job. You'll see, I'll make it work." She sighed. "I don't want to tell Ty who I am. I'm no mother, we both know that. I'd just like to see him, that's all."

He nodded slowly. "You get clean, Angela, you do the things you say you're going to do, and I'll make that happen. But you've gotta be clean, you understand? I don't want him anywhere near you when you're using. And I won't have him within a mile of a man like Vinnie."

She stared up at him. "You'll really let me see him?"

He nodded. "I'm not made of stone. You show me you've really changed and I will."

They were at the car now. She stood near the passenger door, her hand on the handle. "Thank you, Jim."

"Yeah, thank you, Jim."

Jim whirled at the deep, sarcasm-laden voice that came from behind him, but not in time. The tire iron caught him upside the head before he could even blink. His vision exploded. He went to his knees, struggled to stay conscious, but then the second blow landed and he went over onto his side.

"Vinnie, stop it!" Angela cried. You're gonna kill him!"

But the blows kept on coming. Then she shouted, "Vinnie, there's a car coming. Come on, you're wasting time."

Vinnie swore, gripped his arms, and dragged over the driveway, then around toward the back yard. "Go get the kid," Vinnie repeated. "Then we'll see."

God, no. They were going after Tyler. No, it couldn't happen! He had to stay awake, had to get up, had to...

"Will you fucking die, already, Corona?" A boot connected with his ribs, then his head. And blackness descended.

KARA PACED IN the church's tiny rectory, counting off steps across the room. Nine. Nine steps. But she'd traversed it so many times by now that she thought she'd clocked nine hundred.

"Honey, they probably had a flat tire... or something," Maya said.

"Or maybe he's just not coming." Kara closed her eyes, tried to quell the doubts in her mind, but there was no silencing them. Not now.

"Of course he's coming," Maya told her. "Mom's on the phone right now, trying to get hold of someone. And you know the guys were going over there so they could all come to the church together. They'd have let us know if anything was wrong."

The full male contingent of her immediate family, Kara thought. What would they do when Jimmy told them he'd changed his mind? The idea of them going to get him hadn't been to force him to show up. They'd wanted to make him feel a part of the family, surrounded by the rest of the men. An exercise in male bonding, she'd supposed.

Or maybe she shouldn't have believed that lame explanation. Maybe her brothers-in-law had sensed, as she had, that Jimmy didn't love her. That this marriage was based on something else entirely. Probably they'd known from the start—maybe men could see that kind of thing in other men. And most likely they would bring him here on the end of a shotgun barrel if necessary.

She didn't want him like that, though.

From beyond the rectory door she heard her mother cussing at the telephone. Her mother never cussed. Especially not in church.

"It's enough, it's just enough already," Kara said. "He's a half hour late. He's not coming." She reached behind her for the zipper, intending to get out of the gorgeous gown so she wouldn't have to keep pacing back and forth in front of its reflection. It was a sorry, sad reminder of her ridiculous little fantasy.

She couldn't reach the zipper, though, and she sent a desperate look over her shoulder. "Someone get me out of this thing."

"Kara, don't. Just give it a little more time," Edie said.

Kara turned fully and glared at her. "Isn't it obvious to anyone but me? He's not coming!" She hated the tears for burning in her eyes, forcing their way out.

"That's it," Mel barked. "I'm going over there. If this joker thinks he can get away with pulling this kind of crap on *my* sister—"

"Something's wrong."

Everyone fell silent as all eyes turned to Selene, who'd been keeping the twins occupied by playing Chutes and Ladders with them on the pastor's desk.

"What is it, Selene?" Maya asked. "What are you sensing?"

Selene met her eyes, then her gaze slid to Kara's. It was grim and dark. "I don't know, but I know it's not what you think. Something's... wrong. Big and dark and wrong. I think we need to go over there."

Kara felt the blood drain from her face. Guilt swamped her. She'd been pacing and feeling sorry for herself and becoming increasingly angry at Jimmy. What if something had happened to him? Visions of a car accident on the way to the church, of flaming wreckage, suddenly swirled into her mind and terrified her. "What about Tyler?" she whispered. Then she bunched her skirts up in her fists and headed for the rectory door, flinging it open, racing down the aisle of the church, past the pews all draped in pine garland and white roses, toward the tall red double doors that stood at the far end.

Before she got there, the doors opened. Caleb stood there, and the look on his face stopped her in her tracks. She stood four feet from him, her skirts in her hands.

"Caleb, what's happened?" Kara asked, barely aware of her mother and sisters gathering around her, touching her, holding her.

"Jim's been hurt. You'd better come with me, hon. We need to get to the hospital."

"Hospital?" She pressed a hand to her chest and started forward on wobbly knees. "What happened? Is he all right?"

Caleb took her arm and led her through the wreath-decked double doors as the others followed. "We don't know. We found him unconscious in the backyard, just inside the gate. Looks like he took a severe beating."

She frowned. It made no sense to her stressed, overwrought mind. Poor Tyler, he must be scared half to death. Then she lifted her gaze to Caleb's as he opened the passenger door of his car and held it for her. "How bad?" she whispered.

"We don't know, honey. We just don't know. Wade took him to the E.R. and I came right over here."

"Where's Alex?" Edie asked.

Caleb sent her a look. "With the police out at the house."

"Police?" Everything in Kara went icy cold as things began clicking into place in her mind. "Police, Caleb?"

He nodded. "Kara—" He drew a breath, closed his eyes. "Kara, we can't find Tyler."

Her knees buckled. If Caleb hadn't been there, she'd have fallen to the ground.

Her mother was quick to come to her aid, as well, pulling Kara's arm around her shoulders, taking her from Caleb's strong arms and easing her onto the seat of the car. Then she turned and took charge, and Kara was so very glad Vidalia was the way she was. She needed that right now.

"Mel, get over to that house and get to work on this with your husband. It's what you two do, after all. Maya, you take the twins home and get on the phone. I want you to phone everyone we know and get them to call everyone they know to help search for that little boy. Selene, go with her. Get a change of clothes for your sister and bring them to the hospital. Edie, you may as well come with us, since Wade's at the E.R. already." Then she nodded to Caleb. "Get us to the hospital, son, and don't dawdle about it."

Then she got into the front seat beside Kara, closed the door and wrapped her hand around her daughter's.

Kara looked up at her mother, tears in her eyes. "We have to find Tyler."

"By the time we get to the hospital, half the town will be out looking for him, honey. And we'll join them, too. But you have to see Jim first, don't you think?"

"I... " She lowered her head, shaking it slowly. "I'm so torn, I don't know what to do."

"That's why I'm here, child. You just do what I tell you until your head stops spinning and you can decide for yourself again. You have to see him—he may be able to tell us something to help us find the boy."

Kara closed her eyes as Caleb hit the gas. The car lurched forward, spitting gravel in its wake. She saw her sisters behind them, all of them in motion. Maya was explaining things to Reverend Jackson as she gathered the twins in her arms. Kara turned again to her mother, saw the worry in her eyes. "We'll find him. We will find him," she whispered, needing to hear someone— her mother, the strongest woman in the world— confirm it for her.

"Damn straight we will," Vidalia Brand said. "And heaven help any son of a gun who lays a finger on that child until we do. *No one* messes with one of Vidalia Brand's grandchildren."

CHAPTER THIRTEEN

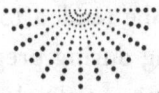

"*A*REN'T WE ALMOST there?"

"Stop whining, kid," Vinnie snapped. "We'll be there when we get mere."

Vinnie wasn't real happy with Tyler, Angela thought. But he hadn't kicked or screamed or cried so far, and she hoped he wouldn't

"So my dad's waiting there already? Why did he leave?"

"Like I told you," Vinnie said, "it was an emergency. We're supposed to bring you to him."

"At the church?"

Angela looked at the boy sharply. "That's where you were going all dressed up, I'll bet. To the church."

"Course it is. You gotta get dressed up for a weddin'."

She shot a look at Vinnie.

"I'm gonna be the ring-bear!" Tyler tugged at his bow tie yet again. He hadn't stopped chattering or fidgeting since they'd put him in the car. She wished he would quit already. He was giving her a headache.

"Do you guys know Kara? She's the lady my dad's gonna

marry. And then she'll be my new mom. Just like I asked Santa for. And it ain't even Christmas yet!"

Ang winced a little. Hell, it wasn't as if being a mother was her life's ambition. Especially not to a disabled kid who never shut up. She'd never wanted him. God, the months of struggling to stay clean while she'd carried him just so he wouldn't be born messed up. She'd slipped a few times. She was only human. But it hadn't hurt him any. She tended to think the bastards who told women to stop living during pregnancy were overdramatizing things. No smoking, no drinking, no drugs. Hell, they didn't even want you taking over-the-counter stuff, aside from those horse-size prenatal vitamins. Her pregnancy had been hell. And in the end, all those months of suffering hadn't mattered—he ended up all screwed up anyway. But it still jabbed her a little to hear Tyler refer to another woman as his mom.

Her buzz was waning. She needed another hit.

"And Mrs. Brand—Vidalia—she'll be my real grandma. I never even *had* a real grandma before. And I'll have all kinds of aunts and uncles, and two cousins and–"

"That's real nice, Tyler," Ang said. He was buckled up in the backseat. She figured she could manage a hit without him even noticing. She reached for the little compact case on the seat between her and Vinnie, but Vinnie covered her hand with his own.

"When I say. Understand?"

She thinned her lips, angry now.

"And as soon as the weddin's over I'm gonna ask for a puppy. Dad will prob'ly say no, but Kara won't. She loves animals, just like me. So I bet she'll get me a puppy. And then everything will be perfect."

Angela turned in her seat, looking back at him with a frown. He wore braces on both legs and couldn't walk without those ugly, cumbersome crutches. In what universe did that qualify as perfect?

"I have to go to the bathroom. Are we almost there?"

"Let's stop for a break," Vinnie said. "I have to call your dad anyway and make sure my directions are all right."

"I don't think they are, mister. I think we must have gone way too far by now."

He was smart, Angela thought. They'd been driving for forty-five minutes. Frankly she'd had enough of it herself. Vinnie pulled into the parking lot of the motel where they'd been holed up for the past three days. Vinnie had barely let her stick her head outside the door of their room. He said the police were looking for them. She thought he'd been making things up just to keep her under his thumb, until she'd spoken to Jim.

Poor Jim. Vinnie didn't have to hit him as hard as he had. She hoped he'd be all right

"Let's go inside," Vinnie said. "I'll give your dad a call, make sure things are on schedule. Don't worry about a thing, kid."

"I'm scared I'll miss the weddin'," Tyler confessed, unbuckling his seat belt, opening his door. Angela got out her own door and headed straight to the room—she had stashed away a little supply of her own and she was damned if she was waiting to use it.

"Angie, what's-a-matter with you anyway?"

She looked over her shoulder to see Vinnie rolling his eyes, then he opened the back door and helped Tyler get out and up onto his crutches. "There's no way your dad would start things without you, kid. Besides," Vinnie added with a look at his watch, "it's not even time yet Don't worry."

"Okay."

He walked beside the boy toward the motel room. Ang stopped watching them and finished unlocking the door. Then she went inside, straight to the bathroom. She slammed the door and locked it behind her. Tyler had to go, he'd said. But hell, he could wait. This would only take a minute.

～

KARA RAN THROUGH the closest entrance to the emergency room, ignoring that its doors were clearly marked as being for E.R. patients only. She looked left and right, spotted a desk and headed for it, still clinging to her skirts. She heard the stampede of footsteps behind her—Edie and Cal and her mother. "Jimmy Corona," she barked at the nurse there. "Where is he?"

The woman blinked at her, probably unused to seeing women in bridal gowns racing frantically through her emergency room. Before she opened her mouth to speak, Wade was there, gripping Kara's shoulders, turning her to face him.

She searched his eyes, desperation and fear clawing at her chest "Where is he, Wade? Is he all right?"

"They're still working on him. Already stitched him up, then took him down to X-ray. Going to run a CT scan and then they'll know more."

"Is he conscious?" she asked.

"No." Wade blinked, lowering his head. "You look so beautiful, Kara. I'm damn sorry your special day got ruined. If the guys and I had arrived five minutes sooner—"

"Don't blame yourself," she said. Then she pulled free of his embrace because a man and a woman in white appeared, pushing a stretcher along the hall and into a room. She glimpsed just one hand—one strong, tanned hand lying still on the white sheets—and she knew it was him. "Jimmy!"

She raced toward him even as they pushed him into a treatment room. Hesitating in the doorway, she sought permission from the faces that surrounded him. A nurse eyed her gown and her eyes turned sympathetic. "You must be Kara," she said. "Wade Armstrong told us you'd be coming."

She returned her attention to Jimmy. She was taping leads to his chest. "Come on in, hon," she said without looking up again. "Sit with him a while. Use the call button if you need us."

"But—but... do you know anything? How is he?"

The male nurse who'd been adjusting the IV line, glanced her way. "The doctor still has to look at his films. We don't know much yet. He's been restless. Muttering. Nothing coherent. You sit with him, talk to him. It can't hurt."

As the two left the room, she moved slowly toward the bed. He lay on his back, his clothes were missing—from the waist up at least. A sheet covered his chest, but his arms lay outside the covers. The leads they had fastened to his chest were connected to a monitor that beeped in a slow, steady rhythm.

There was a huge white bandage plastered to one side of his head. His face was paler than she had ever seen it, except for the purpling bruise that ran from one side of his forehead down to and including his cheekbone. His chest was all taped up.

She swallowed hard, leaned closer, lifted a trembling hand to touch his bruised face. "Oh, Jimmy."

She heard a throat clear. "Excuse me. Mrs. Corona?"

Kara straightened and turned to see a blond woman with a stethoscope draped around her neck over a white lab coat "We didn't get that far," Kara told her. "I'm afraid it's still Miss Brand. But please call me Kara."

"I'm Dr. Miller." The woman held out a hand and Kara took it. "I can't tell you how sorry I am that your wedding day was so thoroughly ruined. Are you all right?'

"I'll be fine. It's Jimmy I'm worried about. How is he, Doctor?"

The doctor looked past her at her patient. "The films don't look bad. There's no sign of any serious damage, but that doesn't give us the whole story. We aren't really going to know anything for sure until he wakes up."

"Is he... is he unconscious or is this—" she could barely say the word. "—coma?"

"The EEG reads nicely. It's not coma. Not yet. He could go deeper or he could come around. No way to predict it. We can really only wait and see." The doctor sighed. "I'll give you a few minutes with him. But then I need to examine him again. All right?"

"Thank you, Doctor."

Dr. Miller left, closing the door behind her. Kara went to the bed. She leaned over it, putting her lips close to Jimmy's ear. "Wake up, Jimmy. Wake up right now. Tyler's in trouble. He needs you. And I need you, too."

She cupped his face with one hand. "Wake up, Jimmy. Come on for Ty."

It didn't evoke a reaction.

Closing her eyes, she fought back a tide of disappointment.

"It's okay. I just want you to know I'm here. We're all looking for Tyler. We're going to find him, I promise you that. We won't give up."

Sighing, Kara got to her feet. She had to clear out, give the doctor room to work. And she had to go looking for Tyler. She kissed his cheek, then turned and walked to the doorway.

"Kara?"

She froze near the door, then turned back around. Jimmy was peering at her, eyes barely open and squinting as if the light hurt them. His brows drew together and he opened his eyes a little further. He seemed to take in her appearance, the dress, and then he closed his eyes again in what looked like anguish this time. "You look—you're beautiful. I'm so sorry...
"

"Don't apologize," she said as she hurried back to his bedside. "I know it wasn't your fault. Jimmy—" She sat down in the chair beside the bed and gripped his hand in both of hers. "Do you remember what happened?"

"They... they took Tyler." He scanned the room. "Angela and Vinnie took Tyler. I need a phone."

"I'll get you one. But I need to ask you something first."

He drew a breath, nodded. "I owe you so much. Ask me anything, Kara, and I'll tell you."

She nodded. "Why you did you really want to marry me?"

His brows drew together. "Kara, believe me when I tell you there's not another woman in the world I would rather have as my wife."

She nodded. "Because there's nothing in the world as important to you as Ty. And I'm the best choice for him." She lifted her head, met his eyes. "It's okay, Jimmy. I know. I've known all along, somewhere inside. This is about Tyler. Not about anything you might... feel for me."

He searched her face. "You were willing to go through with the wedding even believing that?"

She didn't answer. Instead she crossed the room and picked up the cordless telephone. "Here. Make your calls. The doctor said she would be in momentarily to examine you, and Chief Wheatly is next in line. Now that I know you're all right, I'm going out to join the search."

She turned and started for the door, almost tripping over her skirts, having forgotten their presence.

"Kara, please. Please don't go. I need to get out of here, I need to search for my son. But I don't imagine the chief is going to let me until I give him the full account of what happened this morning. And there are things you need to hear, too."

She heaved a sigh, so disappointed she could barely hold her head upright. She had so wanted to think her misgivings were completely off target. She'd expected him to deny it all, to tell her he loved her. But he hadn't done those things. Instead he had only confirmed her worst fears.

Dr. Miller entered, saw him awake in the bed and smiled. "Well, I hope those sharp, clear eyes are a good indication of what's going on behind them," she said. "Good to meet you, Mr. Corona."

"I'll stop in to say goodbye before I leave," Kara told him and she left the room.

Jim threw back the covers and had his legs over the side of the bed before the doctor uttered her first protest.

"No use arguing, Doc. I'm a police officer. My son has been abducted by a felon, and I'm going after him."

"I don't blame you. Can I at least check your pupils? Maybe get a BP and a quick listen to your heart first?"

"No."

"You have thirty-six stitches in your head, Mr. Corona. You're lucky you didn't fracture your skull."

"Very lucky. I know. But since I didn't, I have to leave." He looked down at the trousers he wore and remembered they were part of the tux. The tux he'd been wearing to marry Kara Brand. And now she knew the truth—that he didn't love her—and it made his stomach hurt to realize how deeply he had hurt her.

She didn't deserve that. She'd been nothing but wonderful to him and Tyler. He felt like an assassin.

"Where's my shirt?" he asked the doctor.

"I'll give you your shirt after I check your vitals. Deal?"

He sighed and rolled his eyes but agreed.

The doc made quick work of it, which he appreciated. Then she turned and opened a large plastic bag that had been sitting on the floor, dug out a white shirt and tossed it to him. He caught it and she nodded. "Reflexes are okay."

"Sneaky, aren't you? You have a release form I can sign, Doctor? If you do, bring it now, 'cause in another thirty seconds I'll be out of here."

She nodded. "All right, have it your way." She yanked his chart off the door, flipped it open, scribbled something on it and drew a big X. Then she handed it to him, along with the pen.

She set the bag with the rest of his belongings on the bed beside him.

He scribbled his name beside the X and handed it back to her. Then he pulled on his white shirt. He dug around in the plastic bag for his shoes and socks and she left him alone. But when he bent over to pull on the socks, he was hit with such a rush of dizziness he wound up on his knees on the floor.

And then Kara was there, on her knees, too, gripping his shoulders, helping him to get up again. He met her eyes. They were wet. She'd been crying. Hell, he'd made her cry. She was no longer wearing the wedding gown. God it had just about knocked him out of the bed when he'd glimpsed her in it. Such a powerful image, Kara Brand as his bride. She wore jeans now and a small green sweater.

"You should stay here until the doctor wants to let you go," she said.

"Right. You wouldn't if it was your kid."

"He *is* my kid."

He lifted his head. She blinked, those huge green eyes swimming.

"At least, I'd like for him to be."

She pushed him until he sat on the bed, then she knelt and pulled his socks onto his feet. When she got them on straight, she added the shoes, even tied them for him. "I love him, Jimmy." She couldn't seem to meet his eyes. "And you don't have to marry me to ensure I stay in his life. You really don't."

He didn't even know how to respond to that. The local chief of police came in before he could think of a way.

"Jim. Sorry we're meeting again under these circumstances. I want you to know we're doing everything we can to find your son."

Jimmy nodded, getting to his feet. "I need to be out looking for him. But if you can ride with us to the house, I'll fill you in on the way."

Chief Wheatly said, "I need to take my own car, but we can talk at the house. I've been in touch with your Chief Wilcox in Chicago, and he's already brought me up to date on a lot of this. Have Stefano or Angela contacted you since they took him?"

"No. But I haven't been at the house, and I left my cell phone there, so I don't see how they could."

Jimmy started for the door a bit unsteadily. But then Kara was beside him, sliding an arm around his waist, holding him. She was strong and sure of herself and loyal and determined.

She wouldn't let him down.

For a minute he wondered just why the hell he *didn't* love her. There must be something seriously wrong with his head, and it must have been wrong for a while now. Any normal, sane man would have fallen head over heels for this woman.

As they made their way out of the hospital, Wade came up and handed Kara his keys. "Take my pickup. We'll meet you out there."

"Thanks, Wade."

KARA GLANCED AT the faces surrounding her, saw the love and the strength in each of them. Jim seemed to be avoiding their eyes. He was uncomfortable, and she knew he felt guilty for leading her on the way he had. She'd left his room barely containing her tears, but she'd managed it. Just long enough for Selene to find her and hand her the change of clothes she'd brought.

Selene had taken one look at her and seen the emotional firestorm about to erupt in her, Kara knew she did. But she'd been wise enough and kind enough to say nothing. She'd only given her a hug and pointed to the nearest restroom.

Kara had gone in there to change and lost her battle. She had a full-blown breakdown in ladies room, closing herself in a stall in case anyone came in to witness it. Her dream was shattered. Her heart broken. And yet she still loved him. She loved Jimmy Corona in a way she had never loved any other man, and always would. And she loved Tyler.

Deep down she'd known all along what was happening. She'd chosen to ignore it. Pretended not to see it. But she couldn't lie to herself anymore. Jimmy didn't love her.

When the storm of tears had finally subsided, she'd thought maybe she could get through the next few hours. She'd splashed cold water on her face and reminded herself that her feelings were not important—not now. Now all that was important was finding Tyler. Getting him home safe and unharmed. It was that focus that had allowed her to face Jim again.

She remained in control, exerting an iron will over her emotions as they walked out of the hospital to the parking lot. Kara didn't ask if Jim needed her to drive. He was still having trouble walking, to say nothing of driving. That he even managed to climb into the pickup without help surprised her.

As soon as she put it into gear, he started to apologize again, but she put a stop to it in short order. "Don't," she said. "Don't waste time on what's happened between us or why it happened, Jimmy. Not now."

"But I need to explain—"

"No," she said. "Look, Jimmy, I'm barely holding it together here. I don't want to wallow in this. I need to focus on Tyler."

He was studying her face for a long moment, before he nodded. "Okay."

"Tell me about Tyler's mother. Tell me about Angela. Everything about her."

He licked his lips, lowered his head. "She's a drug addict," he said. "But you already know that. I think she probably was through most of our marriage, though I didn't know about it until it was too late. I was busy with my work, my career. I didn't like to party. She did. So she partied without me. Had affairs. I thought I loved her. Hell, I did love her. I thought a baby would fix things. Give her something to focus on. Settle her down. And at first I thought it had worked."

"But it didn't?"

He shook his head. "I was wearing blinders. She was using cocaine, right under my nose. I should have known, should have seen it. Maybe I did know, deep down and was just in denial."

She lowered her head. "I can't quite swallow that, Jimmy. You wouldn't knowingly subject Tyler to that."

"I wasn't the greatest father back then, Kara. If I had been, I'd have known he wasn't safe with her." He lowered his head, shaking it slowly. "Then I got a call at work one day. My son was in the trauma ward and my wife was in custody. She'd decided to take him out for a walk while she was high. And you know the rest."

Kara had to force her eyes from his tortured face to focus on the road.

"And what happened to her after that?"

He shook his head. "She and her lawyer made a deal with the D.A. She agreed to sign away all parental rights to Tyler in exchange for probation and community service. The alternative would have been jail time. The D.A. said it was my call. I opted to take the deal." He sighed. "Up to now she's stayed away. Kept her promise not to interfere or try to see him. Until she took up with Vinnie Stefano. Now she's letting him use her to get to me."

"That man is dangerous," Kara said. "And he didn't have any qualms about having Colby killed. As far as he knows, he succeeded, and you're the only one left who can put him behind bars."

She turned to look briefly at him, and he met her eyes. "Yeah. He probably intended to kill me this morning. I think they guys showing up were the only reason he didn't. Ang saw them coming, so they grabbed Tyler and booked."

She nodded, but kept her eyes on the road. "How could Vinnie convince her to go along with this? Using her own son this way?"

"He's been filling her head with promises. She thinks he's her knight in shining armor, riding in to save her, make her life like something out of a storybook."

"No one can do that for her. It's something she has to do for herself."

He was silent for a moment, and when she glanced at him again, she found him staring at her. She looked away.

"I imagine he's feeding her all the cocaine she wants, as well. She'd do just about anything for him so long as he dangles the right bait."

"At least Tyler's with his mother," Kara said. "She won't let Vinnie hurt him. She'll... she'll make sure he's okay."

"The last time Tyler was with his mother, she damn near killed him," Jimmy said, his tone grim. "Not every female is kind to children, Kara. I know it's hard for you to comprehend, but the maternal instinct isn't universal. Some animals eat their young. If she was hard up, I don't have any doubt she'd trade Tyler for a line of coke. He's not safe, not with her. He never was."

She tried to hide the horror from her eyes as she drove them back to the house. And then it was shoved to the back of her mind when she arrived there.

"Good Lord, look at all this."

There were vehicles lining both sides of the street. Unmarked sedans, police cars and SUVs with bubble lights, vans marked with official seals. There was yellow tape strung so haphazardly it looked like a Halloween prank the day after, though she was sure the men who'd put it up had some sort of rhyme and reason.

There was nowhere to park the car, so she had to drive past. It was a solid thirty yards before she found a spot along the roadside to pull over. And she was concerned about Jim's ability to walk all the way back to the house.

Sighing, she shut the truck off and opened the door. Jim's hand on her shoulder stopped her from jumping down, and she turned to meet his steady gaze. "I'm sorry I hurt you, Kara."

She shook her head. "You shouldn't be thinking about anything now except Tyler. The rest... the rest can wait"

She got out, then hurried around to his side of the vehicle, intending to help him. He was already out, though. And, putting an arm around her shoulders, he walked back to the house as if he wasn't hurting with every step.

There were police everywhere. Some were flicking brushes over the railing on the front steps and the doorknob. Others were taking plaster impressions of tire marks from the driveway. Another was photographing something on the ground, and it was only when they got closer that Kara saw what it was. A blood trail, where something had clearly been dragged. And that something, she realized with a sickening feeling, had been Jimmy.

"They never touched the door or the railing," Jim said, moving right into the throng. "You won't find any prints." He pointed. "I came out this door, walked with Angela to her car—a late model Ford Taurus, dark blue—there." He moved to the new spot, watching the ground, careful of where he stepped. "I was facing her, talking to her, when he came up behind me. I spun around, and he clubbed me with something. I'm pretty sure it was a tire iron."

"God," Kara whispered, clutching her stomach. She wasn't close enough to Jimmy anymore to be heard, but someone heard. Hands clutched her shoulders, and she turned. It was Edie, and Selene stood beside her. "It's too awful," Kara whispered, and though she fought it, a sob racked her chest

Her sisters held her, then drew her farther away from the police. She glimpsed Wes speaking intently to Chief Wheatly.

She saw a van creeping along the road looking for a spot to stop. It had a TV news logo on the side and a satellite dish on top.

"The press." Then she sniffed and nodded. "But that's a good thing, isn't it?"

"Come on, Kara. Jim's tied up with the police right now anyway, and we have to talk."

Kara frowned up at Edie but didn't argue as her sister tugged her away from the crowd to a small grove of trees where Alex and Mel waited. The others were still with Jim, trying to be of help.

"Okay," Alex said. "Here's what we know. The police aren't releasing any of the intimate details to the press, just your standard Amber Alert—Tyler's photo and description, along with the names and descriptions of his abductors and the suspect vehicle. The last thing they want is a P.I. snooping around, but I was here before them, so I got the freshest information. Turns out Billy Turner drove by here this morning and saw a strange car in the driveway. Dark blue, late-model Ford, Illinois plates."

"That's the same car Jim described," she said. "I don't suppose he got the plate number."

"No. But it shouldn't be too tough to track them down. Neither of them have any personal link to our area, so it stands to reason—"

"Wait a minute. How do you know they don't have any connections here?"

Alex shot a look at Mel. Mel pursed her lips, lowered her eyes. "I was concerned about you, hon. I...we started to run a background check on Jim."

Kara blinked, stunned. "Mel, you shouldn't have done that."

"The hell I shouldn't. You're my sister. And clearly I was right in my assumption that he had a few skeletons in his closet."

Kara shook her head. "You're like a bulldozer, you know that? It was my business, my call. You should have asked me."

Mel sighed. "I'm not used to asking permission to protect my family. Anyway, we turned up the marriage, the maiden name of his ex. So we went ahead and ran a check on her, as well. The woman's a train wreck."

"Yeah, that much I know. We all do—Jim was honest about that."

"Eventually," Mel muttered.

Alex shot her a quelling look. "She's had numerous arrests, including minor drug offenses, prostitution, but nothing to suggest any friends or relatives in Oklahoma."

"So what good does that do us?" Kara asked.

"They have to be staying somewhere," Alex said. "If we work on the assumption that Vinnie has no connections here either, that leaves a hotel, motel, something like that Those kinds of places take license plate numbers down when people check in. So do campgrounds. We can start checking anyone who checked in with Illinois plates. In fact, we've already started—Maya's making calls from the house."

"Won't the police be doing the same thing?" she asked.

"Probably," Alex said. "And they'll probably find them. But I think it would be a good idea for us to be there if and when they do track them down. This guy's dangerous. An armed standoff with Tyler as a hostage would not be in the boy's best interests."

Kara shivered. The image was too much to even consider. Her stomach heaved and she turned away, gripping her belly and doubling over. She vomited in the bushes. Alex swore, and Mel gripped Kara's shoulders, held her hair back.

"Kara?"

She heard Jimmy's voice, closed her eyes and wished she could stop retching, but she couldn't. A second later his hands replaced Mel's on her shoulders. "Kara, are you okay?"

Finally under control, she nodded, tried to straighten. Alex handed her a handkerchief and she wiped her mouth.

Jimmy was searching her face, and his own looked helpless. She said, "Don't. Don't waste a minute worrying about me. You've got more man enough on your plate right now. I'm fine."

He shot a look past her at Alex. "She should be home. I don't want her going through all this and I can't take care of her—"

"You don't need to take care of me."

Her words brought a wounded look to his face. "Please, Kara. Go to your mother's. You're wrung out. You look ready to drop."

She drew a breath, ready to argue with him. But then it occurred to her that she could help Maya track down the lowlife animals who were using a small child the way they were. "What's happening, Jimmy? What are the police doing?"

"Everything that can be done. They're organizing volunteers to search the woods, bringing in dogs to try to pick up Tyler's scent, setting up roadblocks." He looked her up and down. "There's nothing you can do here, Kara. Ty's gonna need you when he gets back. And if he sees you falling apart... "

She nodded. "I'll go home."

"Have some of Selene's special tea. Maybe some chicken soup or something to settle your belly."

"Call the minute you hear anything."

"I'll drive her," Selene said. Her eyes said more, but the look in them was for Kara alone.

Jim nodded. "I'll check in on you." Then almost as if on impulse, he pulled her into his arms and hugged her close. "Thank you, Kara."

"For what? I haven't done anything." But God, his arms felt good around her just then, even though she wouldn't let herself melt into them or embrace him in return. She wished she could stay wrapped in those arms forever. If only he loved her.

"You don't know what you've done," he said. "I'm glad you're here with me. I wouldn't want to go through this without you."

She couldn't say the words that wanted so badly to be said. That she loved him. Always would. Instead she said, "He'll be okay, Jimmy. I know he will."

He walked with her out to the road, put her into Selene's little car and closed the door. Then he stood there and watched until Selene had driven them out of sight.

When she couldn't look back at him any longer, Kara finally turned to her sister.

Selene had that look in her eyes. That intense, almost eerie look she got sometimes. "What is it, Selene?" Kara asked.

Selene blinked and glanced her way, saying nothing.

"You know something," Kara blurted, reading her sister's expression. What is it?"

"I don't know."

"Come on, Selene, spill. You've got an inkling. A feeling. Something."

Selene nodded. "Yeah. I don't think it would be a good idea to let the police be the ones to find him. When Alex was saying what he said, I saw... something. A flash. But there was shouting and gunfire, and I had a terrible feeling about Tyler."

"Any idea where he is?"

Selene shook her head. Kara reached for the cell phone on the dash. When Maya picked up, Kara asked her if she'd found anything yet

"No. None of the local motels or inns have anyone registered with Illinois plates. And I've checked almost all of them."

"There can't be many."

"A dozen. At least within twenty miles. Maybe we'll have to look farther."

"Keep trying, Maya."

"I will. How are you holding up?"

"I'll be fine. Don't worry. Listen, I have to go. Love you, sis."

"Love you, too, Kara."

She disconnected and turned to Selene. "They'd have to be pretty stupid to put Illinois plates on a hotel registry," she said slowly. "I mean, they had to know we'd be looking for them that way."

Selene nodded. "You're right. And it's not like anyone checks. You just write the information in the book and they hand you a room key."

"So chances are Maya's phone calls are useless. The only way we're going to know for sure is to drive to those motels and look for that car ourselves. I just wish I knew where to start."

"Well then let's find out!" Selene pulled the car off onto the shoulder of the road, sending up a cloud of dust. She reached past Kara to open the glove compartment, and from it she took a small velvet drawstring bag. "Grab the map and get out," she said.

Kara didn't question. She knew better than to question her kid sister. She rummaged in the glove compartment for a map of the area and got out of the car. Then she went around to the front, where Selene was already standing, and she unfolded the map on the hood of the car.

"No, no. Spread it on the ground. I don't want the car's electronics interfering. Right here." Selene pointed.

Kara laid the map on the ground, just off the side of the road. The wind kept catching it, so she gathered four small rocks and placed one at each corner to keep it from blowing away.

Selene knelt on the ground in front of the map and opened the drawstring bag. She drew a chain from it, and as it emerged, Kara saw the crystal suspended from its end. "Selene?"

"It's a pendulum," Selene said. "I've been practicing with it. Pick a spot on the map where a hotel or motel is."

"Here," Kara said, pointing. "There are three west of town, right off the highway."

"Okay. Now just think about Tyler. Put his face in your mind, and I will, too."

Nodding, Kara thought of Tyler. His beautiful silky hair. His dimples, so like his dad's. The mischievous twinkle in his eyes. As she watched, Selene held the pendulum perfectly still, suspended over the portion of the map Kara had indicated.

At first nothing happened. The crystal just hung there, motionless. But then slowly, almost imperceptibly, it began to move. The motion was so slight at first that Kara thought she might be imagining it. But she wasn't. It moved faster, its arc growing larger, until it was swinging back and forth, from side to side.

Selene snapped the chain and caught the crystal in her hand. "That's a no," she said. "Tyler isn't there. Where else?"

Kara swallowed hard and racked her brain to think of other hotels and motels within driving distance. She pointed to another spot on the map, and Selene repeated the entire process, getting the same answer again.

And again Kara searched her mind, thought of a motel east of Big Falls and pointed. Selene let the pendulum dangle. This time the movement started immediately. There was no subtlety, no question. It swung, making a perfect and ever-widening circle over the spot on the map.

"That's it," Selene said. "That's a yes. That's where he is." She lifted her eyes to Kara's and probably saw the doubt there.

"It's outside the radius of the search," Kara said. "It's almost forty miles away."

"What can it hurt to drive out there and check?' Selene asked.

"Nothing. It can't hurt anything at all."

CHAPTER FOURTEEN

JIM LOOKED AT the men around him. His own boss, Chief Wilcox, had flown down from Chicago and stood beside the Big Falls police chief, Earl Wheatly, and Colby had checked himself out of the hospital and joined them at the scene as well. Local officers and deputies, men he didn't know, were there, all bonding behind a single cause. His boy. His Tyler.

"We've checked every hotel and motel in the area. None have any record of them under either of their names," Chief Wheatly said.

Jim nodded. "I didn't expect there would be. Vinnie's too smart to use his own name. You'll need to go by the plates."

"Tried that, too," he said. "No Illinois plates."

Jim closed his eyes, fought off the slow-building panic, squelched it and wished to hell Kara were there. Her presence had a calming effect on him, like cool water on a fever. It bothered him, that feeling of needing her.

"Try the campgrounds then." He tried to look more confident than he felt. "They might be holed up anywhere. We should check out any abandoned houses, any homes where the families are on vacation, anything like that."

"I've got some men checking every empty house we know of, others canvassing the residents too," Chief Wheatly said.

"Okay." He walked over to the woman who knelt near the roadside with a matched set of long-eared, sad-eyed bloodhounds, both straining at the ends of their leashes. She was a full-bodied woman with twinkling eyes, currently dimmed by a worried frown. "Any luck?" he asked her.

"They tracked your boy from the house to the driveway. Right where those men were lifting tire tracks. He was taken from here in a car."

"I assumed as much. I'm sorry we got you and the dogs out here for nothing."

"Oh, not for nothing. They can track your son, in a car or otherwise. For a while, anyway." She pointed in the direction her dogs seemed so eager to go. "They took him east."

Jim lifted his brows. He'd never worked with dogs before, had no idea their senses were that keen.

"I just need some men to follow. I'll walk as far as I can. But it might be slow going."

"You can't just let them go at their own pace and follow in a car?" he asked.

She shook her head firmly. "A bloodhound on the scent will walk in front of a bus or off a cliff and be dead before he realizes it. No, Mr. Corona. I stay with my dogs."

He nodded, then waved to some of the officers. When they came over, he repeated what the dog's handler had said, and within a few moments the woman was heading north along the road's shoulder, one cop walking beside her and another following at a snail's pace in a cruiser.

If Vinnie and Ang had taken Tyler more than a few miles... Hell.

Poor Tyler. What must he be going through right now? He

wondered if Angela had tried to tell him who she was. God, how confusing would that be for him? And Vinnie—if that slimebag so much as put a hand on his kid....

"Corona! Phone's ringing!" someone shouted.

Jim sprinted into the house as the telephone jangled and glanced at the officer who manned the wiretap equipment. The phone rang again. The man gave him a nod, and Jim picked up the telephone.

"This is Corona," he said.

"Well, hello, Jimbo. How you doing? You hanging in there?"

Jim saw a haze of red but kept his voice calm. "Missing my kid, Vinnie. Let me talk to him."

"Sure, sure, in a second. Listen, we explained to Tyler how you got called away on an emergency and asked us to bring him along. Only, my directions to the church must have been off. So you ease his mind about that now, so he'll be a cooperative little hostage for us and not have to be punished. All right?"

"You put a hand on him, you son of a bitch, and I'll—"

"I don't have to tell you what I want, do I, Jimbo? The second I hear from my lawyer that the charges against me have been dropped, you and your kid will be reunited. I'll give you eight hours to make it happen. I don't care what it takes. You make it happen."

"I'll do it. You know I will, you've got me where you want me." And for the life of him, Jim couldn't figure out what good Vinnie thought that would do. He had to know he was being recorded right now.

"Glad you realize it. Now talk to your boy and make it quick. I don't plan to keep this call going long enough for you to trace it. And Corona—the better he behaves for us, the easier this will go on him."

"I understand." He found himself looking to his side, automatically seeking Kara's face, her eyes. Damn, he couldn't believe how much he wished she were there right now. He'd vowed never to let another woman mean anything to him. Not a damn thing. So what was going on with his head?

Tyler's voice came on the phone. "Dad?"

"It's me, Ty. Everything's fine."

"Dad! I'm gonna miss the weddin'!"

"No, no, you're not. There was a problem at the church—a big hole in the roof. I think I tree limb fell on it. So we're not having the wedding today after all."

"Oh, no!" Tyler's voice was soft. "Is Kara very sad?"

"She's fine, Ty."

"No way, Dad. She *must* be sad. She looked so pretty!"

Kara's face appeared in his mind's eye, the way she'd looked when he'd seen her before. Pale, shaken, devastated. He'd attributed it to worry over Tyler. And he still thought that was the main cause. But it took Tyler to remind him she'd also been stood up at the altar today. And she'd learned that her husband to be didn't love her.

The woman was an angel. She didn't deserve the hell she was going through right now. Tyler's innocent reminder of that added a layer of pain and a ton of guilt to the burdens already weighing him down.

"It's okay, Dad. I'll make her feel better soon as you come get me."

He swallowed hard and focused on his son. "And I'll come get you just as soon as I can, hon. But it might be just a little while yet. Are they being nice to you?"

"They're okay. Not much fun, though. And the lady—" he lowered his voice to a whisper "—she's kinda *weird*."

"You be a good boy, Ty. Be just as good as you can be, and I'll come for you very, very soon. I promise."

"I wish you could come now. Dad, Kara is still gonna be my new mommy. Isn't sh–"

"Tyler? Ty?" Nothing. Dead air.

"He disconnected," the technician called. "Didn't give us enough time to trace it."

Jim nodded, lifted his head, looked at his chief. "We have to call the D.A. Get him to drop the child pornography case against Vinnie. It's the only way he'll let Tyler go."

The chief pursed his lips. "It's a child-porn charge, Corona. You willing to let him walk on that?"

God, he wished Kara were there.

"We'll get him on kidnapping. Assault. Attempted murder. He tried to kill Colby and he bashed my skull in with a tire iron. Thirty-six stitches, that's gotta be convincing. Attempted murder of two cops is no small potatoes. He'll do more time for that than he would have for the kiddie porn anyway."

Wade shot him a look. "You're kidding me."

"It's true," Caleb said. "Sick system we have, isn't it?"

"I don't like it or agree with it," Jim said. "But it's what we've got." He nodded to his chief. "Get the D.A. on the phone. We have to move on this as fast as possible. I want my kid back."

"Yeah, okay. Just one question, Corona. And.. .hell, you don't know how much I hate having to ask it." He pursed his lips. "Does Tyler realize he's been abducted?"

"No. He thinks I asked those two animals to take him."

The chief nodded. "Then he wasn't blindfolded?"

Jim felt his entire being go cold. He knew what was coming.

"Vinnie isn't stupid. He's not going to go to all this trouble to weasel out of one set of charges only to set himself up with even more serious ones. He thinks Colby's dead so he's in the clear on that. No one to testify. Which leaves you and Tyler as the only witnesses to the kidnapping."

Jim lunged at his boss and had him by the collar before he even realized he was moving. "Don't you even—"

"Ease off, Jim!" Caleb gripped his shoulders and tugged him off. Wade stood beside him, glaring at the six officers about to draw down.

The guys had his back. Hell, that was a shocker.

He released Chief Wilcox.

"I know you don't want to face it, Jim," Wilcox said, smoothing his shirt. "I know, believe me I know. But you can't turn a blind eye to the truth either. There's no guarantee that giving Vinnie what he wants is going to get Tyler out of there alive. He's got to tie up lose ends. Which means Tyler, and then you. Hell, your boy might be safer if you stall a little. They'd have to keep him alive then. And it would buy us some time to track him down."

Jim turned in a slow circle. "I've got to do something."

"Did Vinnie give you a time limit?"

He nodded. "Eight hours."

"Then you've got time. You don't have to make a decision right now. Give it a couple of hours, Jim," Chief Wilcox pled. "Give us time to track them down before you make that call to the D.A. All right?"

Jim pushed a hand through his hair. His pulse was throbbing in his throat and temples, and every nerve ending seemed raw. He looked at Wade, then at Caleb.

And he felt like Caleb read his mind, because he leaned closer and said, "Let's take a ride out to Vi's house. You can talk to Kara."

God that sounded like the answer. "I should be looking—"

"Alex and Mel are working from there. Maya's on the phone, working that angle. You can check and see what they've come up with."

He almost sagged in relief just at the thought of getting Kara's input on this. He sent a look at his chief. "Call the D.A. Tell him what's going on, all of it. Tell him to have things in place, be ready to drop the charges, have the forms ready to file, everything but his signature. And have him get the fax number for Vinnie's lawyer. I want this to go through instantly once I give him the word."

"Okay. I'll do it just as you say."

Jim nodded, turned to Wade and Caleb. They both seemed to understand without a word.

~

TYLER FROWNED AT the phone, then up at the man. "Hey, it stopped workin'!"

"It did?" Vinnie took the motel room phone from him, then messed with it a little. "Hmm, I guess there must be a problem on the line."

The lady looked at the man and rolled her eyes.

"Don't worry, kid, it will be fixed in no time. And then we'll call your dad again."

Tyler pouted and crossed his arms over his chest. "We could use that one," he said pointing to the cell phone on the bedside table. The one with its battery out and sitting beside it.

"'Fraid that one's busted too, kid," Vinnie replied. "Hey, I got some games and stuff. You want to see?"

Tyler lifted his eyebrows. "Sure, I guess."

"Sure. It'll be fun. And we'll get some takeout. Angela, go get us some food, huh? You like pizza, kid?"

Tyler brightened a little more. "It's my favorite. But I don't like onions or green peppers or mushrooms on it."

"Is there anything you *do* like on it?"

"Pepperoni!"

Vinnie smiled at him, seemed more friendly all of the sudden. "Pepperoni it is, kiddo. Angie, go find us the biggest pepperoni pizza you can, huh? Double cheese. And some sody pop, too. What kind you like, kid?"

"Grape!"

"Grape?" Vinnie made a face so funny that Tyler laughed out loud. "Grape then. Get us grape soda, Ang. I'm gonna teach the kid here how to play video games while you're gone."

"I already know how to play video games!" Tyler exclaimed.

The lady heaved a sigh, like she was irritated with him, but she grabbed a coat and went out the door.

"Hey, Tyler, wanna try something fun?" the man said.

"What?" Tyler asked.

"Let's see if you can fit your whole body inside my suitcase. 'Kay?"

Tyler giggled and did as instructed. Of course he didn't fit, not with the leg braces on, but when Vinnie helped him take them off, he fit just fine. Vinnie even showed him how he could close the lid, though he didn't close it all the way tight. Tyler thought it was about the funniest thing in the world.

He heard the door open and he peeked out. The grumpy lady was back, but not with any pizzas. She'd only been gone a minute.

She saw him in the suitcase and he thought she was gonna have a hissy, the way her face changed. Her eyes got kinda big and her skin seemed whiter than usual. Although it was pretty white already. Dad would say she didn't get enough sun.

She looked at Vinnie and then she was yelling, real loud. "What the hell do you think you're doing? What are you doing, Vinnie? What are you *doing?*"

"Oh, knock it off already!" Vinnie snapped.

He sounded mad too, so Tyler cringed a little deeper into that big suitcase. It was kinda like a cave. He could pretend he was a bear and hide out there if he wanted.

Then the lid was flung back suddenly, and he hid his face.

"Get out of there, Tyler. Come on." The lady wasn't yelling anymore. She even put a hand on his shoulder.

Tyler climbed out of the suitcase and sat on the bed. "We was just playin' a game," he told her.

She nodded. "I know." Then she glanced at the suitcase again and frowned. She bent down and picked up a envelope. "What is this? Jesus, Vinnie, this is a one way ticket to South America."

He eyes widened.

"Look, babe, once those charges are dropped, my accounts get unfrozen. I've got a guy ready to transfer everything overseas. And I'm gonna move just as fast as my money, cause you know they'll have a whole new set of charges to file. I gotta get out while the gettin's good."

She blinked. "B-but... it's only one ticket."

"Yeah. But I'll send for you once I get settled."

She looked real sad, then, her eyes got all wet. "And what about Tyler? You promised me he wouldn't get hurt."

"Aw, I wasn't gonna get hurt," Tyler said, wanting her not to cry. "That suitcase is soft, and he didn't close it all the way."

Vinnie and the lady just stared at each other. Finally Vinnie said, "I return him, they file new charges. If they can't find him for a while, that buys me a little time."

She was quiet for a long time. Then she finally handed him the car keys and said, "I think maybe you'd better go get the pizza yourself. I'm not leaving him alone with you."

"You defying me now?"

They were mad again. Tyler didn't like it.

"You don't wanna go," Ang said. "Fine. I will, but I'm taking him with me."

"Not in this lifetime, Angie."

Tyler spoke up. "When my dad wants pizza, he calls and they bring it to us. Can we do that, maybe?"

They both turned their heads toward him. For a minute he thought they were going to yell, but then Vinnie smiled at him. "You're a smart kid, you know that?" Then he crossed the room and opened a drawer, took out a big, fat yellow book and started turning pages. "Someplace around this town has to deliver."

Tyler didn't mention that he really ought to put his leg braces back on. He hated them. Instead he sat where he was, on the bed. The lady got a big shopping bag out of the closet and dumped it out on the bed, and Tyler thought it looked like he was having a birthday party. There was a remote-control race car, a video-game system, a pile of games for it, some books and a lot of other stuff.

"Wow!"

"This is all for you, Tyler," the woman said. "Why don't you pick something out and play for a while, huh?"

"Gee, thanks. And it's not even my birthday."

"Well, it's almost Christmas, right?"

"Yeah, but I didn't ask for any of this stuff for Christmas." Tyler grabbed the box that held the game system and started tearing it open.

"What did you ask for?" the lady asked.

"Just a mommy," he told her.

IT WAS THE third motel they had checked, all of them located in the same little cluster. Kara was so impatient she thought her head would explode. Selene was driving her little car slowly through the motel parking lot when Kara saw it—a car with Illinois plates. Selene saw it at the same moment and sent a startled glance at Kara.

"They're here. That has to be them. They're here, we've found them," Kara whispered. "God, Selene, you're uncanny with that pendulum trick of yours. I can't even believe it."

"Yeah. The question is, now that we've found them, what do we do about it?"

Kara sighed. "I just have to make sure Tyler's okay. After that... we'll figure something out."

"We don't even know which room. And this place is huge," Selene said.

"Pendulum again?"

"I'm not that good. Besides, by the time I get a yes or no answer to every room number in this place, it'll be midnight."

"Then what do we do? How do we find out which room they're in?"

Selene shrugged. "I'm gonna go talk to the desk clerk. You stay here. If Tyler sees you he'll give you away." She opened the glove compartment and took out a notepad and pen. "Jot down the plate number of the car. Just in case they get away from us again."

"Okay. But if you figure out where they are, don't go near the room without me."

"You think we should call Jimmy first?" Selene asked.

Kara thought on it a moment. But God, he was going through so much. "Let's make sure it's really them first. I don't want to get his hopes up only to have them crushed again."

"You really love him, don't you?"

"Yeah. I really do." She wished the feeling was mutual. Sighing, she gave her head a shake. "Park this thing and let's get on with it."

Selene nodded, pulled the car into the first available parking space, then got out and hurried into the motel office.

Kara stayed in the car, her gaze skimming the motel rooms' doors, their windows. She strained her vision until her eyes watered. But there was no sign of Tyler.

Then a pizza delivery car pulled up in front of the row of rooms and a teenager got out with a pizza box and a paper bag. He went to a door and knocked, and Kara watched because it was the only movement she'd seen.

A man opened the door. He looked up and down the sidewalk before his gaze settled on the delivery boy. Kara rolled her window down.

The man took the pizza and the other bag the kid carried, handing them off to someone inside the room, then he dug out some money.

"All *right!* Pizza's here!" someone cried.

It was a child's voice.

It was *Tyler's* voice.

Kara waited until the door was closed, the pizza car gone, before she got out of the car. She glanced toward the office, but there was no sign of Selene yet. As an afterthought she dug a tube of lipstick from her purse and wrote on the side-view mirror, "RM. 15." Then she put the lipstick away and started toward the room.

JIM GOT OUT of the pickup and headed for the Brand house. Before he'd gone two steps, Wade and Caleb were flanking him. He paused, because he got the distinct feeling they were holding him up, even though neither man was touching him. And it was an odd feeling.

He didn't have close friends, other than Colby. Didn't have family. Now all of the sudden he had an entire herd of people who, by all appearances, would be willing to give him a kidney. It was surreal.

Vidalia opened the front door before he reached it and then she was hugging him hard. "Poor man, you look terrible. We're gonna find that boy, you mark my words."

He nodded, but he realized when she said it that he wasn't as certain. A bone-chilling fear had taken up residence deep inside him.

She tugged him inside then, walking beside him. He saw Edie turn around and hug her husband. She'd been standing at the counter, putting on a fresh pot of coffee. It made him ache for Kara.

"Mel and Alex are working on several possibilities," Vidalia said. "Maya's upstairs putting the twins down for a nap. How are the police doing? Any leads?"

"Nothing yet." He looked around the kitchen. He didn't see Kara, and the lead weight of longing in his belly grew heavier. "Is Kara here?"

Vidalia frowned. "Well, no, she never came home. We all assumed she'd changed her mind and she and Selene had gone back over to your place."

"She didn't." He was suddenly worried.

"No doubt she's out looking for that boy herself," Vidalia said. "Land, but I never saw anything like the way she's taken to that child. Not that the rest of us haven't, but Kara... well, she's as smitten with Tyler as she is with you, Jim."

Another guilt arrow stabbed into his chest. It brought company; A new worry. "I don't like that no one knows where she is."

"She wouldn't want you worrying," Vidalia said, "much less diverting any time or attention from searching for Tyler to go out looking for her. She'll call in."

He pursed his lips and sent a look at Wade and Caleb.

"Let's see what Alex and Mel are working on," Caleb suggested. "Give her a little time to call home. Okay?"

Jim nodded.

"They're in the study," Vidalia said.

Jim followed her in, but he couldn't get rid of the niggling dread in his belly.

CHAPTER FIFTEEN

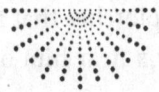

KARA CREPT TOWARD the motel room, but there were only the door and a large window there, curtains drawn. She was afraid she would be spotted for sure if she moved much closer. Biting her lip, she looked around at the way the place was set up. There were three blocks of rooms, two stories each, with pavement and groomed lawn in between. She eyed the room that held Tyler, memorized its position, counted the number of doors from the far end, then crept around to the rear of the building. There were windows in the back, too. Small ones, set high. One for each room, as near as she could guess.

Swallowing her fear, she began counting. When she got to the fifteenth tiny window, she crouched beneath it, then chanced a quick peek inside, quickly ducking down again. A bathroom. She hadn't glimpsed anyone in it, so she rose and took a longer look. The bathroom wasn't neat. There were damp towels piled on the floor, and clothes tossed beside them. The bathroom door was open, though, and she could see into the motel room itself. People moving around—a man and a woman.

221

Then she glimpsed Tyler. He was on the bed and had suddenly slid closer to the foot of it, bringing him into her range of vision. Her heart pounded as she drank in the sight of him. He looked all right. Unharmed. He wasn't wearing his leg braces and she wondered why. Maybe they thought he wouldn't be able to run away if they kept the braces from him. He'd taken off his tux jacket and tie, just wore the pants and white shirt, currently stained in red splotches that made her heart race, until she glimpsed the pizza box near him on the bed, and realized it was just sauce.

Kara backed away from the window, barely able to catch her breath. Quickly, she jogged back around to the front of the building, where she intercepted Selene on her way back to the car.

Selene met her eyes as they drew close. "No luck with them, they don't know... What? What is it?"

"They're in room fifteen. Right there." Kara pointed. "There's a window in the back—it's a bathroom. I saw Ty. I think he's okay."

Selene gripped her sister's hands. "Thank God. What do you want to do? Should we call the police? Jim?"

"Either one amounts to the same thing. And a hostage standoff is the last thing we need here, especially after your...vision. Or whatever. Maybe we can just...spirit him away."

"How?" Selene asked.

"Okay, well. I have an idea."

"Why do I think I'm not going to like this?"

"Because you're probably not. But just hear me out Ty has to go the bathroom sooner or later. He's a kid—they go every ten minutes, right?"

Selene pursed her lips.

"So you pull the car around back. There's more parking back there, so it won't look odd. Leave it running. Then you and I sneak up to that window and we wait. When Tyler comes into the bathroom, we get him to unlock the window, we pull him out and we take off with him."

Selene nodded slowly. "It's risky."

"As risky as having the police surround this place? Besides, who's to say they won't hurt him before they could get here? We can't wait. We have to try this."

Drawing a deep breath, Selene nodded. "Okay, let's do it." She opened the driver's door and got in.

ANGELA WAS IN over her head and she hated it. Vinnie had promised her that nothing bad would happen to Tyler. His plan, the way he'd laid it out to her, had made such perfect sense she couldn't imagine anything going wrong with it. They would take Tyler just for a little while. Just long enough to make Jim withdraw his testimony. When the charges against Vin were officially dropped, every i dotted and every t crossed, his lawyer would call him on his cell phone to let him know, and they would return Tyler and go back to their lives.

Vinnie had painted such a beautiful picture of the way her life would be once he was in the clear and they could be married. His home was like a Hollywood dream house—he'd shown it to her once. He had a pool and everything. And cars and money. He traveled all around the world, could buy just about anything he wanted.

It all seemed so perfect.

But now she was beginning to understand that Vinnie's promises had all been lies. She should have realized he couldn't just go back to his life if Jim pulled his testimony. And then she'd seen him putting Tyler into that suitcase. She couldn't for the life of her think of any reason why he would do something like that, unless it was just to make sure Tyler's body would fit. And that scared her. It scared her enough to make her wonder if

Jim had been telling the truth about what had happened to his partner, Colby. Had the man who'd taken Colby away from there actually murdered him? On Vinnie's order? Vinnie would deny it if she asked and he would probably convince her he was telling the truth.

God, could Jim have been right about Vinnie all along?

She needed to ask Vinnie about it. But she couldn't very well bring the subject up in front of the kid. It would scare him.

She felt bad. The last thing she wanted was to cause her son more pain.

She wished she could get Vinnie alone. Maybe she was reading him all wrong. Maybe he could explain what he was doing, convince her it was all innocent. She wanted to be convinced, she really did.

Licking her lips, she watched the kid playing video games on the TV. He was pretty involved. She sighed and got up, heading into the bathroom and pulling the door shut behind her.

Then she frowned, because she glimpsed something outside. What was that?

She crept closer to the window. Took a quick look outside but couldn't see anyone. Still, when she'd first come in she could have sworn someone was looking into the bathroom window.

Pursing her lips, she looked at the lock on the window. Maybe someone was trying to get in. To rescue Tyler.

She called to Vinnie. She had to talk to him and it had to be now.

He came in, looking at her and frowning.

"Close the door, I have to talk to you."

He didn't. "Just keep it down. I don't want the kid running out the front door on us."

"Hell, Vinnie, he can't even walk without those braces on his legs. Just close the door."

Frowning, he closed the door but not tightly. She drew a

breath. "I been thinking," she said, "about what's gonna happen... after."

"Aw, hon, I've told you over and over what's gonna happen. You're gonna be like a queen. Everything you ever wanted—"

"After you send for me. From South America."

"And you'll have that nice apartment I got you in the meantime."

"Yeah. Okay. But that's not what I meant. I'm talking about Tyler. He's seen us both. I know you've thought of it too. That's why you were making sure his... body... would fit in the case. That's what you were doing, wasn't it?"

He lowered his head. "Just as a precaution, hon. Just in case."

She nodded. "You can't leave him alive, can you, Vinnie? And you've gotta kill Jim too, or go down for that beating you gave him. Right?"

"Angie, Angie, baby, don't you want all the things we've talked about? You don't give two shits for your ex, do you? After how mean he's been to you?"

"No. No, I don't."

"And the kid, baby, that kid's not right. His life is hell anyway. I'll be doin' him a favor."

She felt angry tears spring into her eyes and lowered her head quickly. "I know. I know you're right. I mean, I don't think we have any choice." She lifted her eyes again, searching his. "Do we?"

"If there's another way, I promise—"

"Don't make promises you can't keep, Vinnie."

"You gonna be okay with this?"

She made her face hard, nodded once. "Hell, I'll have to be."

"That's my good girl. Here, babe." He handed her the case. The whole damn case. "Do a little more blow. It'll help." Then he left the bathroom and closed the door.

She looked at the case that held the drug she so craved. Vinnie figured she would snort a line or two and come out of the room too high to care much whether he murdered her own baby boy. Hell, why should he think any differently? She hadn't acted like a mother since Tyler had been born.

She wanted the cocaine so bad her hands were shaking. But not yet. Soon, she promised herself. But not just yet. She set the case down and turned to the window. Then she unlocked it and pushed it open. She still couldn't see anyone, but she whispered all the same. "I'm gonna run Tyler a bath. Then I'm gonna keep Vinnie in the other room and send him in here to take it. Get the kid out of here if you can."

She closed the window again but she didn't turn the lock. Then she brushed the tears from her eyes and returned to the case she'd left sitting on the bathroom sink. She did a line for courage. Then she took the rest with her and went back into the room.

~

KARA WAS STANDING to one side of the little window with her back pressed to the wall, and Selene was doing the same on the other side, when the woman's voice came softly from the bathroom.

They shot each other startled looks, not relaxing until they heard the window close again. Kara closed her eyes.

"It could be a trick," Selene whispered. "We try to get him, they end up with three hostages instead of one."

"She's his mother," Kara said. "I knew she'd try to protect him if she could. Jim didn't believe it, but... She probably finally figured out how dangerous her boyfriend is."

"Even so."

"She has a chance to do something good for her son for the first time in his life. Selene, she put him in those leg braces. She did that. No, I don't think it's a trick. I think she means it."

Kara peered into the bathroom briefly, long enough to see

that water was running into the bathtub and that the latch on the window was open. Then she pressed her back to the wall again. "The window's up high. It's a long way to pull him. I don't know if I'm strong enough. I'm going to have to go in and lift him out to you."

"No, Kara, no, that's too much."

"I'm going to do it Selene, so just deal. When I push Ty out I want you to take him and run to the car. If anything goes wrong—"

"He could catch you in there! Kara, what if—"

"What if," she repeated. "What's the worst that can happen? He kills me instead of a little boy who hasn't even lived five years yet? Come on, Selene, we both know it's worth the risk. Better me than him. We get Tyler out. Period. If anything goes wrong, you take him and you go. Then call Jim and then tell him where I am."

Tears rose in Selene's pale blue eyes. "I'm calling him now. God, Kara, please don't do this."

"I'm doing it. You know damn well if it was your call, you'd do the same. I love that boy, Selene. Do this for me."

The tears spilled over, streaming down Selene's face, but she was tapping keys on her phone rapidly as she did. "You'd better get back out and be right behind me."

"If I'm not, don't come back for me. If he ends up right back in their hands, it will all have been for nothing. Promise?"

Sniffling, Selene nodded and hit Send. "I promise." She dipped into a pocket and pulled out a little pink heart-shaped stone. "Take this. It'll help keep you safe."

"I'll be okay," Kara promised as she closed her hand around the stone. "Thank you, Selene."

"I love you, Kara."

"Love you, too, sis."

~

JIM WAS SITTING in the study, listening to Alex tell him all he'd been doing, which was basically the same things the police had been doing, and feeling more and more restless. Where the hell was Kara? It just wasn't like her not to be there helping, supporting, giving everything she had to help everyone else get through this thing. With every minute that passed he was more and more certain something was terribly wrong.

And this his cell phone chimed, startling him so much that he damn near dropped it. Jim pulled it out to look at the text message. "Kara and Selene tracked them to a motel east of here. She says Tyler's okay, but to hurry. Let's go."

Then he raced to his pickup and took off, dialing his cell phone on the way.

One by one, motors roared to life, headlights flashed on, and Brands sped into action behind him.

~

"LOOK AT THIS," Angela said, staring at Tyler. "You've got pizza sauce all over you." She wasn't seeing the pizza sauce on his face, though. She was seeing the light in his eyes, the way they crinkled at the corners when he smiled, the deep dimples in his cheeks. He really was a beautiful little boy. She wondered why she'd never noticed before. "You should take a bath."

Vinnie frowned at her. She met his eyes, careful to keep her own from showing even a hint of emotion. "He should be clean, Vinnie. I don't want him going... home... with a dirty face. No one should go out like that."

He smiled a little. "Sure. Sure, a bath is a good idea. Why not? We've got time yet. Go ahead, kid. Take a bath."

Tyler pouted, but he didn't argue. Angela picked him up and carried him into the bathroom. She set him on the toilet seat, then leaned in close to him. "I want you to sit right here. I want you to be very quiet, okay? Your friends are coming to get you, but we can't let Vinnie know. So you have to be quiet."

"Is it a s'prise?" he asked, whispering back at her. His eyes got big and the twinkle in them made something knot up in her chest.

"Yeah," she said. "It's a surprise. Now you sit here and be very quiet. Not a peep, okay?"

"Okay," he whispered. "Does this mean I don't really have to take a bath?"

She smiled at him. "Not till you get home anyway." On impulse, she snatched a washcloth from the sink, dampened it and wiped the pizza sauce from his face. Then she wrapped her arms around him and hugged him awkwardly, knowing it would be the last time she would ever have the chance. "I love you, Tyler."

"Really?"

"Yeah. Really." Releasing him, she stepped back. Then she went to the window and slid it open and didn't look at Tyler again when she walked out of the bathroom and pulled the door closed behind her.

Vinnie looked up. "He gonna be okay all by himself?" he asked.

"Yeah. I'll check on him in a minute or two. He's a little shy. Hell, we're strangers to him, right?"

He looked at the door, frowning.

"I wanted a minute alone with you, Vinnie. I wanted to ask... how you're gonna do it."

His brows went up. "He won't feel a thing, I promise."

"How?" she asked again.

He sighed, maybe sensing her hesitation. "I got some sleeping pills. We tell him it's a vitamin or something, get it down him. Hell, we can dissolve a couple in that grape soda he keeps guzzling, for that matter. Make it even easier on the kid. Once he's out, he isn't gonna feel anything."

She blinked. "And then what? Once he's out, I mean?"

"C'mon, Angie, you don't need to know this stuff. I'll send you out to the car. You don't have to see it. Okay?"

She nodded slowly. "Okay."

He looked at the bathroom door again. "He's bein' awful quiet in there."

"I'll go back in," she said, getting up quickly.

Vinnie put a hand on her shoulder. "No. I'll do it."

~

KARA LOOKED THROUGH the window and saw Tyler's eyes light up when he saw her face. She put a finger to her lips, to tell him to keep quiet, and he nodded with a broad smile. Then she put her legs through, sitting on the sill, and slid inside. It was a tight squeeze. It wouldn't be for Tyler, though.

As soon as she was in, she scooped Tyler off the toilet seat and hugged him hard. "Are you okay?" she whispered.

"Uh-huh. I missed you."

"Me, too. Now we have to be quiet."

"I know," he said. "It's a s'prise."

She carried him to the window. He patted her shoulder. "What about my braces?"

"We'll get them later. Come on now, up you go." She hefted him up, and Selene gripped him from outside and drew him easily out through the window.

Kara heard footsteps approaching the bathroom door. "Go!" she whispered urgently. "Go, Selene."

Selene turned and started across the grass toward the waiting car. The bathroom door swung open and Kara spun around, her back to the wall.

The man who stood there had to be Vinnie. He was tall, thin and very, very angry. "What the hell is this!" Even as he said it, he reached for her with one hand while drawing a gun with the other. He shoved her, and she hit the side of the tub so hard she thought her knee cracked. Then he was at the window, pointing the gun. "Stop!" he shouted. "I'll kill you, bitch!"

Kara launched herself at him and a shot rang out "Run, Selene! Don't stop, run!" she shrieked.

The man hit her in the head with the gun. Her head exploded in pain, and she went down hard, her ears ringing. But she heard the sound of squealing tires and she knew Selene was away.

Tyler was safe.

The man leaned over her, swearing brutally. He gripped her by the front of her shirt and hauled her to her feet. "Some kinda hero, aren't you? You're gonna die for this, you realize that, right?"

"I don't care. Tyler's safe and you're going to prison. That's all that matters."

He hit her again—with his fist or the gun, she wasn't sure. But the lights went out, and Kara collapsed to the floor.

JIM WAS SPEEDING toward the motel when he spotted Selene's little car—the one she and Kara had been driving—racing toward him. He flashed his lights, and the car pulled over to the side.

He skidded to a stop, reversed until he was even with it, jumped out of his car and ran across the street.

Selene was already out, opening the passenger door, and then he saw Tyler as she gathered him into her arms. God, he was safe. He was safe! Jim's knees went weak, every muscle turned to water. He managed to go to his son, took him from Selene and held him hard.

"Dad! You're squishing me!"

He eased his grip a little, kissing his son's face, hugging him, rocking him back and forth. "You're okay. Thank God, thank God, you're really okay."

"Sure, I'm okay. Why's everyone keep saying that?"

He pressed Tyler's head to his shoulder and met Selene's eyes. And the look in them made him go cold. "What happened?" he asked. "Where's Kara?"

"I didn't want to let her do it, Jim."

"Do what? Where is she?" Suddenly the ice-cold fear was alive again, clutching his heart in its frigid hands.

"Kara slid in through the bathroom window to get Tyler out. She handed him out to me, but that man came in before she could get back out again. They have her, Jim. God, we have to get her back. You have to go."

"I'll get her," he said and he didn't think he'd ever uttered words and meant them more. "I'll get her back, I swear. How far?"

"Two miles back that way, on the left. Room fifteen. It's in the first block of rooms, ground floor. There's a bathroom window in the back. One door and a big window in front. He has a gun. Took a shot at us as we ran for it."

"Vinnie shot a gun at us?" Tyler asked. His smile was gone. Clearly he was picking up the adults' fear. "Why did he do that?"

"I'll explain later, Tyler." Jim shifted him back into Selene's arms. "They didn't follow you? You're sure?"

"No. I think Vinnie had his hands full with Kara. And, Jim, you should know Angela helped us. She saw us in the back, unlocked the window and kept Vinnie out of the bathroom so we could get Tyler out."

He nodded, but the words didn't matter to him. That his one-time wife had finally, for one moment out of millions, put her son's well-being ahead of her own meant nothing to him. Real parents did it every day of their lives. If either one of them hurt Kara...

He shook off the thought. It wasn't possible to even consider it. "Take Tyler back to your mother's. You'll intercept the guys on the way here. Fill everyone in." Sirens sounded. "The police are already on their way. Go now."

She nodded, putting Tyler back into the car. Then she came out again, a scrap of paper in her hand. "Jim, wait. Here, this is the info on the car they were driving. Just in case."

He took the paper, barely glancing at it before cramming it into a pocket.

Selene got into the car and said, "Save my sister, Jim. Bring her back to us."

"I will," he said, then ran to his pickup, got in and took off.

As he pressed the accelerator to the floor, he realized that in spite of everything—his past his determination, his stubborn-ness—he was sick at the thought of anything hurting Kara. Devastated at the notion of facing a future without her in it, and killing mad at those who were keeping her from him.

He wanted her, he realized. Not for Tyler's sake, not because she would be the perfect mother. But for himself. He wanted to be with her. Always.

And if that wasn't love, he didn't know what was.

Damn, he loved Kara Brand, after all. And he probably had for a while now. He'd been so busy telling himself he didn't—couldn't—that he hadn't noticed that he did. Fine time to figure it out now that he might never have the chance to tell her, he thought. He hoped he would be able to make things right with her.

All along he'd been beating himself up, feeling guilty for not being able to give the woman what she so richly deserved. A husband who loved her. Was devoted to her. Could make her happy.

And now he realized he did. And he could.

But he had to save her life first.

CHAPTER SIXTEEN

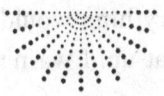

THERE WERE SOUNDS, sickening sounds. Grunts of pain accompanied each one.

Kara opened her eyes and tried to bring the room into focus. Her head was spinning, and so was the room around her. But it slowed, and she found she was lying on her back on a floor, her legs inside the bathroom, her upper body in the motel room. Blinking, she lifted her head, managed to roll onto her side, though the motion brought pain. And then she saw where the sounds were coming from. The man held a woman by the front of her blouse with one fist, and pounded her face repeatedly with the other. He was swearing at her.

Kara pushed up with her hands, managed to get up onto her knees but no further. "Stop. Stop it, you're killing her."

He stopped pounding and swung his gaze her way. Kara didn't look back. She couldn't; her eyes were glued to the woman's battered face. She looked as if she'd lost a battle with a meat grinder. Her neck seemed like rubber. She wasn't holding her head up, and Kara wasn't sure if she was conscious.

The man released his grip on the woman's blouse, and she slumped to the floor. Then he turned and strode across the room to Kara. "You keep your mouth shut, bitch." He kicked her, his foot landing hard in her side. She collapsed flat on the floor, then curled around herself, hugging her middle. God, it hurt.

"You know what you've done, you and your do-gooder family? Huh, you know what you've done to me?"

"It wasn't about you," she whispered. "It was about Ty."

"The kid was fine. You should've kept your nose out of it! I'd have let him go and everything would've been all right. You're the one who screwed that up. I wasn't gonna hurt anyone, but now—"

"Liar."

The tortured whisper came from the other woman, though she didn't move when she spoke. "You were gonna kill him."

"What's-a matter, Ang, you haven't had enough yet?" He started toward her again, and again Kara pushed herself upright. She looked around, spotted a half empty soft drink bottle sitting within reach, grabbed it by the neck and smashed the bottom against the stand. She held the jagged edged remnants as he turned around, shock in his eyes. "She's had enough," Kara whispered. "Leave her alone." Gripping the table with her free hand, she hauled herself to her feet.

"Guess you haven't, though, have you?" he asked.

"You ever beat up on anyone besides women, Vinnie?" she asked. "You kidnap children and pound on women. You're a real man, aren't you?"

"Damn straight I am. And you know what you are? You're a dead woman." He came closer. She saw Angela moving, thought at first she was going to try to help her.

She had a small case, like a square compact, in her hands. Kara didn't know where she'd gotten it. But as she flipped it open, a little white powder spilled out onto the floor, onto her blouse, sticking to the blood there.

Kara frowned. "What is that? What are you doing?"

Vinnie turned, saw the woman and rolled his eyes. "Let her

alone. That's what she does." He smiled at the woman. "Isn't it, Angie? Huh? That stuff might help take the edge off the pain, baby, but don't you worry. It won't last long, and I got a lot of anger to work off yet."

The woman said nothing. Instead she picked up a small straw, held it to her nose and closed off the other nostril. She sucked some of the powder into her nose, despite that it was probably broken.

"Don't," Kara said. "Angela, stop it. Think about Tyler."

Angela looked up, peering through eyes that barely opened at all. "I am," she said. And she sniffed up some more. And then some more. Angela kept it up until there was nothing left in the case, while Vinnie advanced on Kara. Then she backed into a corner, dropped her little gold case and drew her knees to her chest.

Vinnie reached for Kara. "Let's go, sweet cheeks. We need to move. Thanks to your heroics, you're my hostage now."

He hauled Kara to her feet tugged her toward the door, then turned toward Angela. "Angie, can you walk?"

Angela didn't lift her head.

"Hell, you're not going anywhere, are you, honey?" He gripped Kara's upper arm. "Come on."

"Where? Where are you taking me?" Kara was terrified of leaving there. There, at least Jim and the police and her family would know where to look for her. Anywhere else, and, they might never find her.

"To the car," Vinnie said. He opened the motel room door and dragged her across the parking lot. Keeping one hand over her mouth, he yanked out a key ring and pressed a button on it. His trunk popped open.

Kara's blood turned to ice water. She didn't have time to be afraid long, because he looked around, then shoved her into the trunk and slammed it shut. She thought some of the people standing in the parking lot must have seen. They had to have seen. She pounded on the trunk, kicked it. But within a few seconds the car was squealing into motion, turning, and her body rolled and slammed against the sides. It reversed fast, then stopped abruptly. She banged into the front. Seconds later the trunk opened again, and Angela was dropped in beside her. Then the trunk slammed shut, and the car jerked into motion again, slamming Angela and Kara against each other.

Once they got underway, Kara wasn't banged around so much anymore. She put her hands on Angela, curled up beside her. Finding her shoulders, she rolled Ang over onto her back." Angela?" she whispered. She shook her a little. "Ang, come on. We need each other right now. Tyler needs us. We have to help each other get through this."

There was no response.

Kara didn't know a lot about cocaine. But she was pretty sure that what she'd seen Angela ingest was way too much. She smacked Angela's cheek. "Angela?" And when there was still no response, she pressed her fingers to the woman's throat and then her wrist and then she put her ear to her chest to listen.

But there was nothing to hear.

Angela was dead.

JIM WAS SPEEDING toward the motel when another car came careening from that direction, way past the speed limit. The same car Vinnie had been driving when he'd come to the house with his tire iron.

He pulled a u-turn in and pressed the pedal to the floor in pursuit, and it was only when he passed the swarm of screaming black-and-whites that he thought to reach for his cell phone and call in the information.

Chief Wheatly picked up.

"Chief, it's Corona. The suspect vehicle is currently heading south on Cold Springs Road. I'm in pursuit."

"Does he have the boy with him?"

"No. No, Tyler is safe. But he has Kara Brand."

"How the hell... Is she in the car?"

"I didn't see her." His heart turned cold at the implication of that. Vinnie might very well have left her behind, and if he had... he wouldn't have left her alive.

An emptiness yawned in his chest like none he'd ever felt before. Wrong, he thought He *had* felt it once. Four years ago, while he'd paced outside a Chicago emergency room waiting to learn whether his son would live or die.

God, he couldn't believe how much Kara meant to him. How could he not have known? "Denial," he muttered. "Pure self-delusion."

"What's that, Corona?" Wheatly asked.

"Nothing. Just redirect the troops and I'll keep you posted as to where he's heading."

"Already done. I'm sending a separate team to the motel. We'll let you know what we find."

God, he thought desperately, please don't let it be what he most feared. Don't let it be Kara's lifeless body.

The Ford turned off the well-traveled route and onto a side road. "Damn," Jim said into the telephone. "He's onto me. He's turning left onto—" he scanned the roadside for a sign, spotted one half concealed by a tree limb "—Hawthorn Road. Sign's barely visible."

"Got it. I'll advise dispatch. Better stay on the line."

"Will do."

He kept the line open but set the phone down, better to maneuver the car. Vinnie was driving wildly, fishtailing around corners and throwing up dust. The road wound and twisted. A tinny voice came from his phone and he picked it up again. "Sorry, I missed that. Say again."

"Be advised, Corona, that road heads into rough country."

"I can see that. Wait, he's turning again. Hell, this time it's a right onto a dirt road. No street sign." He scanned the horizon for a landmark. "There's a broken-down old barn a quarter mile from the turn."

"Got it."

Jim stayed on the car and when it turned again, he thought Vinnie might flip it right over, but he managed to hold it. Jim took the turn nearly as fast, the pickup rocking onto two wheels.

When he got it under control, he grabbed the phone again. "He turned again. Chief. This time it's barely a dirt track."

He listened for the chief's reply, but there was nothing.

"Chief?" Jim pulled the phone away from his ear and examined its face. The words *No Signal* glowed in green from the panel. Hell. He'd lost the signal. He had no way to direct the cavalry in. Looked as if he was going to have to do this himself.

He opened his glove compartment, took out his sidearm and knew without checking that it was loaded and ready.

KARA FELT AROUND inside the trunk, whenever her body stopped bouncing off the sides long enough, searching for a latch. Didn't some cars have trunk-release buttons inside the trunks to prevent someone getting trapped?

Hell, if a guy like this had one on his car, he'd probably have had it removed.

The roads were getting bumpier, the turns sharper, and her body was being pummeled as if she was riding inside a paint shaker. The beating she took was nearly as bad as the one Vinnie had delivered. And she hurt so much she began to wonder if she was going to survive this.

She closed her eyes. "Tyler survived it. That's what counts."

She consoled herself with the image of Tyler safe in his father's arms. Tyler having a long and happy life.

They hit another bump and Angela's body was jostled even closer against her. Kara pushed it away, wincing at how cool it felt now. It was unnatural. A reminder that she lay there beside death and might soon join Angela in its cold embrace.

The car skidded to a stop. The trunk popped open, clouds of dust rising around it.

Kara didn't wait to see what would happen next. She sprang out of the trunk and hit the ground running despite that every part of her hurt with every footfall. Vinnie must have hit the trunk release from inside the car, she thought, her mind racing. She'd glimpsed him hurrying around the car when she'd landed, but she hadn't looked back. She'd just run.

He was chasing her. She heard his pursuit without looking, felt him close to her and veered off the road into the woods. She couldn't hope to outrun the man, as battered as she was. Her only chance was to lose him in the forest.

JIM'S TRUCK SKIDDED to a halt behind Vinnie's car, which stood cockeyed on the dirt road, the driver's door and the trunk standing open. He dived from his truck, gun in his hand, every instinct alert as he went to the car, circling it, peering inside. No one. Then he moved around behind it, wary that the open trunk could be hiding Vinnie. The bastard could be aiming a weapon at him even now. He took a quick peek around the open trunk, ducking back instantly.

But what he'd glimpsed in that darting glance made his blood run cold. There was a woman in the trunk lying very still.

No sign of Vinnie.

He moved around again, fully this time, praying he wasn't about to find Kara's broken body.

Angela lay there, still and pale. White powder clung to her nostrils and caked in the blood beneath her nose. Her face was swollen from what had to have been a terrible beating.

He didn't need to check her vitals to know she was dead. But he went through the motions anyway.

She was gone. The mother of his child. And though she'd never been a mother to Tyler, he thought maybe she'd tried to be one at the end. She must have tried, just as Selene said she had. And Vinnie had beaten the hell out of her for it

He closed his eyes and shook off the sadness and regret of a life so thoroughly wasted—except it hadn't been a total waste, had it? She'd given him a beautiful son.

"Thank you for that, Ang. Thank you for giving me Tyler. And for giving him back to me today." It surprised him that his throat went tight on those words. He hoped she was at peace somewhere, somehow.

Jim drew himself up, told himself to focus. Then he looked at the dirt around the car and spotted footprints. Two sets led off into the woods. Two sets.

That had to mean Kara was still alive. "Thank God," he whispered. "Thank God almighty." He checked the cell. There was still no signal, but he took it with him all the same as he hiked into the woods in search of the woman he loved.

KARA RAN DEEPER into the woods, zigging and zagging, doubling back and looping around until she didn't even know where she was. Vinnie was still chasing her, but she thought she'd managed to get far enough ahead so he couldn't see her. So she slowed her pace, walking carefully, hoping to make it more difficult for him to hear her, as well.

God, if only it would get dark. The sun was still in the sky, lower than before but not close to setting. Not just yet. She had to keep moving, get away from him, make sure he couldn't hear or see her, and then find a place to hide. It was her only chance.

Every part of her hurt. Her ribs most of all. She was certain now that Vinnie had broken them when he'd kicked her.

She thought about her family, about how losing her would devastate them. About how much she would regret not being able to see the twins grow up, or her mother find love again, or Selene figure out where her life was leading her. She had to stay alive. She had to.

Those thoughts kept her going despite the pain and the way her body cried out for rest, for a break. She crept as quietly as she could through the undergrowth, the thickening woods. She smelled pine and decaying leaves and rich soil. Birds chirped, took flight now and then when she made an inadvertent sound.

A squirrel chattered. She wasn't sure, but she thought the sounds of Vinnie's pursuit were growing fainter.

She thought about Jim. About Tyler. Jimmy didn't love her. But he did like her. And he was attracted to her. She didn't think he'd been faking his desire. And she thought he had fully intended to marry her. Maybe it was only because he knew how badly his son needed a mother. But that was a compliment to her, wasn't it? That Jimmy had chosen her, out of all the women a man like him could have for the asking, to be the one in his son's life. It was an honor. And while Jimmy may not love her, she knew Tyler did. He adored her as much as she adored him. It could be a good life, being Jimmy Corona's wife. Being Tyler's mother. It would be a good life.

If Jimmy still wanted it. And if she could survive long enough to claim it.

She kept going, picking her way, trying not to make a sound as she moved ever deeper into the woods. It was working, she knew it was. She hadn't heard a sound from her pursuer in a long while. Maybe she'd lost him. Maybe he'd given up and gone back to his car. Maybe she could begin to relax now.

She needed to get her bearings, figure out where she was and then find a safe place to stay until after dark. Once the sun went down—and it would only be a couple of hours now—she would make her way out back to civilization. But she'd have to get a solid idea which way to move now, while it was still light enough to see.

She chose a small tree-lined rise and climbed it pulling herself along, still trying to be as quiet as possible. When she got to the top, she found a spot where she could see between the trees and skimmed the horizon in search of rooftops or chimneys or the snakelike cut of a road through the forest.

She was still searching when the distinct sound of a gun being cocked near her ear, made her go ice-cold and still as stone.

"You've really pissed me off, you know that Kara Brand?"

~

IT WAS GETTING dark, and Jim was running out of signs to follow and had no idea which way to go, when he got lucky.

A branch snapped off to his left, so Jim ducked behind a tree and watched, squinting his eyes, until he made out the shapes moving through the haze of foliage. A woman stumbled slowly through the woods. Kara! And Vinnie moved along behind her, his steps stronger and more certain.

Jim swallowed his relief that Kara was still alive and realized from the direction in which they were moving that they must be heading back to the car. He couldn't let them get there. If Vinnie got her to the car, he might take her out of his sight again, and that was not something Jim could allow to happen.

He chose a path that led him at an angle toward the car, and moved as quickly and quietly as he could. He would cut them off before they got there, get Kara out of the line of fire and take Vinnie down, one way or another.

244

Jim's entire focus remained on Kara. He didn't lose sight of her again and he didn't allow any other thoughts to enter his mind. He pushed aside his worry for Tyler. Tyler was safe now, with the Brands, a family who would do anything for him. He buried his concern for Kara's family, who must be going nuts with worry by now, not knowing where Vinnie had taken her. Their concern would be alleviated when he returned their Kara to them safe and sound. He silenced the small voice of mourning he felt over the death of his one-time wife. Angela was in a better place now.

Kara was his focus. Nothing but Kara.

He drew closer to her, close enough now to see that her face looked odd, and then he realized that was because it was bruised. Vinnie had hit her. The thought made his stomach heave. But he had to stay in cop mode now or he'd blow any chance of getting Kara away from Vinnie alive.

He managed to get nearer, and still nearer as they hiked toward the road and the waiting car. He lifted his gun and said a brief silent prayer.

KARA LIMPED THROUGH the woods seeking a way out of this mess, but she saw no means of escape. The maniac walked two steps behind her, his gun in his hand, pointing right at her. She kept feeling the phantom sensation of a bullet blazing into her back, burning through her flesh, shattering her bones, piercing her vital organs. She knew he wouldn't hesitate to pull that trigger if she tried to escape. And she kept jerking and wincing as she thought of him tripping over a root or stepping in a hole and shooting her accidentally.

She searched the forest, hoping for some kind of help to arrive, for some kind of sign to show her what she was supposed to do. She kept one hand in her pocket, where she clutched the pink stone Selene had given her, and prayed for a miracle.

Closing her eyes, she thought of Jimmy. She wondered briefly if she would ever see him again. Swallowing hard, she stopped walking.

"What are you doing?" Vinnie demanded. "Get moving, woman."

She straightened to her full height and turned to face him. "You're going to kill me, aren't you?"

He looked her squarely in the eyes. "Not just yet. Unless you push it."

"Then what are you going to do?"

He pursed his lips. "Use you. You're my passport out of here." Then he lowered his head, though he kept his eyes on hers. "I'm going to have to leave the country. That kid was my ticket. Now you're taking his place."

"So you knew you never had any chance of staying here, a free man. You assaulted a cop. Kidnapped his son, and now his fiance." She swallowed hard. "Angela's dead."

"I didn't know that when I tossed her into the trunk with you. Sorry about that."

She narrowed her eyes on him. "Don't you even care that she's dead?"

"Why should I care? She was worthless. Loved cocaine more than she loved her own kid. Helped me kidnap him for God's sake. All I had to do to coax her along was keep feeding her that damn powder. Freaking junkies. They're all the same."

Kara closed her eyes.

"I don't have to kill you, you know. Doesn't matter much that you know who I am. Like I said, I gotta skip the States anyway. And I don't plan to come back. You cooperate with me, be a good hostage, get me out of here, and I might just let you live."

She opened her eyes again and searched his. "Do you mean that?"

"I do. I get clear of this place and I'll let you go. You can run right back to that hole-in-the-wall town of yours. Put on your white dress. Have the wedding you were planning to have, the life you were planning to have. You can be Tyler's mommy. Hell, you'd be a million times the mom Angie ever could have been. It'll be great. You'll have a husband who loves you. A great kid to raise. A happy little family, just like you've probably been dreaming about your whole life."

Kara frowned. "You're doing to me just what you did to Angela, aren't you?"

"What are you talking about? I'm offering you a deal. Cooperate, don't give me any trouble and—"

"And you'll give me the drug I crave, right?" She shook her head slowly. "You're good at reading people, I'll give you that much. You know how bad I want that pretty picture you've painted for me. That happy dream. And you're using it to make me do what you want me—what you *need* me to do."

He shrugged. "I get what I want, you get what you want, right? What's so bad about that?"

"It's not going to work, Vinnie. Not with me. Jimmy doesn't love me. All he wants is a mother for his son."

He lifted his brows. "You sure about that?"

She nodded.

"You were going to marry him anyway, though."

"Yeah, I was. For Ty's sake. But it's far from my dream come true. If I die out here, Jim will just find some other woman to help him raise Tyler. And he'll pick a good one, too."

"So you're saying no deal?"

She lifted her chin. "I'm not going to help a man like you get away with murder, "Vinnie."

"Murder. What murder? Angie killed herself."

"You fed her the drugs. You ordered the murder of Jim's partner, Colby. You deal in child porn and you kidnapped a little boy—would have killed him, too, if I hadn't got him away from you." She shook her head. "Sorry, Vinnie. No deal. If you're going to kill me, do it and get it over with. I'm not walking another step to help you."

"Hell." He lowered his head, shaking it slowly. Then he raised it again and lifted the gun.

Something flew out of the trees and hit him hard, knocking him to the ground. The gun went off, but the bullet flew wild, hitting a tree near Kara's head. She ducked instinctively, then realized the missile had been Jimmy Corona. He was rolling on the ground and wrestling with Vinnie, who was still clutching his gun.

When they stopped twisting, Vinnie was on the ground on his back and Jimmy straddled him, pinning his hands to the ground above his head. Vinnie still held the gun in his right hand, and that was the one he was struggling to raise.

"Drop it. Just let it go," Jim told him. His lip was bleeding.

"Thought you didn't love her," Vinnie said, grinding out the words.

"You thought wrong. Drop the gun, Vinnie."

Kara looked around for a weapon—a stick or a club she could use to help—but saw nothing... and then she saw a gun lying on the ground a few feet away. It had to be Jimmy's. She went to it, picked it up, but then the men were in motion again. Vinnie got a leg up between them and kicked Jim off him. Jimmy landed on his back, and Vinnie sprang to his feet and pointed the gun at him.

Kara aimed and fired.

The shot rang and echoed amid the trees, and for a moment everything seemed to freeze in place. And then slowly Vinnie dropped to his knees. She saw the dark spot on his shirt. It was spreading. His hands went limp and his gun fell from his grip, and then he toppled forward and lay still.

Jim got to his feet, picked up the fallen weapon, tucked it into his jeans and then he came to her. She stood there shaking, holding the gun on Vinnie still, even though he was no longer moving. Jim put his hands over hers, gently took the gun away. "It's okay. It's all right, Kara." He started to pull her into his arms, but she tugged herself away from him.

"Is he...? Did I...?"

Jimmy nodded, understanding her question, and he went to lean over the fallen man, touched his neck. After a moment he gripped Vinnie by one shoulder, lifting him off the ground enough to get a look at the front of him, though she couldn't see past him. His body blocked her line of sight. A second later he let the man drop back onto the ground facedown and he rose and returned to Kara. His hands closed around her shoulders. "He's dead, Kara."

"Oh, my God."

"You didn't have a choice. He would have killed me. Both of us."

"I know that." She met his eyes, staring into them for a long moment. And then she just gave in to the shock that was fighting to take over and hurled herself into his arms. The tears came, the sobs with them.

Jimmy wrapped his arms around her and he held her so hard she didn't think he would ever let go. His hands stroked her hair, his lips touched her cheek, her jaw. He kept telling her it was going to be okay, and before long she realized they were moving. He'd picked her up in his arms and was carrying her through the woods.

They emerged onto the dirt road just as police vehicles came screaming onto the scene. Tires skidded, dust clouds rose, men emerged from cars and fired questions.

He told them where to find Vinnie, but he never let go of Kara, not once. And then he was putting her into his pickup and driving her away from there, from the horror, from the death.

CHAPTER SEVENTEEN

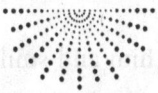

$\mathcal{T}$HE HOSPITAL'S WAITING room was decked with red and green paper chains and popcorn garland, courtesy of the kids in the pediatric unit. It was also was full of Brands. Vidalia hadn't stopped pacing since they'd arrived, even though Kara's injuries were minor. Kara hadn't wanted to come to the hospital at all, but Jim had insisted. She needed checking out. And he needed some kind of validation that she really was okay.

So Vidalia paced. Selene sat on the floor outside the treatment room, legs crossed, eyes closed. He didn't know what she was doing, but he knew she was definitely doing something. Maya and Caleb had a row of chairs to themselves. They had their hands full trying to manage the twins, but nothing had wiped the worry from their eyes. The kids were on the floor—Dahlia, Cal and Tyler—up to their elbows in the toy chest some helpful nurse had brought out for them. Mel and Alex sat quietly waiting, holding hands. Mel looked mad enough to do someone serious damage. The fact that Vinnie Stefano was already dead didn't dampen her anger a bit. Edie and Wade were coming down the hall now, each carrying a cardboard tray full of foam cups. Six each. Nine cups held coffee and three, hot cocoa for the kids. Jim took his from Wade's hand, then returned to his post near the treatment-room door, trying to get a glimpse inside.

He'd taken no more than three sips from his cup when the door nearly hit him in the nose as it opened. He stepped back, startled.

The doctor looked at him and smiled, then looked past him at the others, all of whom were jumping to their feet and rushing forward.

The doctor held up two hands. "Kara is fine. The most serious injuries are two cracked ribs. She's going to be sore for several weeks, but there's no other damage, aside from various bruises."

"Can we see her?" Jim asked. He had unfinished business with Kara Brand and he'd waited about as long as he could stand to get on with it.

"She's getting dressed. Says she wants to go home."

Jim nodded. "All right. Okay."

Kara came out of the room then and he was pushed aside by the oncoming tide of bodies, each rushing to get to her, to hug her gently, to touch her.

Hell, he couldn't blame them. He'd been burning to do the same things, so he understood. They had the right. He didn't. He'd managed to convince Kara that he didn't even love her just before realizing that he did. So he stood out of the way and let them all hold her, assuring themselves that she would be okay.

But eventually, after she'd spoken to each of them and the sea of bodies parted, she looked up and met his eyes. "Take me home."

He was so surprised he stammered at first. "I... I thought you'd be going to your mom's tonight."

"If you want me to... I mean—"

"I don't," he said quickly. He couldn't take his eyes off her. There was a bruise on her jaw and she still had twigs in her hair, but aside from those and a few scratches, there was little sign of the horror she'd been through. Much less the heroics she had displayed tonight. "The chief's going to need you to give a statement but I convinced him to hold off until tomorrow."

"I appreciate that."

"You call us if you need anything," Vidalia said.

"I could take Tyler for the night if you want," Maya offered.

Jimmy glanced at Kara, but before he could say a word, she shook her head. "We want to keep him close to us tonight. After what happened—you understand."

"Sure I do." Maya gently hugged Kara again. "Have a good night honey. Feel better."

"I will."

Kara started for the door, and then Tyler stepped into her path, handed his crutches to his father and wrapped his arms around her legs. She held him to her, and her eyes welled up with tears. "I didn't know he was a bad man, Kara. I'm sorry I went with him."

She shot Jim a look, clearly unsure how much he'd told the boy. "It's all right Ty. Everything's all right now."

"I know."

"Come on, son. Let's get home, huh?"

Tyler nodded, and Jim scooped him up and carried him to the door, across the parking lot to where he'd left the pickup. The whole clan walked them out and then waved as they drove away.

TWO HOURS LATER Tyler was finally asleep. Kara has taken a soothing hot shower and sat wrapped up in her most comfy robe. She sat in the living room nursing a glass of wine and staring at the twinkling lights of their Christmas tree.

Jimmy came from Tyler's bedroom, filled his own wineglass and sat on the sofa beside her. The Christmas tree's lights were the only lights still on and the whole room smelled like pine.

Time to get things said, Kara thought. She sat up a little straighter, set her glass aside. "We need to talk."

"I know we do." Jim licked his lips. He seemed nervous for some reason. Then he said, "I heard what you said to Vinnie out there in the woods."

She lifted her brows, not meeting his eyes. "I said a lot of things out there. You're gonna have to be more specific."

"Okay, I will." He set his glass down. "You told him you knew I didn't love you. That I only wanted a mother for Tyler."

"Oh." She said it softly. Then she took a deep breath. "Well, I told you pretty much the same thing in the hospital. And... it's okay, Jimmy."

"No, it isn't."

"It really is. I... I can live with that. I can be his mother. I can give you both everything you need. If... if you still want me to," she said, warily meeting his gaze.

He searched her eyes, his own intense and probing. "I still want you to, Kara. But not because Tyler needs a mother."

"I don't under—"

"Shh." He pressed a gentle finger to her lips. "Let me talk, okay? You've been through enough today. I don't want you to worry or think or try to be selfless. You do far too much of those things anyway. Just relax and listen, okay?"

Kara blinked and nodded. "Okay."

He took a deep breath. "Angela burned me. I stayed with her way longer than I should have because I loved her. It nearly cost me Tyler. And it cost Tyler more than any kid should have to pay for his father's mistakes."

"You couldn't have known—"

"Uh-uh. You're listening, remember?" He said it with a gentle smile.

Kara nodded and let him continue.

"I made up my mind that I would never love another woman. Not when it messed up my judgment to the point where I put my own child at risk. When I came here, when I started... pursuing you, that was the attitude I was clinging to. That I wouldn't love you. That I was incapable of loving you. But you were... you were just too good to pass up. If I could have started from scratch and created the perfect mother for my son, she would have been you, Kara."

She nodded. "I understand."

"No, you don't. I thought I'd stick around here maybe for a year or so and then talk you into coming back to Chicago with me. That I'd pick up my life right where I left off. But something happened while I was wooing and winning you, Kara Brand. Something happened to me. *You* happened to me. You made me fall in love with you."

She drew in a soft breath, because those were the last words she had been expecting him to say to her tonight.

"I love you. It took me way too long to realize it. But I did, and when it hit me, it hit me hard, Kara. I love you. I want you to marry me because I love you. And the fact that you're the best woman in the whole world and the perfect woman to help me raise my son—those are just bonuses."

Tears welled in her eyes. She tried to blink them back, but they spilled over all the same. "I can't believe—"

"Well, you will, because I intend to spend the rest of my life proving it to you. If... if you're willing to let me after I botched this so badly the first time. So let me ask you again, Kara, for the right reasons this time. Will you marry me?"

She smiled through her tears and met his eyes, stunned to

see they were damp as well. "Yes. I will. And if you really want to go back to Chicago, then I'll go with you. I'll go anywhere you want me to, Jimmy."

"Stop sacrificing yourself, will you? You don't want to go to Chicago. Kara, you deserve to ask for what you want. So tell me the truth. Where do you want to live?"

She blinked and searched his face. "I... I want to live here. Right here in Big Falls."

He smiled and seemed to drink in her face with his eyes. "I don't want to go back to Chicago either. My life is here now. With you and this town and your family." He looked around the house. "This is the first place I've lived that... that feels like home."

"That's because it *is* home," she whispered. "For you and Tyler and for me."

"And it always will be," he promised. And then he pulled her close and kissed her gently. "Always."

"Dad? Kara?"

They pulled apart almost guiltily. Through the slightly open bedroom door, they could see Tyler awake and sitting up in his bed, watching them. They got up quickly, and went to him.

"What is it, Ty?"

He looked from one of their faces to the other, and smiling, said, "This is best Christmas ever."

"It's not even Christmas yet," Kara said. "It's still a week away."

"But I already got just what I asked for. Santa did it. He did it. He got me a mommy for Christmas."

He opened his little arms, and Kara hugged him to her, with tears streaming like rivers. When he let her go, he looked at his dad seriously. "Since I already got the mommy I asked for, and it's not Christmas yes, do you think I could ask Santa for a puppy?"

Laughing, Kara looked at Jimmy, her husband and her son, laughing with her, and through tears, she said, "You're right Ty. This *is* the best Christmas ever!"

Click here for an excerpt from Selene's book,
One Magic Summer

ONE MAGIC SUMMER

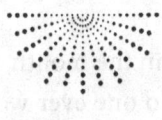

CHAPTER 1

"*T*HERE'S SOMETHING INCREDIBLY freeing about being naked outside," Selene said.

She adjusted the sarong skirt where it was knotted at her side. It was the only piece of clothing she wore. "Well, *nearly* naked."

"Naked enough to get the idea," Marcy said, giggling as she spun with her arms open wide and her head tipped back beneath the stars. "This is awesome. It's...primal."

"I'm not sure I like it so much." Helena had finally stopped crossing her arms over her chest, but it had taken the better part of the ritual before she'd let the energy take away her inhibitions. "I mean, among you guys, sure, but I don't know that I'd do it with anyone else.

"Well, we couldn't have known what it would be like unless we tried it," Erica said, and she whipped off the skirt and stood in the moonlight, completely naked, while the others gasped and laughed. "And I *love* it. It's like—a rebellion. It's like shouting in the moonlight, 'Take your stupid phony standards, society, and cram them where the sun don't shine!' Who the hell ever decided clothes were necessary, anyway?"

"Probably the first caveman to get caught naked in a snow-storm," Selene said. Everyone laughed, and the ring of that laughter, feminine and secretive, filled the clearing. Beyond it the thunder of the nearby waterfall pounded. It was constant and powerful, and the main reason the women—Witches all, and every one of them completely hidden within the depths of the proverbial broom closet—had chosen this spot for their secret gatherings.

They came here once in the month, when the moon was full. And no one else knew. No one ever would. They had too much to lose. Here they came, to cast a circle of invisible power. Here they called on the elements of nature to meld with their own energies, so that they could be closer to the Whole. Here they worshiped the Moon Goddess. They called her Diana, visual-ized her as a powerful huntress. They saw her not as a separate being, or a deity dwelling somewhere in the cosmos. To these women, Diana was the deepest, most powerful part of them-selves. And she was also the collective soul of womankind. The secret rituals they held here were sacred and beautiful.

Trying the nudity was an attempt to learn to see and love the beauty of their own bodies—a direct challenge to the way society taught women to think of themselves. And it was also to satisfy the curiosity they'd all felt when reading that some Witches practiced their rites *only* in the nude.

"Magical requests, before we close?" Selene asked. She felt incredibly free and slightly wicked standing bare-breasted in the moonlight. Not that she hadn't done ritual in the nude before. She had. But only when she was all alone and certain no one would ever find out. This was entirely different.

Marcy raised her hand, even knowing it wasn't necessary. "I know I ask every month, but could we just *try* to turn my ex into a toad?"

Selene shook her head slowly. It was an old joke, but still funny. They didn't do harm. They just didn't.

"Fine. Then let's work to ensure my custody battle gets settled in the best possible way for the boys."

"Works for me," Selene said, and she stepped aside. Marcy moved to the altar at the center of the circle taking with her a photo of her sons, Jack and Joey, both blond, blue-eyed angels, six and eight respectively. She removed the drawstring pouch from the sash at her waist, and laid that beside the photo. Everyone knew it contained a lock of each boy's hair. Then she stood, hands extended to feel the energy, and she led the chant.

"Be it me or be it him, give my boys the best for them."

"Be it her or be it him," the women repeated, "give her boys the best for them."

The others began to move in a clockwise circle around the altar, chanting with Marcy in a slow and steady rhythm. Selene picked up a rattle. Erica kept time on a small drum. Their movements grew faster as the rhythm picked up. Faster. Louder. The rattle became more urgent, the drum more frantic. And the energy rose. Marcy's hands rose with it, and when she sensed the power peaking, she shouted "Release!"

At the moment of that shout the others went still and silent, expelling their breath and relaxing their bodies with such a rush of release that two of them even sank to the ground. And in the same instant, Marcy drew her hands downward quickly, aiming them at the photo on the altar, pushing all the energy they had raised into the photo and hair, which stood in as representatives for the boys themselves.

She sighed, and let her head fall forward, spent. "That was intense," she muttered.

"I sure felt it," Helena said. She was one of those on the ground, but she got up now, smoothing her sarong and brushing twigs and leaves from it. "You're selfless, Marcy, you know that? Most people would be working magic to win custody. Not to do whatever's best for the boys."

"They're what matter, "Marcy said. "They're all that matter."

The others nodded. If the doe-eyed brunette, Helena, felt the energy, it had been real, Selene was sure of that. Helena was the most sensitive, and her impressions were usually accurate. As for Marcy, she came off as the most fiery, the most hot-tempered and impulsive, and her coloring matched her personality. Flame-red hair, bright-green eyes. But there was nothing she wouldn't do for her kids. Nothing. And inside a circle, she could generate magical energy like nobody's business.

"Anybody else have magic they need done tonight?" Selene asked, looking around the circle. "You, Erica? How are things with your father?"

"He's still the local minister," she replied, as she gathered up her sarong and tied it around her waist again. "And I'm still keeping the truth from him."

Selene had to wonder how. Erica with her dyed black hair, straight down her back to her waist, and her overly dramatic application of eyeliner, her Stevie Nicks wardrobe and her collection of goddess-symbol jewelry, seemed to be doing everything except painting the word *Witch* across her forehead. But her father didn't see it, or didn't want to. And she didn't come out and tell him. Mostly, they didn't communicate at all.

She was the youngest of them all, still in college, living in her own apartment with some other juniors, and having as little as possible to do with her father, though she still went home on weekends.

"You, Tessa?"

The butterscotch-blonde sighed. "I just want to keep this part of myself private. Chet would never understand."

They'd been married less than a year, and Tessa lived in fear of losing her new husband. Selene thought he would understand, and was probably much more deeply in love with Tess than Tess could comprehend, but she was going to have to come to that conclusion on her own.

"I just want to keep this part of my life secret. Just a little bit longer."

"And anything else?" Selene asked.

No one had anything, until Marcy said, "What about you, Selene? Isn't there something you want to work for?"

"Yeah, or maybe someone?" Helena added.

The others laughed softly. Selene rolled her eyes. There were no secrets in this circle, that was for sure. "I want to find the love of my life. The perfect mate for me. The man I'm destined to be with. But I don't want to work magic for that. I know he's out there, the Universe has been telling me so my whole entire life. I want him to come to me exactly when and where and how he's supposed to. And until then, I can wait."

"How can you be sure he hasn't already, though?" Tessa asked. "I mean, how can any of us be sure the one we pick is the right one? You should at least ask for a sign."

"I agree," Marcy said. "A clear, unmistakable sign to let you know when he arrives."

Selene smiled. "That wouldn't be a bad idea. What kind of a sign though?"

"Have him fall at your feet the first time he sets eyes on you," Helena said with a breathy sigh.

"Have a fork-tailed comet shoot through the sky when you meet."

"And make sure he absolutely can't live without you," Erica tossed in. "We like our men a bit needy, right?"

"You guys are a riot. What do you say we just do the secrecy charm and close the circle?"

"Fine," Marcy said. "Have it your way. But remember we're between the worlds. Whether we cast a spell or not, we've created a thought form. You're going to get a sign."

Helena nodded her agreement, went to the altar, knelt beside it and took the wine from the ice bucket nearby. She poured it into five wine glasses, and each woman came forward to take one.

They returned to their positions around the circle, then. Selene in the west, probably because her silver-blond hair, pale-blue eyes and even her name corresponded with a moon goddess, and because the moon was most closely associated with the west, and with water. Helena stood in the east, home of the element of air. Marcy was in the south with fire, and Tessa in the north, the home of earth. Erica took center, and the position of spirit, though her own spirit seemed awfully unsettled tonight. Probably she was excited about the four-day camping weekend she'd be spending at a Pagan festival, down at Merry Meet Campground in Texas. She was leaving right from here. And only her fellow Witches knew where she would be.

They lifted their glasses as one, and Selene said:

"Elements and Deities gathered this night, we bid you farewell and give thanks for your light. Our secrets we ask that you help us to keep, until the time comes when fate deems we must speak. Hail and farewell."

The others repeated, "Hail and farewell," and then they gathered closer to the center, clinked their glasses together with their favorite toast, "May you never thirst," and drank deeply.

But Selene stopped with her glass halfway to her lips and lifted her head, her eyes probing the darkness beyond the altar and the ring of candles that marked the boundary of their circle on the ground. "Someone's coming," she whispered.

Marcy shot her a look, then quickly grabbed the double-edged dagger from the altar, and thrust it into Selene's hand. "Better open the circle, hon, so we can get this site cleaned up and get out of here."

She nodded and moved to the edge of the circle, lifting the blade, and trying to keep her focus on the task at hand, rather than out there, in the night, where something was happening; something that made her stomach clench tight, and her nerves tingle. She pointed the blade outward and moved slowly, counterclockwise—or what the Witches called *widdershins*—around the circle, drawing its energy into the blade. When she returned to the north, she pointed the blade down, intending to send the excess power back into the earth mother as she prepared to drive the athame's tip into the ground at her feet.

But before she could bring it down, someone came. Crashing, stumbling, careening, he came and he fell. Right there: right at her feet at the edge of the circle's boundary. He rolled onto his back, knocking lit candles over in the process, and she stood blinking down at him even as he opened his eyes. He gazed up at her, his unfocused eyes on her body, her unclothed breasts and then her face, and finally, as they found the blade in her hands, his eyes went wide.

Something flashed overhead, so bright she jerked her head up and she saw the comet, its forked tail glittering behind it as it jetted across the sky. "Ohmygoddess," she muttered, and, as she lowered her head again, Selene realized that the man was bleeding. And not just a little bit. His shirt was soaked in blood.

He'd fallen at her feet. A fork-tailed comet had shot across the sky. And he would almost certainly die without her.

"Damn," Selene muttered. "As much as I tell myself I believe, it still gives me goosebumps the way this shit works." She drove the blade into the earth beside him and whispered, "The circle is open. So mote it be."

HE'D FOUND HIMSELF stumbling through the woods, a burning pain in his gut, his shirt and his hands soaked in blood. And he'd known—though he wasn't sure how—that someone was chasing him. He had to run. He needed help. He was injured. Those were his thoughts then. And those were the thoughts that had driven him down from the steep, wooded hillside into the clearing.

He'd heard them, clearly. Voices, like tinkling bells: women, laughing and talking, chanting and singing. Beyond the voices there had been a roar, like rushing water, but it was the voices that drew him.

They held in their female lilt the promise of aid, so he'd fought his way clear of the undergrowth, pushing aside branches to try to catch a glimpse of his salvation, better to pick his way closer.

The women danced in a circle of candles, bathed in moonlight, naked, except for sarong skirts, and one hadn't even been wearing that much when he'd first glimpsed them. For a moment he thought he must be hallucinating from the blood loss, imagining he'd stumbled upon an enchanted grove full of fairies. Their backdrop was a thundering waterfall, the source of the rushing, roaring sound. But the women were far more interesting. Their bodies swayed and moved in time with the haunting and primitive sounds of rattle and drum, and their voices rose in some mystical cadence, though he couldn't make out the words. The sight of them, the feeling of something primal and forbidden, something *powerful*, sent chills racing up his spine.

But he needed help, he couldn't be choosy. If they were real and not just a delusion, they would help him. God, please, he thought, let them help him.

A branch snapped behind him, and that, if nothing else, propelled him into motion once again. He headed down the hillside, in far too much of a hurry to pick his way with care, so he slid and stumbled often.

Finally, he was there, on level ground, in the clearing. The women—and he was fairly certain now that they were women, not fairies—at least he didn't *see* any gossamer wings sprouting from their backs—didn't see him. They were too involved with whatever it was they were doing. He fell to his knees, and darkness closed in around the edges of his vision. He'd lost too much blood. He wasn't going to last much longer. No time for caution. Dragging himself to his feet, he lurched forward, making it almost to them before he fell again, landing hard this time.

Silence. Dead silence.

Forcing himself to make his body move, he pushed, rolled over onto his back and blinked up at the woman who stood over him. He saw wide, surprised eyes, their color nothing more than a reflection of the candlelight around her, so they seemed to blaze with an inner flame. Her hair was long, perfectly straight and very pale. The spun silk of angel hair, he thought. Her breasts were small and unclothed, round and perfect, her waist, just the right size to hold in his hands, and her arms were slender but strong.

He saw the rest and sucked in a breath, a *painful* breath. She had a blade raised up above him, its tip aimed squarely at his chest. And the way she clasped its handle in both fists suggested she was about to bring it down *hard.*

"HE'S HURT! HE'S bleeding!" Selene drove the blade of her athame into the earth beside the fallen man as his eyes fell closed again, grounding the energy it held and freeing her hands at the same time. She dropped to her knees, tore his shirt open. "Get a light over here. And someone grab my cell phone."

Marcy came running with a candle, and held it up high as the others gathered closer. At some point she'd tied her sarong back around her waist. The man had a hole in his belly and spurts of blood pumped out of it in time with his pulse. Someone handed Selene something, a small T-shirt, she thought, and she wadded it up and pressed it hard against the wound, then focused there to keep him from bleeding to death. "What's the chant? What's the damn Pow-Wow bleeding chant?"

"Um—uh, wait, lemme think," Marcy said.

Helena leaned closer. "Blessed Mary, Mother of God, who stoppeth the pain and stoppeth the blood," she whispered. "What's the rest?"

"Women's mysteries fine and strong, stop this blood by female song," Selene said as the rest of the charm, long used by the Pennsylvania Dutch Pow-Wow Healers came back to her. She nodded hard, and repeated the words, pressing against the wound and falling into a steady cadence. "Blessed Mary, Mother of God

"Here," Helena said, drawing Selene's gaze upward. She was holding out a cell phone. Selene kept chanting as she took it. She chanted and chanted and the blood slowed more and more.

"Put the phone away," Marcy snapped.

Selene shot her a look, breaking her chant. "I have to get him some help."

"You make that call and we're all outed as Witches, Selene. There's no way we'll have time to clean up the site and get out of here."

"We're talking about a man's life," Selene said softly.

"We're talking about me losing custody of my kids." Marcy looked at the man, her expression torn. Then she glanced at the others. "And about Helena losing her job. How many Oklahoma schools are going to employ a kindergarten teacher who's known to frolic naked in the moonlight? And what about Erica? Her father's the town minister for goddess' sake."

Selene looked from one of them to the next, then nodded slowly. She had no small stake in keeping this secret herself. Her mother was going to have a freaking breakdown over this. But she didn't see that she had a choice. "Look, this is my problem, not yours. I'll cover you."

"What makes it your problem?" Marcy snapped.

"Marcy, hell, didn't you see the comet?" Helena whispered.

Erica nodded. "He's the one. Fell at her feet. Going to die without her. We asked for the signs, and we got 'em in spades," she said. "Poor guy probably doesn't even know he just fell into his destiny."

"Just go," Selene said. "All of you. Gather up as much of your stuff as you can and get the hell out of here. But hurry. I'm making that call right now. You should have a good ten minutes before they get here."

The women scattered, gathering clothes, handbags, ritual tools even as Selene punched buttons on the cell phone. She gave the information calmly and slowly and then disconnected. Helena came to her as she folded the phone and set it down. The others were already running along the path back to the road where their cars were parked.

"You should go, too. They'll be here soon."

Selene looked up at her friend, then down at the man, at his face, for the first time. "I can't leave him. I can't."

"Well at least gather up the rest of the ritual gear, hon. Good luck."

"Merry part, Helena."

"Yeah, and merry meet again—I hope," Helena said. She handed Selene her blouse. "Better put this on before they get here." And then she hurried away.

Selene told herself to follow her friend's wise advice, and she got as far as pulling her blouse on before she got distracted. But then a candle flickered in the breeze, and painted the fallen man's face in amber glow. He wore a day's growth of beard. Some men thought that look was sexy.

She thought it was sexy. Even lying there, unconscious, he was sexy. Hair cut short, kind of brushed back on the top. Dark, dark hair. And a luscious, thick brow line. Everything in her was drawn to him, physically drawn, as if he were magnet pulling her body closer. And even as she wondered whether that was only because she knew he was fated for her, she gave in to it. She leaned closer. She closed her eyes and inhaled him, and something in her knew that scent. She ran a hand over the smooth, strong chest, and something in her knew that silken steel against her palms. Something in her knew the pounding of the heart that beat beneath his skin.

He opened his eyes, dark like his hair in the light of the candle glow, and he stared into hers, but he was unfocused, blinking, clearly confused and in pain.

"Don't be afraid," she told him. "Help is on the way. I'm not going to let anything happen to you."

"You...you...." He gave up his effort at speech, his eyes falling away from hers, sliding over the athame that was thrust into the ground near his head.

"What's your name?" she asked.

He jerked his eyes back to hers. "I...I don't know," he whispered. And then he looked panicky again. "I don't know—"

"That's okay," she told him, keeping her voice calm, soothing. "I know who you are."

That thick brow bent in the middle. "Who...am I?"

"You're the one," she said softly. "You're the one I've been waiting for."

His confusion didn't ease. In fact, it seemed to increase as he stared up at her. And then she heard sirens wailing, vehicles arriving, doors slamming. Feet came running in time with the bounding flashlights. Paramedics were pushing her out of the way, and kneeling around the man. She stood a few feet away, watching them, willing him to be all right. And then a hand fell onto her shoulder.

She turned, startled.

"Ma'am, do you mind telling me what's—" The police chief stopped there, pushed his wide-brimmed hat back on his head, and blinked at her. "Miz Brand? Selene Brand?"

She nodded. "Hello, Chief Wheatly."

"Well now, what in the name of all that's—"

"Chief, he's trying to say something," one of the medics called.

Chief Wheatly sighed. "You stay right here, Selene," he said, patting her shoulder. Then he went to where the medics worked on the stranger. They spoke in low tones. She heard her beloved's voice, strained and whispering. When they all kept looking back at her, and then around at the circle with its candles and its altar full of Witch tools, she felt a ripple of warning move along her spine, and she went closer to try to hear what was being said.

The chief pulled her athame from the ground, eyed it and dropped it into an evidence bag.

Uh-oh.

Then Chief Wheatly turned toward her, holding up the bag. "This your knife, little lady?"

"Yes, Chief, it is, but it's not—"

"So we'll find your fingerprints on it, then."

"Of course you will, but not because I—"

"You do realize that young feller over there has been stabbed, don't you, Selene?"

She blinked. "Not by me," she said.

"Well, now, that's good to know. Good to know." Chief Wheatly took her arm, and drew her with him as he moved closer to the altar, and nodded at the tools there. There were a goblet full of moon-water, a silver censer, still emitting a thin spiral of fragrant sandalwood smoke, a magic wand, unmistakably phallic in shape and size, a candle snuffer that looked like a Witch's hat dangling from the end of a broomstick handle, a dinner-plate-sized crystal pentacle, a hollow half sphere of quartz-lined stone called a geode with a few pinches of sea salt inside, a statue of a beautiful naked woman, with hounds at her sides and a bow in her hands, a statue of a beautiful, naked man with a full beard, horns on his bushy head, and hooves instead

MAGGIE SHAYNE

of feet. They were Diana, the Huntress, and Pan, her lover. They were images representing the Goddess and God.

Selene doubted the chief would see them that way, though.

After looking the items over carefully, Chief Wheatly turned to face her. "You care to tell me what's been goin' on out here tonight, Selene?"

She pursed her lips and tried to swallow against the dryness in her throat. "I'll be happy to tell you, Chief. I was here minding my own business when this man came stumbling out of the woods bleeding, and fell at my feet." She shrugged. "I called you. End of story."

"That's not the way he tells it."

She lifted her brows, her eyes shooting back to the man. They were lifting him onto a gurney and then hauling him toward a waiting ambulance. "How *does* he tell it?"

"Someone stabbed him. He thinks it was you."

She thought she could have fallen over dead from shock. "Why would he say something like that?"

"Well, now, that's a mighty good question, Selene. You were here alone, you say?" Even as he said it, he was looking around at the ritual site. Without even trying, Selene could find evidence of others there. Two pairs of shoes, a couple of blouses. She prayed her friends had taken everything that might possibly identify them by name.

"Do you see anyone else?" she asked, not exactly lying.

"No, ma'am, I don't." Chief Wheatly clearly saw everything she did, though. "But uh, this ground is gonna give up plenty of footprints, you know. And if there were cars parked nearby, we'll know. Looks to me like there were at least a few others out here with you."

She glanced at the chief, met his eyes, and lowered her own. She couldn't understand why the wounded man would think— then again, he was hurt, confused, and he'd looked up at her to find her standing over him with a blade poised over his chest.

"He's confused, Chief. I would never hurt anyone. And as to what the ground is going to give up, there has to be a trail of blood leading from the woods to this clearing."

"That there is. I've got men on it already."

"Doesn't that prove my story?"

"Only proves he was stabbed elsewhere. Doesn't prove you weren't the one who did it, though frankly, Selene, I'd be pretty shocked." He shrugged. "You didn't see him until he came out of the woods, you say?"

She nodded.

"Fella says you told him you know who he is. That true?"

She pursed her lips. "I think maybe I'd better shut up now. Chief. I'm awful sorry and I hate to be rude. But you know, my brother-in-law, Caleb, would be pretty mad at me for talking to you without him here, given what you think might have happened out here tonight, him being a lawyer and all."

"Uh-huh."

"You wanna do me a favor and call him for me?"

The chief eyeballed her. "You could call him yourself from the station, Selene. I'm gonna have to call your mamma anyway." He pursed his lips, shook his head. "And I don't mind tellin' you, that's one call I don't look forward to makin'."

No, she wasn't looking forward to that, either. Her mother was going to have an absolute hissy over this. She would never understand.

"I suppose you're going to confiscate all my things," she said, nodding toward the altar.

"Afraid so, Selene. This is a crime scene."

"It's not, really. I told you, he was stabbed somewhere else. He just stumbled in here."

"Still—"

"Yeah, I know." She stared at the statues on the altar. "These things are...they're sacred objects, Chief. This spot is as holy to me as a church is to other folks. I don't expect you to under-stand that, but—"

"So then this was some kind of...occult ritual?"

She wasn't about to answer that one. "I'm just asking you to take care with my things, is all. Maybe...maybe you could have Jimmy take charge of collecting the evidence? As a favor to my family?"

"That would put him in an awful position, Selene, him being your brother-in-law. Suppose he finds something incriminating?"

"You know Jimmy Corona, Chief. He's a good cop. He wouldn't tamper with evidence—not even for me."

"No, I don't suppose he would. All right, out of respect for your family, Selene, I'll have Jimmy oversee things here. He's off duty so I'll call him in. And...." the chief thinned his lips, sighed, "while I'm at it, I'll have him tell Caleb to meet us at the station."

"Thanks, Chief Wheatly."

He harrumphed, taking her gently by one arm, and leading her toward his black-and-white SUV. "I've known your mamma a long time," he said. "It's not her fault if you've fallen into some kind of satanic cult, girl."

"I have not fallen into any—"

"She's done the best she could by you girls. It can't have been easy raising five kids all alone. I just hope we can find a way to get you back on the straight and narrow. Vidalia Brand is a good woman. She doesn't deserve this." He opened the door, eased her into the passenger seat, closed the door and then got behind the wheel. He took his radio mike from the dashboard. "Sally, I need you to put in a call to Jimmy Corona. Tell him to meet me at the station and to bring Caleb Montgomery with him. Tell them Selene Brand is being brought in for questioning in relation to an attempted murder with...ties to the occult. And uh, maybe you'd best put in a call to Reverend Jackson, as well."

Selene shot him a look. "You ever hear of separation of church and state, Chief?"

"Aw, c'mon, Selene. Your mamma would want him there."

She pursed her lips, folded her arms across her chest, and leaned back in the seat. This was going to be a hell of a long night.

One Magic Summer

ALSO AVAILABLE

The Oklahoma Brands
The Brands who Came for Christmas
Brand-New Heartache
Secrets and Lies
A Mommy For Christmas
One Magic Summer
Sweet Vidalia Brand

The McIntyre Men
Oklahoma Christmas Blues
Oklahoma Moonshine
Oklahoma Starshine
Shine On Oklahoma
Baby By Christmas
Oklahoma Sunshine

www.ingramcontent.com/pod-product-compliance
Lightning Source LLC
Chambersburg PA
CBHW010737130726
47899CB00015B/3298